"Gun!" Walker said sharply. "Everybody down!"

As shots cracked, people flung themselves to the floor. Walker somersaulted, covering most of the distance between Paco and himself as the gang leader's bullets whined over him. As Walker came up from the roll, he thrust his foot out, driving the heel of his boot into Paco's belly.

Walker leveled his gun and snapped, "Drop it!" Paco stumbled against the bar, caught his balance, and started to jerk the pistol up again. Walker sprang forward, striking with his own gun. The barrel cracked across the wrist of Paco's gun hand. Paco howled in pain, and the Saturday night special slipped from his fingers.

WALKER, TEXAS RANGER™

THE NOVEL

James Reasoner

BERKLEY BOULEVARD BOOKS, NEW YORK

WALKER, TEXAS RANGER: THE NOVEL

A Berkley Boulevard Book / published by arrangement with
CBS Enterprises

PRINTING HISTORY
Berkley Boulevard edition / April 1999

The Penguin Putnam Inc. World Wide Web site address is
http://www.penguinputnam.com

ISBN: 0-425-16815-8

BERKLEY BOULEVARD
Berkley Boulevard Books are published by The Berkley Publishing Group,
a member of Penguin Putnam Inc.,
375 Hudson Street, New York, New York 10014.
BERKLEY BOULEVARD and its logo
are trademarks belonging to Berkley Publishing Corporation.

PRINTED IN THE UNITED STATES OF AMERICA

10 9 8 7 6 5 4 3 2 1

This book is dedicated to Chuck Norris,
who made it possible in the first place

ACKNOWLEDGMENTS

Special thanks are due to the following people: Aaron Norris, Gordon Dawson, and Lisa Clarkson, of *Walker, Texas Ranger*, for their advice and encouragement; John Lansing and Bruce Servi, authors of "Codename: Dragonfly," and Gordon Dawson, again, author of "El Coyote," for the inspiration; Jeff Nemerovski and Mary Ann Martin of CBS Television, Inc.; Leslie Gelbman and Kimberly Waltemyer of The Berkley Publishing Group; my agent, John Talbot; and Livia, Shayna, and Joanna for everything else, including all the Saturday nights we sang the theme song along with Chuck.

PROLOGUE

The five men burst out of the bank doors. The last one to emerge paused for a second, turning to spray the lobby of the bank with automatic weapon fire from the ugly gun in his hand. Then he joined the other men sprinting toward the van waiting at the curb.

The robbers wore green camo flak jackets and black hoods over their heads. They carried Uzis and canvas bags full of the cash they had looted from the bank. As they piled into the van, a security guard stumbled out of the building, one hand pressed to his bloodstained side while the other fumbled at the holstered revolver at his hip.

The wheelman, who wore a baseball cap and had a thatch of bright red hair sticking out from underneath it, pounded his heels on the steering wheel. "Come on, come on, you guys," he implored the robbers. "We got to get out of here!"

The man who had fired back into the bank lobby squeezed off another burst at the security guard. The guard went over backward as bullets stitched into his body.

For several blocks along the downtown Dallas street, people heard the shooting and reacted by screaming and ducking for the nearest cover. Traffic screeched to a stop as panic set in.

As brake lights flared in front of him, Texas Ranger Cordell Walker reacted with smooth efficiency and brought his high-powered pickup to a skidding stop in time to avoid rear-ending the vehicle in front of him. Riding next to Walker, Ranger James Trivette was thrown forward against his seat belt by the abrupt stop.

"What in the world—!" exclaimed Trivette.

"Trouble up ahead," Walker said as he flipped on the flashing lights on the front of his pickup. The window beside him was rolled down, since this was a warm spring day in Texas, and he heard the racket of gunshots. Without hesitation, his booted foot tromped down on the accelerator as he wrenched the wheel to the side.

The pickup shot out from behind the stalled traffic into the oncoming lanes. Expertly, Walker dodged the cars coming toward him and powered the pickup toward the scene of the shooting. It wasn't hard to find. Walker just backtracked the frightened people fleeing from the violence.

A siren wailed from somewhere up ahead. Walker's keen eyes spotted a van coming toward him at a high rate of speed. A block behind it was a Dallas police car. A man leaned from the passenger side window of the van and fired an automatic weapon back at the police cruiser.

Walker hit the brakes and swung the wheel again. The rear end of the pickup slewed around so that the big vehicle was broadside across the street, blocking the two middle lanes. Walker and Trivette piled out, leaving the doors open as they grabbed for the .45 semiautomatics clipped onto their belts.

The driver of the van saw the obstacle in front of him and tried desperately to send the careening vehicle through the narrow gap between the front end of Walker's pickup and the cars parked along the curb.

He didn't make it.

The van sideswiped some of the parked cars, rebounded,

2

and skidded at a sharp angle toward the other side of the street. With a grinding and crashing of metal, it impacted some of the cars parked there and came to a shuddering halt.

Walker and Trivette stayed well away from each other, approaching the wrecked van from different angles with their guns leveled. "Texas Rangers!" Walker shouted. "Come out with your hands up!" No sooner were the words out of his mouth than the side door of the van was thrown open and two of the robbers leaped out, firing at the lawmen.

Walker went to one knee and drew a bead on the first gunman, then quickly squeezed the trigger of the .45 twice. The bullets slammed the robber off his feet, though Walker couldn't tell if they penetrated the flak jacket or not. The second man swung his chattering Uzi toward Walker, forcing the Ranger to roll swiftly to the side to avoid the slugs chewing up the concrete surface of the street.

Trivette fired three times. The shots threw the second man back against the side of the van. He hung there for an instant, then flopped forward on his face.

As Walker came up on his feet, the slap of running footsteps drew his attention to the sidewalk. The driver and another man had gotten out of the van on the far side and were trying to escape. Walker broke into a run and angled to cut them off. He jammed his gun back into its clip, then leaped onto the hood of a parked car and threw himself into the air.

His flying tackle took down both men. Walker's black Stetson went sailing off his head as he and the two robbers sprawled on the sidewalk. Walker scrambled back to his feet first, with the black-masked robber right behind him. The driver stayed down, groaning.

The robber had dropped his gun, so he came at Walker with his fists. Walker blocked the punches easily, shot a blow of his own into the middle of the man's face. The robber's head rocked back, but he recovered quickly and with a growled curse charged Walker like a bull.

Walker pivoted and brought his right leg up to meet the rush. The heel of his boot thudded against the robber's chest, stopping the man as if he had run into a wall. Walker continued his turn, his leg swinging out and coming up even higher. As he completed the turning kick, the side of his foot slammed into the robber's head and flung the man backward a good ten feet. He was out cold when he crashed to the sidewalk.

Meanwhile, Trivette was pulling another of the robbers from the van. The man was groggy and barely able to stand up. The fifth and final holdup man was still inside, lying with his head at an unnatural angle. The crash had broken his neck, but he might still be alive. Trivette turned over the half-conscious robber to several uniformed Dallas police officers, who'd rushed up with guns drawn, then leaned into the van to check on the last man. Trivette pressed a couple of fingers to the man's neck, then straightened and shook his head. "Dead," he told the officers.

Walker used a booted toe to prod the side of the man he had just knocked out. The man's head rolled back and forth loosely. He was still unconscious. Walker turned toward the driver, the only one of the robbers not wearing a hooded mask and flak jacket. Walker drew his gun and said, "On your feet."

The driver pushed himself shakily upright and held his hands toward Walker, palms out. "Don't shoot!" he begged. "I'm unarmed. Please, don't kill me!"

"I'm not going to kill you. You're under arrest."

Walker put his gun away and stepped toward the driver, reaching for the handcuffs attached to his belt. An evil grin suddenly split the man's face as he jerked a knife from behind his belt at the small of his back and slashed at Walker's face with it.

Walker ducked and let the blade pass harmlessly above his head. As he straightened, he brought his right fist up in an uppercut. The blow landed against the driver's jaw with

4

a sound almost like an ax chopping into a tree. The driver's head jerked to the side, his eyes rolled up in their sockets, and he crumpled like a puppet with its strings cut. The knife clattered onto the sidewalk as the driver's suddenly nerveless fingers released it.

Walker stepped back, opening and closing his right fist several times. His hand would be a little sore in the morning.

But it would be worth it.

"Good job, Rangers," one of the uniformed officers said as Walker picked up his hat and rejoined Trivette on the other side of the street. "These boys robbed the bank up the street. Got away with a wad of cash and killed a guard."

"Was anyone else hurt?" asked Walker.

"Not seriously. A couple of minor wounds."

Walker nodded. "Good. Come on, Trivette."

"Wait a minute." The cop looked surprised as he spoke. "Aren't you going to stick around while we take these prisoners in?"

"You can handle that." Walker settled the Stetson on his head. "We have to be somewhere else—and we're already late."

ONE

The seemingly abandoned warehouse had seen better days, but then, so had this entire section of Dallas. The side streets were lined with blocky, run-down buildings like this one, while the boulevard that ran through the center of the area was a haven for dingy bars, strip joints, and adult video stores. Despite the fact that it was the middle of the day, there was not much traffic along the boulevard, nor on the side streets. The high windows in many of the warehouses were boarded over with pieces of plywood.

Walker and Trivette sat in the back seat of a nondescript car parked in front of a pawn shop. Two men sat in the front seat, and the one behind the wheel, a DEA agent named Davis, turned his head to talk to the two Rangers.

"That's it, there on the other side of the street," he said. He was a thin man, slender almost to the point of gauntness, with longish, fair hair and intelligent eyes behind a pair of glasses. He looked more like a bookstore clerk than what he actually was, a very competent federal agent.

Davis's partner, a younger agent named Brennan, added, "We were afraid you weren't going to get here in time, Ranger Walker."

"Trivette and I ran into some trouble along the way," said Walker.

"That bank robbery downtown?" asked Davis. "We heard about it on the scanner."

"That's right," said Trivette. A grin flashed across his face. "It was like an Old West shoot-out for a few minutes there. Come to think of it, it happened right about high noon, too."

"Tell us what you've found out about the warehouse," Walker said to Davis.

"It's owned by a company called Pilgrim Realty, but that's just a blind," Davis explained. "Pilgrim is owned by another company, which is owned by another company, and so on and so on."

Walker nodded. He knew how criminals could pile up layer after layer of lies and deceptions to hide their activities.

"We were able to follow the paper trail across the border into Mexico, but that's where it ran out," Davis continued. "That was enough to get some of our contacts across the border involved, though, and that's how we found out about El Diablo."

Trivette laughed, but he didn't sound particularly amused. "El Diablo," he repeated. "Are we supposed to take that name seriously? It sounds like something out of a hokey old movie."

Davis grimaced. "That's what we thought at first, too, before our agents in Mexico realized just how frightened some of their contacts are of El Diablo. The Mexicans take him seriously, that's for sure."

"El Diablo," Walker mused. "The Devil. As if Satan himself has gone into the drug-smuggling business."

"Or someone almost that bad," said Davis. "Anyway, we started tracing the pipeline back this direction, and this warehouse"—he nodded toward the ugly building half a block away, diagonally across the street—"is a major distribution center. At least, we think it is."

"We'd better find out," said Walker.

Brennan looked at his watch. "The rest of the task force ought to be along right about . . . now!"

Even as he spoke, a pair of vans swung into the side street and gunned up to the warehouse, screeching to a halt beside the loading dock with its closed and locked overhead doors. Davis cranked the engine of the car, dropped the engine into gear, and sent the vehicle spurting up the street. He brought it to a stop in front of a smaller door leading into the warehouse's office area.

"We have men covering the back," Davis called over his shoulder as he hurriedly got out of the car. He was shrugging into a lightweight black windbreaker as he moved. The letters *DEA* were stamped boldly on both the front and back of the windbreaker. Brennan was quickly donning an identical jacket.

Federal agents wearing body armor and helmets and carrying automatic weapons sprang from the vans and jumped up onto the loading dock. One of them had his weapon slung on his back and was carrying a pair of bolt-cutters instead. He used the powerful cutters to snip through the padlock fastened in the hasp of one of the overhead doors. Then he ducked back out of the way as other agents threw the door up and charged into the warehouse. Their shouts of "Federal agents!" echoed from the high ceiling of the building.

Meanwhile, Davis and Brennan hit the office door with a ram they had taken from the car. The door looked flimsy, but it resisted the efforts of the federal officers at first. Wood splintered and fell away from the door, revealing a core of steel. The jamb was not strong enough to stand up to the repeated battering, however, and after a few swings of the ram, the door popped open.

The frenzied *pop-pop-pop* of gunfire filled the ware-house. Walker and Trivette ran into the office area with Davis and Brennan right behind them. A couple of men had been sitting there behind desks, but now they were on their feet and clawing for guns hidden under their coats.

Walker identified himself and added, "Don't try it!" but the men didn't listen. Their hands came out of their coats holding guns. Walker waited a beat longer, just to be sure the men intended to resist arrest, then fired.

One of the men howled in pain and fell, clutching a bullet-shattered shoulder. The other man dropped his gun and thrust his hands into the air in surrender.

A connecting door led from the office into the warehouse proper. It was closed, but that didn't stop Walker, didn't even slow him down. His heel drove into the door just below the knob and knocked it open. He went through in a rush with Trivette close behind him. Davis and Brennan stayed behind to take the two office workers into custody and see to the wounded man.

Stacks of boxes filled the warehouse, except in the center, where a long table was covered with bags of heroin that was being cut down to street potency. Several roughly dressed men, probably illegal aliens from Mexico who were working in the warehouse for a pittance, came running toward the office door, evidently hoping to escape the federal agents that way. They stopped short when they saw the two Texas Rangers. None of the men were carrying guns. One of them, a huge, bearded man almost as wide as he was tall, hesitated for a second, then continued the charge, running at Walker with a bull-like bellow.

The man was faster than he looked, but his speed was no match for Walker's, who darted out of the way. The drug smuggler ran past Walker before he could stop and start to swing around. Before he could manage that, Walker chopped down at the back of his neck with the butt of the .45.

The blow made the man stumble and shake his head, but he threw off the effects and swung an arm like the trunk of a small tree at Walker's head. Not expecting the man to still be on his feet, Walker was caught slightly by surprise, and as he swayed backward, the man's fist clipped him on the side of the head.

Walker was thrown off balance for a moment, but he recovered almost instantly, in time to block the next punch the big man threw. He hooked a blow of his own into the man's stomach, which was hard with muscles despite its girth. That barely slowed down the big man, who looped his arms around Walker in a bear hug.

The drug smuggler's arms closed, trapping Walker in a vicelike pressure. Walker still had his gun in his hand, and he could have pressed the barrel into the man's side and started pulling the trigger. He wanted to take as many of the smugglers alive as possible, though. Each prisoner would be a potential link to someone higher in the chain of evil bringing the poison into the country.

Walker dropped the gun and head-butted the man instead, driving the crown of his head into the middle of the man's face. That loosened the smuggler's grip enough for Walker to pull his arms free. He clapped his cupped hands over the man's ears, drawing another howl of pain. The potentially deadly embrace slackened even more, and Walker twisted loose. He swung three punches—a right, a left, and another right—then came up off his feet in a flying kick that sent both feet crashing into the man's chest. With an impact that seemed to shake the entire building, the big man went backward and slammed to the floor.

Scooping up his gun, Walker covered the man and glanced around the rest of the huge, high-ceilinged room. Gunfire was still going on in a couple of the corners. Walker saw Trivette crouched behind a crate, trading shots with two of the smugglers.

A flash of movement caught Walker's eye. More men were making a break for the rear of the warehouse. They would have a surprise waiting for them back there, thought Walker.

But before the fleeing smugglers could reach their goal, the young DEA agent called Brennan stepped out of the

11

office and shouted, "Stop! Hold it right there!" He squeezed off a warning shot with the pistol he held. The nine-millimeter slug whined over the heads of the smugglers.

As several of the criminals turned sharply toward the federal agent, Walker yelled, "Brennan! Look out!"

The warning came too late. One of the smugglers had an automatic pistol in his hand, and it moaned like a bull fiddle as hundreds of rounds spewed from its muzzle. Brennan danced backward, his black windbreaker jerking as slug after slug hit him. His face was twisted in a mask of horror and agony as he fell halfway through the open door from the office area.

Davis dropped into a crouch next to his young partner. "Brennan!" he shouted, his voice a mixture of sorrow and fury.

Walker snapped a couple of shots toward the fleeing men, driving them back away from the rear of the building where they wanted to go. Davis had men back there waiting for anyone who tried to escape that way, but suddenly, after seeing what had happened to Brennan, Walker wanted to finish this job himself.

Several of the helmeted, flak-jacketed DEA agents ran around a tall pile of wooden crates and opened fire on the men who had been trying to escape out the back. A couple of the smugglers fell, but the rest came toward Walker. He went into a crouch and fired at their legs, taking down two more of the men. The rest threw their guns down and thrust their arms into the air in surrender.

Elsewhere in the warehouse, the gunfire was dying away to nothing. The smugglers had been taken by surprise, and they were outnumbered and outgunned. With at least half of them already wounded, the others were not going to continue putting up a fight.

The surrender came too late to help Brennan, though. Walker and Trivette walked over to join Davis, who was standing beside Brennan's body.

"He was wearing Kevlar under his shirt," Davis said in a voice choked by emotion, "but those bastards were using armor-piercing rounds. Poor Matt never had a chance."

Walker nodded grimly. "I'm sorry, Davis."

The DEA agent sighed and rubbed his lean jaw. "Well, at least we put a stop to the flow of drugs through this warehouse. That'll help . . . for a while."

"We have to find El Diablo," said Walker. "Then we could shut off the pipeline at its source."

Flanked by Trivette and Davis, Walker strode over to the group of prisoners who had not been wounded in the firefight. They stood there under the guns of the other federal agents. Some of the smugglers looked cowed, while others glared defiantly at Walker.

He raised his voice slightly as he said, "Who can tell me about El Diablo?"

The very mention of the name made some of the more frightened-looking men cringe even more. But one of the more defiant ones spat on the cement floor of the warehouse and glowered even more darkly at the Ranger.

"You will never stop El Diablo!" he said. "None of us would dare risk his vengeance by telling you where to find him, and even if we did, you could not catch him!"

"Want to bet?" asked Trivette.

"El Diablo is everywhere! He sees everything, knows everything. Even now, he knows what has happened here today . . . Ranger." The smuggler's voice practically dripped with contempt. "He cannot be seen unless he wishes it to be so, and he strikes out of the darkness and kills! If you try to find El Diablo, he will kill you, too!"

"We'll take our chances," said Walker. He jerked his head toward the open roll-up door. "Get them out of here," he said to the federal agents.

The prisoners were herded out of the warehouse at gunpoint. The wounded men were given first aid, then they, too, were gotten on their feet and marched out. As Walker, Trivette, and Davis watched them go, Trivette said, "Do

13

you believe all the stuff that guy was saying about El Diablo, Walker?''

''You mean about him knowing everything that's going on and not being able to be seen unless he wants to be?'' Walker shook his head. ''Sounds like some sort of demon to me—which is probably exactly the image El Diablo wants to project.''

''I thought the Cherokee were a mystical people and believed in spirits and things like that.''

''There are things in the spirit world that are beyond our understanding,'' Walker said, ''but that's not the same as a bunch of drug smugglers. That sort of evil is in *this* world—and that's too bad.''

TWO

Rancho Vega Garcia,
near Nuevo Laredo, Mexico

Young women in bikinis so small as to almost not be there lounged around the large, kidney-shaped swimming pool. Blondes, brunettes, redheads—white, black, Hispanic, Oriental—the only thing they had in common was that they were all stunningly, breathtakingly beautiful.

Don Carlos del Vega Garcia looked at the young women as he sat at a table under a spreading umbrella and sipped from a glass of tequila. In the midst of such loveliness, he wondered, why was he not happy?

He knew the answer.

Walker.

Carlos sighed, and his younger brother, Ramon, looked up from the other side of the table. "What is wrong?" he asked.

A slender man with graying dark hair, dressed in an elegant, expensive sports shirt and slacks, Carlos did not look like the popular conception of a drug lord. Neither did Ramon, who was slightly taller and more muscular than his older brother but equally suave. Judging from appearances, Carlos could have been any successful, middle-aged businessman, while Ramon might have been taken for a professional soccer or tennis player. In reality, however, until a few years earlier they had run the most successful drug smuggling cartel in all of northern Mexico.

Then Texas Ranger Cordell Walker had entered the picture.

"I was just thinking of Walker," said Carlos.

Ramon waved a skillfully manicured hand. "Forget Walker," he advised his brother. "He thinks we are still in prison. He has no idea what we are doing—and even if he did, he could not stop us."

Carlos brooded into his glass of tequila and said, "That is what you said when we hired Shrader."

Ramon looked as if he wanted to spit, as if the name Shrader put a vile taste in his mouth. "Shrader paid for his incompetence . . . with his life."

Carlos nodded, but his mind was miles away and years in the past. Randy Shrader, the hotshot mercenary pilot who claimed that he could fly anything, had been right about that. Shrader had succeeded in stealing the United States military prototype helicopter known as Dragonfly. The high-tech chopper, with its nearly unstoppable firepower and stealth technology, had enabled Shrader to break Ramon out of the country club federal prison in which the American authorities had placed him after his conviction. Then, with Shrader at the controls, Dragonfly had been placed in the service of the Vega Garcia cartel, and an already successful operation had quickly become even more dominant in the drug trafficking between Texas and Mexico.

But then Cordell Walker, a Texas Ranger and a man with an old grudge against Shrader that dated all the way back to Vietnam, had gotten involved in the case. Shrader had wound up dead, and the Vega Garcias' operation was left in tatters. Demoralized and strapped for cash, Carlos and

Ramon had been unable to avoid arrest by Mexican authorities. Even the sometimes corrupt and frequently inefficient Mexican courts had to function correctly on occasion, and in this case, the unthinkable had happened to Carlos and Ramon del Vega Garcia.

They had gone to jail.

Luckily for them, that situation had not lasted very long. A few well-placed bribes with what was left of their fortune had freed them and left two other men behind bars in their place. They had returned to their rancho near Nuevo Laredo, not far from the Rio Grande, which they had managed to hold on to despite their legal troubles, and had spent the past couple of years trying to build their organization back up to what it had once been. They were on the verge of success. . . .

But past failures still rankled in Carlos's mind. He and his brother had a score to settle with Walker. Honor demanded it.

Sometimes honor had to take a back seat to the needs of business, however. When they were solidly established again, then would be the time to strike back against the Texas Ranger.

Thinking of time reminded Carlos to look at the watch on his wrist. It would have cost several thousand dollars, had it not been stolen.

"He should have been here by now."

"Don't worry. El Diablo has never failed us yet."

Carlos grunted. El Diablo . . . such a name. He was not sure why their associate had adopted it. A fondness for melodrama, perhaps.

A servant in a short white jacket came out of the hacienda onto the terrace next to the swimming pool. He bowed slightly to the Vega Garcias and announced, "Señor El Diablo is here, don Carlos, don Ramon."

"Excellent," said Ramon. "Send him out here."

The newcomer was already striding boldly onto the terrace from the hacienda without waiting to be invited. Carlos's back stiffened. El Diablo was arrogant, no question about it. But as long as he was getting results, his arrogance could be tolerated.

El Diablo nodded curtly to the Vega Garcias. "Don Carlos. Don Ramon."

Carlos waved a hand at the two empty chairs sitting by the glass-topped table. "Sit down," he said. "Lupe will bring you a drink."

"Thank you," El Diablo said with a smile. The expression did little to soften the hard lines of his face or relieve the icy coldness of his eyes. He pulled back one of the chairs and sat. His eyes went briefly to the dozen or more young women around the pool.

Carlos noted the glance and said, "If you would like to stay overnight, I could have one of them sent to your room. Or two or three, if that is your pleasure."

El Diablo hesitated, then shook his head. "Not this time. I have much work still to do."

"You are a dedicated man, Diablo," Ramon said, a hint of mockery in his voice, perhaps unwisely. Despite his childish name, El Diablo was not a man to be trifled with. Ramon went on, "You spend all your time working for the success of the Vega Garcia cartel."

"The success of the cartel is my success as well," El Diablo pointed out.

Carlos cleared his throat. "Ah . . . yes, that is true," he admitted. It still bothered him to do so. El Diablo was more than an employee; in order to secure his help in their unofficial release and the rebuilding of their drug smuggling empire, they had been forced to make him a partner.

El Diablo reached for the briefcase he had brought with him, lifted it onto the table, and snapped back the catches. He lifted the lid. "These are the latest profits from our distribution centers in San Antonio, Houston, Dallas, and Fort Worth." He began taking stacks of currency, all the bills neatly banded together in thick bundles, from the briefcase. Carlos and Ramon both smiled in satisfaction as they saw the money piling up on the table's glass top.

Suddenly, a ringing sound came from inside El Diablo's perfectly cut coat. He stopped taking money from the briefcase and reached for the cellular phone instead. "Yes?"

For a moment he listened, and as he did so, the planes of his face grew harder and sharper. With no warning, he violently swept his arm across the table, knocking the case and the bundles of money to the ground. Both Carlos and Ramon jumped in their chairs, shocked by El Diablo's reaction to what he was hearing.

"What!" he exploded. "Everyone? They got them all?" He spent a moment cursing fluently and fervently in Spanish, then rubbed a hand over his face in exasperation and asked, "What about the merchandise?"

The answer clearly displeased him. He stood up and began stalking back and forth. "Call our lawyers immediately for the supervisors," he told whoever was on the other end of the connection. "No, they can forget about the workers. Let them rot in jail. They know nothing that can damage us."

Carlos and Ramon were watching El Diablo intently, and they did not see the bikini-clad young woman who slipped up behind them. She bent, reaching out for one of the bundles of bills that El Diablo had knocked off the table. The Vega Garcias still did not notice as she picked up the money and began to back off. She looked down at her outfit—three tiny triangles of fabric—and frowned as if she were wondering where she was going to hide the cash.

She didn't have to worry about that for long. Still barking orders into the cell phone, El Diablo suddenly stalked around the table and snatched the bundle of money out of the hands of the surprised young woman. Using the same hand that now held the money, he gave her a tooth-rattling slap that sent her backward, arms flailing, into the pool. Water splashed high into the air, but El Diablo had already turned away, the incident forgotten, before the drops pattered back into the pool.

El Diablo thumbed a button on the phone, ending the connection, then tucked it back into his pocket as he turned to the Vega Garcias. He tossed the bills he had taken from the young woman onto the table.

"Bad news?" Carlos asked, rather unnecessarily.

"Our warehouse in Dallas was raided by American federal agents earlier this afternoon," El Diablo said.

"But . . . but how did they find out about it?" sputtered Carlos.

"That doesn't matter," Ramon said tightly. "What happened?"

"Several of the men working there were killed," said El Diablo. "All the others were arrested. No one got away."

"And the heroin?"

"Confiscated. All of it."

Ramon ground out a curse. Carlos propped his elbows on the table and dropped his head into his hands. He felt like sobbing, but he would not. Not in front of his brother and El Diablo.

"We can absorb the loss," Ramon said. "It will hurt, but we can do it."

"This time," El Diablo said. "But that is perhaps not the worst news."

"What else could be worse?" Carlos practically moaned.

"There were two Texas Rangers in the raid with the federal agents. One of them was—"

"Walker," Carlos breathed in a hushed voice.

"Walker," confirmed El Diablo, clearly irritated at being interrupted.

Carlos came to his feet. The feeling of despair that had washed over him a moment earlier was gone as rapidly as it had come, to be replaced by a sense of outrage. "This man Walker has been alive for too long," he said. "I want him dead!"

Slowly, El Diablo nodded. "When the time comes, he will die. But there are more important matters right now."

"What could be more important than our honor?" demanded Carlos.

"We have to move to a different plan for our Dallas operation now. The police and the DEA will be looking for any traditional means of moving the merchandise in."

"You have an idea?" asked Ramon.

El Diablo nodded again. "Two, in fact. One that we can implement almost immediately, and another that will take a bit more time to arrange."

"Does either of them include killing Walker?" Carlos asked harshly.

El Diablo shrugged. "Perhaps. As I said, when the time is right . . ."

THREE

Phyllis Harrison said to the little boy, "Say 'ah.' "

He stuck his tongue out farther than seemed humanly possible. "Aaaaahhhh!"

Phyllis shone the light she was holding past the tongue depressor and studied the small white ulcerations on the back of the boy's throat. Then she took the tongue depressor out and said, "All right, you can close your mouth now."

"Did I do all right, Doctor Phyllis?" the boy asked eagerly. "Did I say it okay?"

"You did just fine, Juan," she assured him.

Juan's mother leaned anxiously toward Phyllis. "He will get well, Doctor?"

Phyllis smiled tolerantly. She had long since given up on getting her patients to understand that she wasn't really a doctor and never had been. She had spent her entire career as a nurse. But she had spent most of that career working next to the best doctor she had ever known.

Her husband, Keith.

Phyllis pushed back the graying brown hair that always threatened to fall into her face. "Juan will be fine, Mrs.

Lopez," she told the boy's mother. "He has a bad cold, that's all. He's not running a fever, so I don't think there's any infection or strep throat. Give him a few days to get over it on his own. If he doesn't, you can bring him back to me."

A brilliant smile flashed across the young woman's face. *"Gracias,* Doctor. *Muchas gracias."*

Phyllis returned the smile and ruffled the black hair on Juan's head. *"De nada."*

Mrs. Lopez opened a threadbare purse and took out a couple of crumpled dollar bills. She held them out. "Is enough?"

Phyllis started to tell the woman to put her money away. She knew how poor the Lopezes were. Nearly everyone in this part of Dallas was poor. But the payment would go for a good cause and would satisfy Mrs. Lopez's pride, too, so Phyllis took it. "It's fine," she told Mrs. Lopez. "Thank you."

The mother and the little boy went out, leaving Phyllis alone in the small room. She remained for a moment on the stool where she had sat as she examined Juan. She was tired after a day of seeing patients. She was getting too old for this, she told herself, not for the first time.

But somebody had to do it.

That was what Keith had always said, too—somebody had to take care of folks when they got sick. Only he had said it with a smile and with the enthusiasm that had made him such a dedicated physician for thirty years.

Until the night that noble heart of his had given out, dropping him in a heap on the kitchen floor of their north Dallas home, practically at her feet. She had been at the counter chopping celery to put in a salad, and she could still remember the feel of the knife's wooden handle in her fingers, the smell of the celery, the crisp sounds the blade made when it cut through the stalk, punctuating Keith's voice as he told her what had happened in the office that day, as he had always told her ever since she had finally retired six months earlier.

But he hadn't retired, oh, no, he had gone on pushing himself, working the long hours, tending to his own practice as well as trekking out to the free clinics in all the worst parts of town. . . .

"Oh, Lord. Phyl—"

And that was all the warning she'd had, all the warning either of them had. By the time she had dropped the knife and turned around, he was gone, slumping to the floor, and she had dropped to her knees with him and caught hold of him and tried to pull him back up and called his name as if that would will him back to life. . . .

She pushed her hair back again, took a deep shuddery breath, and told herself aloud, "Stop it. Just stop it." She stood up and went out into the waiting room.

Actually it was just the living room of this tiny rented house. The examining room had originally been a bedroom. There was a kitchen and a bathroom to the rear, and that was all. The house sat on a small, bare lot. Several of the other houses on the block were abandoned and partially boarded up. But the crackheads and the other drug addicts got into those houses anyway, tearing the boards off the windows if they had to. Those other houses were falling apart, and a couple of them were nothing but burned-out husks now.

Not this house, though. The word had gone around. This house—and the woman who came here nearly every day— was to be left alone.

After Keith's funeral, Phyllis had had to make up her mind what to do next. Their two children were grown and married, one in Weatherford, one in Corsicana. Phyllis could have gone to stay with either of them and would have been welcomed. But she wasn't ready yet to sell the house and leave Dallas. She felt as if there were still something that needed to be done. . . .

Finally, it had come to her that what she needed to do

25

was to continue Keith's work. She couldn't do anything about his private practice, of course. She wasn't a doctor, and she had retired from nursing. Still, she knew as much about medicine as many of the doctors currently practicing. Her years with Keith had seen to that. And he hadn't been some crusty old reactionary who was unwilling to change with the times. He read all the medical journals, attended all the seminars, kept up with all the latest techniques. And so had Phyllis. She could set a bone, diagnose an earache, even deal with more complicated problems as well as anyone else.

So she had come here to one of the worst areas in Dallas, a neighborhood beset by poverty and gang violence, and let it be known that she was willing to provide medical help to anyone who needed it, whether they could pay or not. She had rented this house and fixed it up with her own two hands, despite the fact that her son and daughter did everything in their power to convince her that she was crazy to risk her life like this.

So far, during the six months that the unofficial, unlicensed, one-woman clinic had been open, things had gone surprisingly well. The place had been broken into a few times in the first couple of weeks, but then she had helped the little sister of a Latino gang leader recover from pneumonia, and he had shown his gratitude by making it known that Doctor Phyllis was under his protection. Unwilling to be outdone, the leader of the local black gang had issued the same directive to his followers. Phyllis was as safe here as anyone in this part of town could be.

She took off the white coat she wore to the clinic— Keith's coat, because when she wore it, she always felt as if he were somehow here with her—and hung it up, then turned off the lights. It was past six o'clock, and she didn't think anyone else would show up looking for help.

As soon as she stepped out onto the porch of the small house, she knew she was wrong.

A car was roaring down the street, weaving back and

forth slightly as it came. It skidded to a stop in front of the clinic, and the driver's door was thrown open. A young man stumbled out of the vehicle and started up the cracked concrete sidewalk that led from the curb to the porch. His hand was pressed to his chest, and Phyllis saw a dark stain on the shirt underneath his splayed fingers.

"You the . . . doctor lady?" he asked in a hoarse voice as he staggered up to the porch. He was probably eighteen or nineteen, Latino, muscular. He would have been handsome, had his face not been so pale and haggard from pain. Phyllis had never seen him before.

She caught hold of his arm and helped him up the crumbling steps onto the porch. "Let's get you inside," she said in a calm voice. Even though she hadn't yet gotten a good look at the injury, she knew it had to be either a gunshot or a knife wound. It had bled too heavily to be anything else.

This wouldn't be the first time she had treated such an injury. The gangs were starting to understand that they could come to her for help, just as she had hoped they would.

Before she could lead the young man inside, another car screeched to a stop in front of the clinic. The Latino jerked his arm out of her grasp and reached behind him to pull the revolver that was tucked behind his belt in the small of his back. Several young black men piled out of the second car, and in the fading light, Phyllis saw the guns in their hands.

"No!" she cried out as the Latino started to raise his weapon. She caught at his arm and forced it down, something she might not have been able to do under normal circumstances. He was weak from loss of blood, however.

"Stop it!" he gasped. "Get outta here, lady—"

"Stop!" Phyllis thrust her other hand out toward the black gang members. Her voice was loud and clear. "I won't have any violence here!"

"Better watch out, bitch," snapped one of the newcomers. "We gonna do this dude—"

Another of the young men said, "Shut up," and shoved the loudmouth to the side.

"Hey, man, wha'chu doin'—"

The second gang member stepped forward, ignoring the angry protest. He looked at the two people on the porch of the house and said, "You Doctor Phyllis, ain't you?"

"That's right," she said.

"Heard 'bout you an' this place." The young man waved the hand that held the gun to indicate the house. "Word is we gots to steer clear of you, lady." He turned his head and barked at his subordinates, "Put them guns up."

"Thank you," said Phyllis. She took a risk by asking, "Did you shoot this young man?"

The spokesman for the gang just smiled. "He been shot? Wouldn't know nothin' 'bout that. We be movin' on now." He angled his head toward the car in which he and his companions had arrived.

They went, their attitudes mostly surly and reluctant, but the important thing, thought Phyllis, was that there had not been any shooting here. She had to keep a low profile with the authorities if she was going to be effective in this poverty-stricken, high-crime neighborhood.

"Should've let me . . . shoot 'em," mumbled the wounded Latino.

"And what good would that have done?" Phyllis demanded crisply as she steered him toward the door. "That would have just gotten us both killed. Have you been shot or stabbed?"

"Shot," the young man answered through gritted teeth. "It went on through, came out the back."

Phyllis glanced at the back of his shirt, saw the bloodstain and knew that he was telling the truth. "We'll get you fixed up," she said. "The bullet doesn't appear to have hit any major organs, so we'll clean and bandage the wound and get you started on antibiotics to prevent infection.''

"I'm gonna . . . pull through?''

"I certainly hope so,'' she said as she took him into the waiting room and flipped on the light switch.

"Me, too. Got to live so . . . I can kill those bastards. . . .''

With a groan, he passed out. Phyllis caught him, lowered him to the floor. She would get started on his treatment right here in the waiting room, she supposed. She had to save him. . . .

So he could kill other young men.

That thought plagued her all the time she was working over him. As she had thought, the wound, while serious, looked somewhat worse than it actually was. With any luck, he would live.

But for how long? Would he be gunned down in an ambush before this wound was even fully healed? Would he kill the ones who had hurt him, only to be killed in turn? How many more would die because, on this day, this particular young man was going to live?

Phyllis told herself sternly not to dwell on those questions. No one could predict the future. All she could do was deal with the present.

He regained consciousness while she was bandaging the wound. After a few minutes, he felt strong enough to help her lift him onto the battered old sofa. When he was stretched out and resting, he looked up at her and said, "*Gracias.* I knew if I could . . . get here . . . you would help me. Enrique told me . . . about the gringa *curandera.*''

"You know Enrique?'' Phyllis asked in surprise. "Enrique Guzman?''

"*Sí. Mi hermano. . . .*'' His eyes closed, but he was sleeping this time, instead of unconscious.

He must not have meant that in a literal sense, thought Phyllis. She knew Enrique Guzman, knew that he did not have any brothers, only sisters. Had this young man meant that Enrique was a member of the same gang? That was a troubling thought. Phyllis had been convinced that Enrique was no longer involved with any of the gangs, now that he had become involved in an antidrug program that also taught the martial arts. Enrique had told her as much, and she believed him.

She was going to have to have a talk with Enrique, she decided, and perhaps with the man who helped run the antidrug program.

He was a Texas Ranger named Cordell Walker.

FOUR

C. D. Parker uncapped the bottle of beer, shoved it across the hardwood bar that was polished to a high gleam, and said with a snort of contempt, "El Diablo? What the hell kind o' name is El Diablo? Sounds like somethin' out of a funny-book."

Walker sipped from the bottle, then said, "It's serious, C. D."

"Yeah, from the looks of things, he's the head of the operation that was bringing drugs into that warehouse we busted a couple of weeks ago," added Trivette, who was sitting beside Walker at the bar. "But that's all we've been able to find out about him. And let me tell you, we've been beating the bushes for him, too."

C. D. grunted. "Yeah, I knew you boys hadn't been in here much lately. Figured you were pullin' some long hours on some case. I remember doin' the same thing when I was a mite younger."

"Yeah, I imagine you did," said Walker.

C. D. was a retired Texas Ranger—not that there really was such a thing—and one of Walker's best friends. He ran this honkytonk bar known, appropriately enough, as

31

C. D.'s Place, but he was always ready to help out Walker in time of need.

"Yes, sir, we'd stay with it until we had everything run to the ground," C. D. went on. "Lots of times, pure-dee persistence was what broke a case wide open."

"Well, if persistence is what it takes, we ought to have El Diablo wrapped up any day now," said Trivette.

Someone fed coins into the jukebox in the corner, and a Western swing tune started playing. Walker was glad he and Trivette had taken a few minutes off to come over here to C. D.'s. These moments of relaxation were valuable, he was convinced of that. They let a man refresh his mind, maybe look at all the angles of a difficult case from a little different perspective. . . .

"There you are," a woman's voice said from behind him.

Walker swiveled on the bar stool and smiled at the beautiful blonde in a charcoal gray jacket and skirt. Assistant District Attorney Alex Cahill had the prettiest blue eyes Walker had ever seen, but right now her expression was solemn and those blue eyes were bright with excitement.

"I thought I'd find you here," Alex went on. "Agent Davis gave me a call when he couldn't locate you."

"Davis has something?" asked Walker.

Alex nodded. "A possible line on El Diablo." She handed Walker a piece of paper. "He said he'd meet you at this address."

Walker reached for his hat, which was sitting on the bar next to the forgotten bottle of beer. "Thanks, Alex. Come on, Trivette."

"You know," Alex said, "I'm not your answering service, Walker."

"I know," Walker replied with a grin. "I couldn't do this to an answering service."

He kissed Alex, taking her by surprise, then headed for the door of the bar. Trivette followed, grinning as well.

Alex watched them go, then said, "That's an exasperating man."

C. D. wiped the bar with a rag. "You mean Cordell? Yeah, he's got his own way o' doin' things, that's for sure. But it usually works."

Alex had to nod and smile a little herself. "Yes, it usually does."

Walker wheeled his pickup into the parking lot of a convenience store. Trivette said, "There's Davis."

The DEA agent got out of his car and came over to Walker's pickup. He stood beside the open window on the driver's side and said, "I see you got my message."

"You've found out something about El Diablo?" asked Walker.

Davis looked terrible. His features were even more drawn than usual. He took off his glasses and rubbed at his eyes. "Yeah," he said as he settled the glasses back on his nose. "Got a tip from a source of mine that a house down the block is being used for cutting the stuff El Diablo's shipping into Dallas."

"This house replaced the warehouse we busted?" Walker said.

Davis nodded. "That's the idea. I've set up a raid. We'll be hitting the place in a few minutes."

Walker and Trivette exchanged a glance. "This is the first we've heard about it," Walker pointed out to Davis.

The DEA agent shrugged. "I didn't know I had to clear everything with you, Walker."

"You don't, but we've been working together on this, Davis—"

"Maybe I wanted to move a little faster," Davis cut in. "I haven't been sleeping much since Matt was killed. He was a good kid, would've made a good agent—if he'd had the chance. If those bastards hadn't killed him."

"Look, Davis," Trivette began, "you can't take these things personally. You didn't let Brennan down—"

"The hell I didn't!" Davis stuck his hands in his pockets. "The raid's going down in five minutes. Are you in or not?"

Walker sighed, then nodded. "We're in."

The house was a nondescript brick structure in a middle-class neighborhood, one of thousands of similar houses in this residential area, which was quiet and peaceful in the middle of a weekday. Oak trees dotted the front yard, and in a few weeks, flowers would be blooming in the bed that ran across the front of the house. A couple of blocks down the street, a church and a school sat across from each other, and there was a convenience store on a nearby corner. Nothing out of the ordinary marked the neighborhood or this particular house where a man pulled a late-model car into the driveway. He killed the engine, got out, and walked to the front door of the house as if he belonged here. When he rang the bell, the door was opened almost immediately.

"Good," said El Diablo to the Anglo man who had opened the door. "You were expecting me." He swung the storm door aside and stepped into the house. The other man backed off. El Diablo shut the door behind him.

All the curtains were tightly pulled over the windows. In just about every room of the house, the work of cutting heroin with baby powder and laxative went on. A low-pitched chattering came from the men and women who were doing the cutting. Several of them cast nervous glances toward the man who had just come in.

El Diablo looked around, nodded with approval. This house had been rented less than a week earlier, after the first shipments had reached Dallas following the raid on the warehouse. What was coming in now was just a trickle compared to the earlier traffic, but that would change soon enough.

"Any problems?" El Diablo asked.

The man who had let him in shook his head. "Everything's running smoothly. The man who rented this place for us has been paid off, and he's out of the picture. The neighborhood's quiet. Nearly everybody works, so there's not many people around during the day to get nosy.''

El Diablo nodded. "Good, good. No one has noticed the comings and goings?''

"Nope. If anybody's curious, I guess they just think the missus and I have a lot of friends.''

At that comment, a woman sitting at one of the tables with several bags of heroin in front of her looked up and smiled.

"Ah, if you don't mind my asking,'' the man went on, "why are you here? There haven't been any problems with our work, have there?''

"Not at all,'' El Diablo assured him. "I just wanted to look things over for myself. You see, in a short time, the volume of merchandise coming into Dallas is going to increase, and I have to make sure you can handle it.''

"We can handle it,'' the man declared. He grinned. "So, the boys are about to get back into business in a big way, huh?''

El Diablo frowned. Only a few of the higher-level people knew that the Vega Garcias were involved in this operation, and he did not want this loudmouth mentioning any names that should not be mentioned. "That is none of your business,'' snapped El Diablo.

"Hey, no offense. I know you're in charge of the operation.''

El Diablo forced himself to relax. This fool might prove to be a liability in the long run, but right now he was not worth worrying about. And even though he was talking to a nobody, El Diablo could not resist a moment of boastfulness. "And it is an operation the likes of which no one has ever seen before.''

"That good, huh?''

El Diablo was debating whether or not to elaborate and had just about decided not to reveal any more to this Anglo, when the decision was taken out of his hands. A man hurried into the room and said in a loud, frightened voice, "Hey, I think there's cops out there!"

Davis brought his car to a halt opposite the house he had pointed out to Walker and Trivette. Walker stopped the pickup right behind him. From each end of the block, Dallas police cars were entering the street, running with their lights flashing but no sirens.

Already wearing his DEA windbreaker, Davis bolted out of the car with his service revolver drawn. Walker and Trivette hurriedly got out of the pickup and joined him. The police cars screeched to the curb, followed by an unmarked van that belonged to the narcotics detail. Black-jacketed officers from that detail sprang out of the van and raced toward the house with the uniformed officers.

"I'll take the back!" Davis called to Walker and Trivette. He ran along the narrow space between the wall of the house and the hedge that marked the property next door.

"If they have a lookout, they know we're coming," said Trivette as he and Walker drew their guns and started to follow Davis.

Suddenly, one of the front windows in the house exploded outward under a burst of gunfire. Walker and Trivette flung themselves off their feet, diving for cover as high-powered slugs chewed up the grass of the front lawn.

Walker rolled behind an oak tree while Trivette scrambled behind some garbage cans. The cans weren't going to be much protection against such potent firepower, but they were the closest cover available. The trunk of the tree behind which Walker crouched was too narrow to conceal all of his body. It was better than nothing, though. He snapped a couple of shots at the broken window, hoping to drive the gunner back. The fire from the house ceased momentarily.

"I'd say they know we're here," Walker called dryly to his fellow Ranger.

Trivette raised up quickly and fired twice at the window.

36

He ducked back down and said, "Davis is back there by himself!"

The racket of automatic weapons fire filled the afternoon air again. Walker turned sideways, making himself as small a target as possible behind the tree trunk as slugs smacked into the wood. "I know he is," he said to Trivette during the next lull, "but there's not much we can do about it now!"

Both of the Rangers were pinned down, good and proper.

El Diablo moved quickly through the house, leaving the sounds of battle behind him. His car was still parked in the driveway, but he was going to have to abandon it. It was a rental, anyway, he told himself philosophically. And any of his fingerprints they might find in it would not be on file in any computer database in the world. He had made certain of that by wearing flesh-colored latex gloves, complete with false fingerprints, that were indistinguishable from his real skin unless one looked closely.

Let these fools fight it out with the gringo police, he thought. Their resistance was serving as a delaying tactic that would give him a chance to get away. He ran through a small kitchen and out the back door of the house.

At that moment, a thin man in a black windbreaker came charging around the rear corner of the house. "Federal agent!" he yelled as he jerked the barrel of a pistol toward El Diablo. "Hold it right there!"

El Diablo let his instincts take over. He went down, diving forward into a rolling somersault. The gringo lawman fired, but the bullet did not come anywhere close to its target.

As he came back up into a crouch, El Diablo lifted the gun he had snatched from under his jacket and fired twice. Both slugs punched into the chest of the federal agent, rocking him backward. The man tried to lift his weapon for another shot, but his mortally wounded body betrayed him.

His knees folded up, and he crumpled to the ground, blood spreading wetly and thickly over his chest.

The sounds of gunfire from the front of the house intensified. El Diablo straightened and ran across the backyard toward a hedge that bordered an alley. He bulled his way through a narrow opening in the growth, paused briefly to weigh his options, then pelted down the alley to the right, toward a cross street. He turned before he reached it, though, cutting through another backyard.

In less than five minutes, he was three blocks away from the house where the shoot-out was taking place, driving off in a car he had hotwired and stolen from its parking place along the curb. His hands clasped the wheel tightly.

He waited until he was well away from the neighborhood before he gave in to his rage and began to curse. . . .

More glass shattered as tear gas grenades were fired through the windows of the house by members of the DPD tactical squad. That was what Walker and Trivette had been waiting for. As clouds of the choking, stinging stuff began to fill the house, the two Rangers left their cover and sprinted along the side of the building toward the backyard.

Walker was slightly in the lead. He stopped short as he saw Davis's body sprawled on the grass. Green shoots were beginning to poke through the brown, winter-dried lawn, but now some of them were stained with red.

Walker's gaze traveled quickly around the yard. No sign of whoever had shot Davis. Grim-faced, Trivette dropped to one knee beside the DEA agent and used his free hand to check for a pulse. After a moment, Trivette said, "He's dead, Walker."

Quickly but cautiously, Walker moved toward the rear hedge. He saw where someone had pushed through the growth into the alley behind the house. Walker followed suit, gun held ready for instant use. He grimaced in disappointment as he looked up and down the alley. No one was in sight.

The shooting had died away. Walker figured that the tear gas must have done its job. He pushed back through the hedge and met Trivette and several of the police officers.

"Get a search going along this alley and all around the neighboring streets," Walker said briskly to the officers. "Whoever shot Agent Davis may still be around here somewhere."

The cops hustled to carry out the Ranger's orders, leaving Walker and Trivette to stand beside Davis's body with bleak expressions.

"He should have waited," said Trivette. "He rushed things too much."

"He was anxious to find the man who was responsible for the death of his partner."

"El Diablo. Do you think he was here, Walker?"

"Doubtful," Walker said. "But you never know." He turned toward the house. "Did everyone inside surrender?"

Trivette nodded. "The tear gas did the trick. A couple of the men tried to come out shooting, but the tac squad was able to wound them and take them into custody without killing anybody."

Walker settled his pistol back into the clip holster on his belt. "Come on. I want to talk to them."

He strode purposefully around to the front of the house, where handcuffed prisoners were being loaded into a police van that had pulled up to the curb. Walker motioned for the officers to wait a minute, then faced one of the prisoners, a frightened-looking man in a black T-shirt and jeans. There was a smear of blood on his face from a cut that had probably been inflicted by flying glass.

"What do you know about El Diablo?" Walker demanded.

Surprise flickered for an instant in the man's eyes, but then he shook his head stubbornly. "El Diablo?" he repeated. "Never heard of him."

Walker took a shot in the dark. "He didn't happen to be here today, did he?"

"I don't know anything about somebody named El Diablo," the man insisted.

One of the other prisoners in the back of the van, a woman with lank, fair hair, suddenly said, "Damn it, Jerry, don't you know how much trouble we're in? If you won't tell him, I will!"

The man's head swiveled toward her. "Shut up!" he said raggedly. "Don't you know what's good for you?"

"I think she does," said Walker. He looked at the woman and went on, "Tell me about El Diablo."

She swallowed hard, then said, "He was here, just like you thought, Ranger. I don't know how you knew about it, but he was here."

Walker exchanged a glance with Trivette, but neither of them said anything. When good luck fell into your lap, it was best just to keep quiet and accept it.

"He said we were doing a good job," the woman babbled on, ignoring the hostile glares the other prisoners were giving her. "He was glad, because there's a big shipment coming in soon."

Walker stiffened. "How big?"

"He didn't say. But I got the feeling it was going to be a lot."

"Can you describe El Diablo?"

The woman nodded eagerly. "He's Hispanic, about six feet tall, and real strong-looking. He was wearing a suit."

"No other marks or distinguishing characteristics?"

The woman frowned in thought, then shook her head regretfully. "Not that I can think of."

"All right," said Walker. To one of the officers, he added, "You'd better isolate her when you get them all booked. The rest of them won't like the fact that she talked."

"Got you, Ranger," the cop said with a nod.

The rest of the prisoners were herded into the van, then the doors were closed. Walker and Trivette stepped back and watched the vehicle pull away.

"So El Diablo *was* here," said Trivette. "Good guess, Walker."

"As C. D. would say, even a blind pig finds an acorn every now and then."

"That wasn't much of a description to go on, though. It could fit thousands of men in this area."

Walker nodded. "We'll get him anyway." He turned to watch as a gurney carrying a figure zipped up in a body bag was wheeled from the backyard by a team of paramedics. Walker's face was grim as he went on, "We'll finish the job—and we'll finish it right."

FIVE

Phyllis Harrison knocked on the door of the apartment. This apartment complex was rather run-down, with peeling paint on the walls of the buildings and jagged cracks running through the concrete walks. The swimming pool in the center of the courtyard was half full of slimy green water that was mostly concealed by the dead leaves floating on its surface.

The door was opened by a short, slender young man who looked surprised to see Phyllis. "Doctor!" he exclaimed. "What are you doing here?"

"I came to see you, Enrique," Phyllis said. "I have some questions, and I want answers."

Someone called a question in Spanish, and Enrique turned his head to reply briefly. Then he stepped out of the apartment and pulled the door shut behind him. "My sister, she don't have to know about this trouble," he said.

"How do you know it's trouble?" asked Phyllis.

He shrugged. "Why else would you come to see me?"

"Because I'm worried about you." Phyllis's stern expression softened a little. "You were the first one to listen to reason, Enrique. You managed to quit the gangs without anyone coming after you."

Again, his narrow shoulders rose and fell in a shrug. "What you said to me made sense. Sooner or later, if I kept runnin' with the gangs, I was gonna get hurt."

"But now you're back with them."

"How'd you know that?" The question was surprised out of him.

"I nearly had a shoot-out at the clinic yesterday afternoon. A young man who was wounded showed up on my doorstep, and the ones who had shot him were right behind him."

"Oh, man, Doctor Phyllis, I'm sorry! I told the others they could trust you if they ever needed help, but I warned 'em not to take their trouble there to the clinic."

"Did you honestly expect gang members to heed that warning?"

Resentment flared in his dark eyes. "You don't turn away no gang members when they come to you for help."

"That's true," she admitted. "I don't. But I still don't like what happens when you join a gang."

"Don't seem too picky about it when we're givin' *you* a hand, bringin' that stuff in and all—"

Phyllis shook her head. "I told you," she said sharply, "that's just between the two of us."

"Can't be that way. I got to have contacts who can help me get it."

Phyllis took a deep breath. She shouldn't have come here. For one thing, Enrique had a point. She herself made use of the gangs when they could help her get what she needed. The pills were smuggled in from across the border, brought here to Dallas, then delivered to her by Enrique. She had purposely never asked too many questions about the process; if she didn't know all the details, it didn't seem as much like she was breaking the law.

She was a hypocrite, she told herself. So be it. The cause was a good one.

"All right," she said. "I'll leave you alone. I just hope you know what you're doing." She hesitated, then added,

"Does Ranger Walker know about any of this?"

Enrique snorted. "You think I'd tell Walker about our arrangement?"

"Are you still involved with his program?"

With a somewhat nervous shifting of his feet, Enrique shook his head. "Had to give it up."

"The other gang members made you give it up, you mean."

His pride kicked in. "Nobody *makes* me do nothin' I don't want to!"

"I hope that's true, Enrique," Phyllis said softly. "I certainly hope that's true."

Phyllis drove back to the clinic, sighing heavily several times as she did so. Her visit to Enrique had done no good at all. If anything, she had probably made the situation worse and driven the young man even more deeply into the gang he had rejoined. She had been totally unfair, telling him not to associate with such people when she herself was making use of them.

But she had to have those pills. She simply had to.

When she arrived at the clinic, she found two people waiting patiently on the front porch. She recognized Silvia Rodriguez and her son Manuel. The little boy was eight years old, and cute as he could be. He was sitting on the steps next to his mother, but he hopped up and greeted Phyllis with a big smile.

"*Hola,* Doctor Phyllis," he said.

"Hello, Manuel," she replied. "Why aren't you in school?"

"Manuel is sick," Silvia said. She pointed to her son's left ear. "His ear hurts."

Phyllis nodded. "Well, let's go inside and take a look at that ear, shall we?"

She unlocked the door and let the young woman and the little boy inside. A quick examination confirmed what Phyllis expected: Manuel had a middle-ear infection. His temperature was 101 degrees, and there were bright red streaks running through the walls of the ear canal. He was sniffling a little, too, aftereffects of the cold that had developed into an infection.

"We can take care of this just fine," Phyllis assured Silvia and Manuel. "Some antibiotics will get rid of the infection."

Silvia shook her head sadly. "No money for pills."

"You can afford these," said Phyllis. "I promise." She unlocked a drawer in the cabinet that sat against one wall of the examination room.

This could get her in a lot of trouble with the law, she thought as she counted out twenty capsules from a large bottle, emptying it, and placed them in an envelope with ten capsules she took from a fresh bottle. She had no license to practice medicine, certainly no legal right to dispense medication like this. But the people in this neighborhood didn't care about that. All that mattered to them was that she would help them without worrying about whether or not they could pay her. That meant more than any questionable legalities.

She closed the flap of the envelope and handed it to Silvia. "Give him one of these capsules three times a day. Do you understand?"

Silvia bobbed her head. "One pill, three times each day," she repeated.

"That's right."

"How . . . how much?"

Phyllis smiled. "Whatever you can afford, just like all the other times."

In this case, it was a crumpled five-dollar bill that Silvia took from the pocket of her dress. Phyllis hated to take even that much, but she did. All the money went for rent and upkeep on the building, along with more medicine. The money Keith had left her financed most of the clinic's work, but that money would run out eventually. By letting the patients pay a little as they could, Phyllis hoped to make things last as long as possible.

She ruffled Manuel's thick black hair. "You're going to feel better really soon," she told him. "But if you're not better by tomorrow, you come back and see me again, all right?"

"Can I come see you even if I feel better?"

"Sure," she said with a grin. "I'm always happy to see you, Manuel."

Silvia thanked her again, then left with the boy and the antibiotics. Phyllis watched them and felt good about what she was accomplishing here. True, a simple ear infection was only very rarely a serious illness. Manuel might have been all right without any medical attention. But there was always the chance that the condition could have turned into something bad and cost the boy his hearing—or worse.

Now if Phyllis could just stop worrying about Enrique. . . .

Though the young man was never far from her thoughts, Phyllis was too busy the next day to brood too much about the situation. She was wrapping up an ugly cut on the hand of a man who worked in a nearby auto body shop when the front door suddenly slammed open. The door between the examination room and the waiting room was open, so Phyllis had no trouble hearing the panic-stricken voice calling, "Doctor! Doctor!"

Phyllis hurried into the other room and found Silvia Rodriguez standing there with Manuel cradled in her arms. The little boy's arms and legs hung limply down, and his head was thrown back. For one horrible moment, Phyllis thought he was dead. Then she saw the shallow rise and fall of his chest and heard the quick, raspy breathing.

"Oh, my God!" she exclaimed. "What happened?"

"Manuel is sick! I give him the pills, and he seem to be better las' night, then today I give him another pill, and he get so sick!"

The body shop worker, a burly black man, said, "Let me help, Doc." He stepped past Phyllis and took Manuel from Silvia.

"Put him on the table in the exam room," said Phyllis. When the man had gently placed Manuel on the table, Phyllis leaned over him and rested her stethoscope against his chest. His heart was racing madly. His face was cold and clammy, and even though he was unconscious, he was shaking. Phyllis rolled back first one eyelid, then the other, and studied the pupils, which had shrunk almost to pinpoints.

"What is wrong, Doctor? What is wrong with him?" Silvia asked frantically.

Phyllis swallowed hard. "You say this started after you gave him one of the antibiotic capsules?"

"*Sí, sí,*" Silvia replied, nodding. Tears rolled down her cheeks. "My little boy, he will be all right?"

The body shop worker had stepped back, but now he said with a frown, "That kid looks like he's in pretty bad shape, Doc. You want me to call an ambulance?"

Phyllis took a deep breath and then nodded. Manuel's life was at stake. She couldn't waste time worrying about herself or anything else.

"Yes, we have to get him to a hospital right away," she said.

Silvia caught hold of Phyllis's arm. "My boy, my boy, what is wrong with him?"

"I think . . . dear God . . . he looks like he's overdosed on heroin."

Phyllis and Silvia waited tensely in the hallway outside the swinging double doors that marked the entrance to the emergency room at Parkland Hospital. Manuel had been wheeled through those doors on a gurney nearly forty-five minutes earlier, still unconscious and suffering mild convulsions. The fact that the convulsions hadn't been any worse than they were gave Phyllis a slight reason for hope that the boy would be all right.

She prayed that would be the case. For Manuel's sake—and for her own.

Not that her situation really mattered now, she reminded herself. She had a feeling that she was already in such deep trouble that she would never see the end of it. None of that was important, though, when it was stacked up against the life of a young boy.

"M-Manuel will be all r-right?" Silvia asked tearfully for what must have been the twentieth time since her son had been taken into the ER.

"I'm sure he will be," said Phyllis, but the lie sounded hollow even to her own ears. She wasn't sure of anything anymore.

Suddenly the emergency room doors swung open, and a tired-looking woman in a white coat stepped through. She looked around, caught sight of Phyllis and Silvia, and came toward them. There had been a time, thought Phyllis, when she had known most of the staff at every hospital in town, but that was in the past. This doctor was a stranger to her.

"Mrs. Rodriguez?" the doctor asked Silvia.

"*Sí, sí.*" Silvia's head bobbed up and down quickly, revealing her desperate need to hear whatever news the doctor had to give her.

"I'm Doctor Sommersby. We've stabilized your son Manuel, but he's still in critical condition. He suffered an overdose of heroin."

"How much?" Phyllis asked.

Dr. Sommersby gave her a curious frown. "Who are you?"

"Phyllis Harrison. I'm a . . . a friend of the family." *And the one who nearly murdered that poor child,* she thought. *The one who may yet wind up responsible for his death.*

"Well, he's a small boy," said Dr. Sommersby. "Does he have any history of drug use?"

"No, no!" Silvia shook her head emphatically. "He is only a child!"

The doctor shrugged. "These days, you never know. At any rate, given his age and size and medical history, I'd say . . . no more than two hundred milligrams."

That was just about the answer Phyllis had been expecting. She fought back a moan of dismay.

"One odd thing, though," Dr. Sommersby went on, "there were no needle marks anywhere that I could find on Manuel. I'm wondering how he ingested the drug."

Silvia just looked baffled. "I . . . I do not know. Manuel was with me all day, and he had no medicine except the pills for his ear."

"Pills for his ear?" The doctor seized on that immediately. "Prescription medication?"

"I . . . I do not know what you mean. . . ."

Phyllis was staring down at the tile on the floor of the hospital corridor. She had stood just about all of this she could stand. It was time for the truth.

She looked up and said, "I gave him the pills."

"You?"

Silvia said, trying to be helpful, "Doctor Phyllis, she give Manuel the pills because his ear hurts."

"You're a doctor?" asked Sommersby.

"An R.N. . . . retired. And the pills were supposed to be antibiotics," Phyllis said.

The doctor looked confused, but she said, "I'm afraid I'm going to have to call the police."

"Yes, I know," Phyllis said with a nod. "That's exactly what you have to do."

SIX

"They're singing like canaries," said Trivette, "but the trouble is, they only know one song."

"El Diablo," said Walker.

They were sitting in their office in the courthouse. Trivette had just gotten off the phone with a contact in the local office of the Drug Enforcement Agency. He nodded and said, "That's right. They all heard their boss refer to the man who came there not long before the raid as El Diablo, but they don't really know anything about him except that he seemed to be in charge of the whole operation. *And* he was bragging about how a big shipment of the stuff was coming up from Mexico."

"How big?"

"Bigger than ever before."

Walker leaned back in his chair and frowned. He remembered how much heroin had been confiscated at the warehouse a couple of weeks earlier, as well as in other raids in recent months. If a shipment was coming in that would dwarf those, then it would be huge indeed.

"We've got to get a line on that somehow," Walker said. "Stop it before it gets into the country, if at all possible."

Trivette grunted. "The border between Texas and Mexico is awfully long, Walker. How are we going to cover all of it?"

"We're not. Not without some help, anyway."

Before Trivette could ask what Walker meant by that, the phone on Walker's desk rang. He scooped it up. "Walker."

Alex Cahill's voice sounded in his ear. "There's a prisoner at the jail asking for you, Walker. Do you know a woman named Phyllis Harrison?"

Walker cast his memory back over the hundreds of friends and acquaintances—as well as enemies—he had made in his life. The woman's name was familiar, but he couldn't place her at first. Then, like a light being turned on, the proper information popped out of Walker's brain.

"Phyllis Harrison," he said. "The widow of Dr. Keith Harrison?"

"I wouldn't know about that," said Alex. "All I know is that she's been arrested, and she wants to see you. That information was passed along to our office along with the report on the arrest."

"Arrested?" Walker repeated in surprise. Trivette looked puzzled, so Walker held up a hand and signaled for him to hang on for a minute. "Why in the world would a woman like Phyllis Harrison be arrested?"

"Possession and distribution of illegal drugs, specifically heroin."

Walker sat forward sharply. "What!"

"That's not all, Walker. She's charged with attempted murder, too—and that charge will be upped to murder if a little boy who's in the hospital right now doesn't pull through."

"I'm on my way, Alex. I'll stop by your office after I've talked to Phyllis." Walker hung up the phone and reached for his hat.

"What's going on?" Trivette asked as he picked up his own hat and prepared to follow Walker.

"Something that doesn't make any sense at all," Walker said.

It had been a couple of years since Walker had seen Phyllis Harrison, but he recognized her immediately as he stepped into the interrogation room at the county lockup. Her hair had a little more gray in it, and there were a few more lines on her face, but basically she was still the same attractive, middle-aged woman Walker remembered from their last meeting. Her husband had still been alive at that time, Walker recalled. The occasion had been a dinner honoring some of Dallas's prominent citizens, among them Dr. Keith Harrison. Walker had been there to introduce one of the other dignitaries, and during the course of the evening he had spoken to both Dr. Harrison and Mrs. Harrison.

There had been one more change in her since he had seen her last, Walker realized as she lifted her head and looked at him, but he didn't know how recent the change was.

Her eyes were haunted now.

"Ranger Walker," she said, her voice low, husky, and controlled, just the way he remembered it. "Thank you for coming. Did they tell you why I'm here?"

"They told me," said Walker.

"Then I'm a little surprised you came. It's not often that a Ranger answers a plea for help from someone accused of drug trafficking and attempted murder."

"Are you guilty?" Walker asked bluntly as he placed his hat on the scarred wooden table that was the main item of furniture in the room.

Phyllis Harrison looked down at the table and didn't answer.

Walker hesitated. Phyllis's silence implied that she *was* guilty . . . or she at least thought she was. But the instincts Walker had developed over years as a lawman told him that there was more to this story than was apparent.

"I can't help you if you don't talk to me," he said quietly.

Phyllis took a deep breath. A shudder ran through her. "I gave him the pills," she said.

"The little boy?"

Phyllis's chin went up and down in a nod. "Yes. They were supposed to be antibiotics, for his ear."

Walker pulled back a chair and sat down opposite Phyllis. He glanced toward the large mirror on one side of the room. Trivette was on the other side of that one-way glass, he knew, along with a couple of detectives from the Dallas police force.

Clasping his hands together in front of him, Walker leaned forward slightly. "You've been told your rights?" he asked. Until he knew exactly what was going on, he was going to play this by the book.

Phyllis nodded again. "Yes, they read me my rights. I called my lawyer . . . our lawyer, the one who handled everything for Keith and me . . . and he's advised me not to say anything."

"Maybe you'd better follow your attorney's advice," Walker suggested.

Adamantly, Phyllis shook her head. "No, I want to tell the truth. But I want to tell *you*, Ranger Walker, because Keith always said you were a good man. He knew you enjoyed working with children, and so did Keith."

It was Walker's turn to nod. "I remember," he said. "Dr. Harrison was always volunteering his time and medical skills to help kids who didn't have anywhere else to turn."

"And I've tried to follow in that tradition."

Walker curbed the impatience he felt. He sensed a certain brittleness about Phyllis, and he knew that if she was rushed, she might simply shatter into a million pieces emotionally. "Tell me about the little boy," Walker said.

"His name is Manuel . . . Manuel Rodriguez. He came

to me . . . that is, his mother brought him to me . . . because he had an earache.''

"I didn't realize you were a doctor, too, Mrs. Harrison."

"I . . . I'm not. But I opened a clinic, anyway. Unofficially, you understand. I was able to put the word out that I would try to help anyone who needed it, whether they could pay or not."

"There are already free and low-cost clinics for that," Walker pointed out.

"Yes, and I probably should have volunteered at one of them. I can see that now. But at the time, I thought I would be doing some good for the community . . . that I would be carrying on with the work that Keith started."

Her husband's death must have hit her pretty hard, thought Walker. It was conceivable that in her grief she had thought she was doing the right thing.

"So the boy's mother brought him to you . . ."

"Yes, and I diagnosed an ear infection. I gave him some antibiotics to clear it up."

"But if you're not a doctor, you couldn't write a prescription for him—"

"I mean it literally, Ranger Walker, when I say I gave him the antibiotics," Phyllis said. "I had the pills in my office."

"And where did you get them?"

"Mexico."

That simple, one-word answer was enough to send Walker's mind leaping ahead. He said, "It's illegal to bring drugs like that across the border without a prescription."

"I know, but they're a fraction of the price in Mexico that they are here. People walk across the international bridges in El Paso and Laredo and buy amoxicillin all the time, even if they don't have a prescription for it."

"They risk being sent to jail if they bring it back across the river without one," Walker pointed out.

"People do it anyway. That's why Mexican pharmaceuticals are so easy to obtain along the border. That's why I was able to buy them in large quantities and have them brought up here so I could use them in my clinic."

"Be careful," warned Walker. "You're admitting to possession of illegally obtained drugs and possibly even being an accessory to drug smuggling."

"That's what I am!" Phyllis said. "And if Manuel dies, I'll be a murderer, too!" Her head dropped forward as she covered her face with her hands. Sobs shook her slender body.

Walker gave her a few moments to get some of the pent-up emotions out, then, as Phyllis dried her face with a tissue she took from the pocket of the jail coveralls she was wearing, he put the theory he had formed earlier into words.

"The heroin Manuel overdosed on . . . it was in one of the antibiotic capsules, wasn't it?"

Phyllis nodded shakily. "It had to be. I . . . I don't know if there was only one like that in the capsules I gave him. Some of them had to be all right, because his mother gave him one the night before that didn't hurt him. The pills I gave him came from two different bottles. I emptied one bottle and opened a new one. Since nobody else has gotten sick, it must have come from the new bottle."

Walker stood up, went behind the chair where he had been sitting, and rested his hands on the back of it. The wheels of his brain were spinning so furiously that he could no longer sit still. "It makes sense," he said. "Open the capsules, empty out the antibiotics, and replace them with heroin. They would probably do that with one box in each case of antibiotics, then mark it so they could tell it apart from all the others. Once the drugs are on this side of the border, someone else in the pipeline retrieves the box that's been tampered with . . . but in the meantime, all the packaging and the capsules themselves look like standard antibiotics. And while those could be illegal, too, the authorities aren't going to be nearly as worried about stopping them from getting across the border."

"I . . . I suppose you could be right. . . ."

Walker reached over and picked up his hat. "You shouldn't have gotten mixed up with contraband pharmaceuticals, Mrs. Harrison, but I don't think you meant for any harm to come to that little boy."

"I didn't! I swear that, Ranger."

"I believe you," Walker said with a nod. "Someone slipped up, and some of the pills that had been tampered with got mixed in with the real antibiotics." He clapped the black Stetson on his head. "What I have to do is find out who did the tampering."

Phyllis's fingers knotted together. "I . . . I'm thankful you know I didn't hurt Manuel intentionally."

"I know that," said Walker, "but what you have to do now is tell me how you got those capsules up here from the border."

"I don't know if I should . . . ," Phyllis said miserably.

"Mrs. Harrison." Walker's voice was low, intense. "You're not the only one using those Mexican antibiotics. Like you said, people walk across to the border towns and buy them all the time. If we're going to stop what happened to Manuel from happening to anybody else, we have to get on the trail of the people who are really responsible."

She nodded slowly. "I know. And I did have help. A young man . . ." She looked up at Walker. "You know him. His name is Enrique Guzman."

SEVEN

Trivette was waiting when Walker left the interrogation room. "Do you believe her story?" he asked solemnly.

Walker nodded and said, "I do. Mrs. Harrison was too upset about the little boy to lie."

One of the Dallas police detectives with Trivette said to Walker, "We've already charged her with possession and attempted murder. When we searched that so-called clinic of hers, we came up with a dozen more capsules of heroin."

"You heard her explain how that happened," said Walker.

The detective shrugged. "Even if she was telling the truth, she still had the drugs in her possession. And that kid's still in the hospital." The man gave a harsh laugh, then added, "I can't believe you're sticking up for this woman, Walker. I thought you were so gung-ho about cracking down on drug dealers."

"I wouldn't call Mrs. Harrison a drug dealer," Walker said. "Come on, Trivette."

"Where are we going?" asked Trivette.

"To see Alex."

• • •

Alex laid the open file folder on her desk and said, "Detective Potter is right about one thing, Walker: Mrs. Harrison *did* have the heroin in her possession. We'll have to present that charge to the grand jury."

"You'll never make an attempted murder charge stick," said Walker. He had one hip perched on a corner of the desk.

Alex nodded. "You're right. I've already spoken to the district attorney about that, and the charge is going to be lowered to involuntary manslaughter . . . if the child doesn't survive."

"I hope he makes it," said Trivette, who was sitting in front of the desk. "For his sake, and for Mrs. Harrison's."

"That leaves us with the most important question," said Walker. "How did the heroin get in those antibiotic capsules?"

"It had to have happened on the other side of the border," Trivette theorized. "Once the capsules were on this side of the Rio Grande, there wouldn't be any point in making the substitution."

"Could you smuggle enough heroin that way to make it worthwhile?" asked Alex.

"As a stop-gap measure, maybe," replied Walker. "Remember, we disrupted the regular pipeline a couple of weeks ago with that raid on the warehouse."

Trivette leaned forward. "So to keep a little cash flowing, the people responsible for the heroin traffic fall back on using the antibiotic gimmick until they have everything in place to launch a bigger operation."

"That's the way it looks to me," Walker said with a nod.

"Then the one behind the tampering with the capsules could have been . . ."

"El Diablo," Walker concluded.

Alex looked up at him. "You really think this mysterious El Diablo exists?"

"He exists, all right. He's the one who killed Davis when we raided that house the other day."

"There's no proof he had anything to do with these tampered capsules, though," Trivette pointed out.

Walker straightened. "That's why we're going to see Enrique Guzman. I hope he has some answers about where exactly the capsules came from."

"Who is this Guzman character, anyway?" asked Trivette.

Walker's jaw tightened grimly as he settled his hat on his head. "Someone I thought better of."

Even in the middle of the day, there were quite a few people around this run-down apartment complex on the edge of the barrio. The North Texas economy might be booming, and unemployment might be low overall, but that didn't always extend into all sections of the community. Several young men were lounging on the steps that led up to the second floor of the complex. They watched Walker and Trivette with narrowed eyes and suspicious expressions as the two Rangers walked past, bound for the apartment where Enrique Guzman lived with his sister and mother.

"I really thought Enrique had turned things around for himself," Walker said. "He came to the dojo and worked out regularly for a while, and he said he was out of the gang he'd been running with."

"What about drugs?" asked Trivette.

"He claimed he never used them, and I believed him." Walker shook his head. "Now I don't know what to believe."

Behind the Rangers, the young men who had been sitting on the steps got up and sauntered after them. Walker knew they were there, but he wasn't going to do anything about it—yet.

"I checked with the other instructors at the dojo," Walker went on, "and they said Enrique hasn't been working out for several weeks now."

"His old gang probably lured him back in."

"We're about to find out," Walker said as he and Trivette stopped in front of one of the ground-floor apartments. Walker raised his hand to knock.

Before he could, the door opened. The young woman who had opened it stopped short as she was about to step outside. "Oh!" she exclaimed. "I didn't know anyone was—Who are you?"

"Texas Rangers," Walker said. "I'm Cordell Walker, and this is James Trivette."

The young woman's dark eyes widened slightly. "You're señor Walker. Enrique told Mama and me all about you."

"Is Enrique here?"

She shook her head. "No. I don't know where he is." She added wistfully, "I wish I did."

She was a very attractive woman in her early twenties, which made her a year or two older than her brother, Enrique. Her long black hair was pulled into a ponytail that came halfway down her back. She wore a long-sleeved white silk blouse over a short, tight black skirt. Her legs were sleek in black stockings. But despite the somewhat provocative attire, she didn't look like a prostitute.

"Can I help you?" she asked Walker and Trivette. "I have to get to work, but if it doesn't take long . . ."

"Where do you work?" asked Trivette.

"I'm a waitress at the Olympia."

Walker knew the place. It was a combination restaurant and bar sometimes frequented by shady characters, but overall its reputation was not too bad. He was glad that Enrique's sister wasn't working as a hooker.

"What's your name?" he asked.

"Elayna. Like I said, I'm in a little bit of a hurry. What's this all about?"

"We have some questions for Enrique."

"It's about him being back in the gang, isn't it?" Elayna caught her lower lip between even white teeth. "I told him.

I warned him not to have anything to do with those . . . those . . ." She spat out a Spanish curse.

"Hey, *chica,* that's no way to talk about your *hermano*'s amigos."

At the sound of the harsh, mocking voice, Walker and Trivette turned and saw the half dozen youths who had followed them from the stairway. They were all grinning, but there was nothing pleasant about the expressions.

"Go away, Paco," snapped Elayna. "This has nothing to do with you."

"Enrique's my friend," said the largest of the young men, the one who had spoken a moment earlier. "These gringo lawmen come onto our turf, start pushing you around—"

"They're not pushing me around," Elayna said. "We were just talking."

"Our business is with Miss Guzman right now," Walker told the young men, keeping his gaze leveled at the one called Paco as he spoke.

Trivette added, "If we want to talk to you, we know where to find you."

Paco stepped forward, and he stopped grinning. "You come in here and start throwing your weight around. We don't want you here. If you got no warrant, get out."

"We're just talking to Miss Guzman—" Walker began again.

Paco interrupted with a torrent of curses. He sprang forward, swinging a fist at Walker's head.

Well, he had tried to do this without any trouble, Walker thought as he easily blocked the punch and moved aside so that Paco's momentum carried him past. Paco stumbled but caught his balance and whirled around, then launched another attack, sending a flurry of punches at Walker this time.

Walker dropped underneath the blows and thrust his leg out, sweeping it around in a move that knocked Paco's feet right out from under him. This time, Paco had no chance

63

to prevent himself from falling. He crashed hard onto the cracked cement walkway.

That was enough to galvanize his companions into joining the fight. One of them sprang at Trivette, only to run into a short, powerful jab from the rock-hard fist of the former professional athlete. Meanwhile, Walker let himself fall lightly to the ground, only to roll over and use the motion to power himself back upright. He grabbed the shoulders of one of the young men charging him and pivoted at the hips, throwing the man past him. At the same time, Walker's right foot came up and drove into the belly of another attacker. That man stumbled backward, doubling over in pain.

One of the men grabbed Walker from behind in an attempt to pin his arms. Walker drove an elbow back sharply into the man's gut, breaking the hold. He spun, rapping the back of his right fist against the man's nose as he did so. Cartilage crunched under the blow.

Trivette used some of the kicks Walker had taught him to knock another of the young men head over heels. By that time, Paco was up again, and he had a knife in his hand this time, a switchblade he had jerked from the rear pocket of his jeans. Sunlight flickered on the blade as he slashed at Trivette from behind.

The potentially deadly strike never landed. Walker threw himself into a flying kick that sent him crashing into Paco from the side. Both men went down. Walker chopped at Paco's wrist with the side of his hand and heard a satisfying clatter as the knife fell from suddenly nerveless fingers and went bouncing away. With a roar of anger, Paco rolled into Walker and reached for the Ranger's throat with his good hand.

Paco moved fast. Walker couldn't stop the man from clamping hard fingers around his throat. Walker rolled onto his back, using Paco's bullish strength against him. Walker's knee came up into Paco's unprotected groin.

Paco gave a high, thin scream and fell away from Walker, clutching himself. Walker came up on his hands and knees and then up onto his feet. One of the men Trivette had knocked down was still down, and the other four had backed off, their expressions a mixture of anger and fear. One of them held up his hands, palms out, and said, "Hey, no more, Rangers. We don't want no more trouble."

By now people were peering out cautiously from doors and windows all over the apartment complex, their attention caught by the commotion. Elayna Guzman looked around and flushed, humiliated by the brawl that had taken place in front of the apartment she shared with her mother and brother. "You and your amigos get out of here, Paco," she snapped.

Paco was hauling himself onto his feet, still bent over from the pain that coursed through him. He glared at Elayna and said, "You can't talk that way to me, bitch—"

"The lady can say whatever she wants, Paco," said Walker. "And unless you and your friends want to be arrested for assault and attempted murder, you'll take her advice."

Paco switched his glare to Walker and held it for a moment, but clearly, most of the fight had been knocked out of him. He jerked his head at his companions, then trudged toward the trash-littered alley that ran along the far end of the apartment complex. The others followed him, and they disappeared around the corner of the complex a moment later.

"We could have arrested them," Trivette pointed out.

"Probably should have," agreed Walker, "but that's not why we're here." He looked meaningfully at Elayna again.

She shook her head helplessly. "I told you, I don't know where Enrique is. I'm so mad at him for getting mixed up with an animal like Paco again that I'd tell you if I knew. I swear it."

Walker picked up his hat and brushed some of the dust from it. "So Paco is a member of the gang, is that right?"

"Paco *runs* the gang," said Elayna. "He won't forget what happened here today, either."

"I hope not." Walker smiled. "Maybe he'll learn a lesson from it."

Elayna's eyes rolled and expressed plainly how likely she thought *that* possibility was.

A new voice came from down the sidewalk. "Hey, what's going on there?"

Walker and Trivette turned and saw another young man walking hurriedly toward them. He wore a white T-shirt, black jeans, and a black leather jacket.

"Nice retro look," muttered Trivette. "It's 1957 again."

Walker ignored his partner's comment. He had recognized the young man as soon as he saw him. "Hello, Enrique," he said.

"Ranger Walker?" Enrique's eyes widened in surprise. "What are you doin' here?"

"They're looking for you," Elayna said before Walker could reply. "What have you done now, Enrique?"

"Nothin'," he snapped at her. "Nothin' that's any of your business. I thought you had to be at work by now."

Elayna turned back to Walker. "Here he is. Now you can ask him your questions yourself."

With that, she stalked off toward the street, probably heading for the bus stop at the end of the block so that she could go to her job at the Olympia.

Enrique looked uncomfortable under Walker's calm, level gaze. "Hey, I'm sorry I haven't been showin' up lately at the dojo, Ranger," he began. "I been busy, you know. But I promise I'll try harder—"

"Busy doing what?" cut in Walker. "Smuggling drugs for El Diablo?"

EIGHT

If Enrique had been surprised before to see Walker, now he looked absolutely shocked. "What?" he exclaimed.

"El Diablo," Walker repeated. "Does the name mean anything to you?"

Enrique shook his head. "Never heard of him, man."

The frightened look in his eyes told a different story.

Since Enrique was already shaken, Walker decided to keep the young man off balance. "Phyllis Harrison is in jail," he said.

"Doctor Phyllis? In jail? I don't believe it."

"Believe it," said Trivette.

"And she's not a doctor," Walker said. "She was a nurse, but her late husband was the doctor."

"Doesn't matter." Enrique was angered by what the Rangers had just told him. "You shouldn't put somebody in jail for tryin' to help people, and that's all that Doctor Phyllis ever did."

His voice deliberately harsh, Walker said, "She helped one kid right into the hospital by giving him an overdose of heroin."

"No! Doctor Phyllis hates drugs, hates the gangs! She

wouldn't have anything to do with that stuff! That was why she got so mad at me when I—'' Enrique's protest stopped short, but he didn't need to continue.

''When you went back into the gang,'' Walker finished for him. ''Imagine how she would have felt if she had known you were smuggling heroin in those antibiotic capsules you got for her.''

Enrique took a step back, as if Walker had just punched him in the stomach. ''There was heroin,'' he whispered, ''in those pills?''

''She gave some to a little eight-year-old boy named Manuel Rodriguez to cure his earache,'' Trivette said. ''Instead they put him in the hospital and nearly killed him. He may not make it yet.''

Enrique put a hand to the side of his head. ''Oh, man,'' he said softly. ''I didn't . . . I can't believe . . .''

''If you're not to blame, Enrique,'' said Walker, ''then tell us who is.''

''I . . . I can't. . . . I gotta think about this. . . .''

With no warning, Enrique suddenly spun around and broke into a run. Trivette started to go after him, but Walker quickly put out a hand and stopped him. ''Let him go,'' Walker said.

''But he knows something, probably a lot more than he's telling us.''

''We've stirred the pot enough for now,'' said Walker. ''We'll just wait and see what boils up.''

When they left their office late that afternoon, Walker and Trivette swung by the hospital to see how Manuel Rodriguez was doing. The little boy was still in critical condition, a nurse explained to them, but he was stable and perhaps even a little improved from when he had been admitted earlier in the day.

''That was good news,'' Trivette said as the two Rangers got back into Walker's pickup.

''Yeah, but he's a long way from being out of the

woods.'' Walker wheeled the pickup out of the parking lot onto the street and headed for C. D.'s.

Alex was waiting for them there, a meeting that had been arranged earlier. Walker slid into one of the hardwood booths next to her, while Trivette sat across from them.

"What did you find out from Enrique Guzman?'' Alex asked.

"He knows something about El Diablo,'' said Walker. "I could tell that by the way he reacted to the name. But I don't believe he knew anything about the heroin being in some of those antibiotic capsules.''

"Did you bring him in?''

Trivette spoke up. "Walker let him go. I'm still not sure why.''

C. D. had come up to the booth in time to hear the last exchange. He laughed and said, "Cordell's just playin' that boy like he was a fish, gettin' the bait set good before he tries to reel him in. Ain't that right, Cordell?''

"Something like that,'' Walker said.

C. D. was wearing a long white apron and carrying a tray with three bowls on it. He set them, one by one, in front of Walker, Alex, and Trivette. Steam rose from the bowls.

"What's this?'' asked Trivette, peering down at the one in front of him.

"A new addition to the menu. Thought you'd be perfect to try it out on.''

Trivette picked up a spoon from the table, poked it into the contents of the bowl, stirred, and sniffed. "What's in it?'' he asked.

"Dang it, Jimmy, there's no need for you to be so blasted suspicious. Shoot, you act like I'm tryin' to slip somethin' past you. I ain't ever poisoned you yet, now have I?''

"I don't know,'' Trivette said dubiously. "Some of that chili you've tried out on me in the past would have been better if you'd used it for paint remover.''

"Just eat the blamed stuff!''

"All right, all right." Trivette.pointed the spoon at C. D. "But if I keel over dead, Alex, I expect you to prosecute this . . . this culinary culprit."

Stifling a laugh, Alex said, "All right, Jimmy, I promise." C. D. glowered at her for a second, then turned his attention back to Trivette.

Walker sat back, grinning, and waited to see what Trivette's reaction would be.

Gingerly, Trivette dipped his spoon into the stew and brought a little of the stuff to his mouth. He tasted it cautiously, with a frown on his face. He licked his lips, took another small bite, and the frown disappeared. Trivette spooned up more of the stew, ate it, and gave an enthusiastic nod.

"Hey, this is really good, C. D.," he said. "I take back all the terrible things I said about your cooking. What do you call it?" He leaned forward and reached for another spoonful.

Proudly, C. D. said, "I call it C. D.'s Possum Stew."

Trivette froze with his mouth about to close around the spoon, which was brimful and dripping with the concoction. He lurched upright, dropping the spoon into the bowl, and yelped, "Possum! You mean there's possum in this?"

"Well, I couldn't very well call it possum stew if it didn't have any possum in it, now could I?" demanded C. D.

Walker and Alex were both laughing as they pushed their bowls away. "No offense, C. D.," said Alex, "but I think we'll pass on this little taste-test."

"But it's good," C. D. insisted. "Jimmy said so."

Trivette was wiping frantically at his mouth with a napkin. He stopped and looked up at C. D. "That was before I knew it had possum in it!"

"Ain't you ever heard the old sayin' about how what you don't know won't hurt you?"

"Why don't you just bring us some chili, C. D.?" suggested Walker. "There's another old saying about the devil you know being better than the one you don't."

C. D. squinted at him. "I reckon after I think on that for a while, I'll be downright insulted." He sighed. "All right. Three bowls o' red, comin' up." He turned and went back toward the door at the end of the bar that led to the kitchen.

Trivette's face contorted in a grimace as he said, "Possum stew. I can't believe he snookered me into eating possum stew! That's almost as bad as that snipe hunt you took me on a few years ago."

Alex changed the subject by saying to Walker, "What *are* you going to do about Enrique?"

"I'm hoping that once he thinks about everything that's happened, he'll come to us and tell us what he knows about El Diablo and that heroin."

"And if he doesn't?"

"Then we'll still find out," said Walker, "one way or another."

Enrique walked down the alley behind the abandoned supermarket. A streetlight at the far end of the alley cast a watery glow into the darkness, but the light was faint here as Enrique approached the concrete dock where once crates of food had been unloaded. Several figures were sitting on the dock. Enrique recognized the broad shoulders of the largest one.

"Paco," he called.

Paco pushed himself off the dock and landed lightly on his feet. He sauntered toward Enrique. "Hey, 'Rique, what you know, man?"

Enrique stabbed a finger in the air toward Paco. "I know you been tryin' to pull something," he accused.

"What are you talkin' about?"

"Those pills." Enrique's voice was low and intense. "Those pills you helped me get. There was something wrong with 'em."

Paco shook his head. "I don't know what you're talkin' about. You came to me and asked me if I could help you get some medicine for that doctor lady. That's what I did, man. Got in touch with some people I know in Laredo, and they sent 'em right on."

"There was drugs in some of the pills! Heroin. In pills for little kids!"

One of the gang members on the loading dock laughed and said, "Why you worried about some brats, 'Rique?"

Ignoring the question, Enrique stepped closer to Paco and said, "You been tellin' me about somebody called El Diablo, all about what a big, important man he is and how you're gonna work for him, Paco. Is *he* responsible for this? Did El Diablo put that junk in those pills?"

Paco grimaced and gave Enrique's shoulder a hard shove. "Back off, man. An' you better shut up about El Diablo, too. You don't go 'round talkin' about his business."

"Then he is to blame for that kid being in the hospital!"

"What little kid?" asked Paco.

"The one who accidentally got one of those capsules filled with heroin."

An obscenity burst from Paco's mouth. He grabbed Enrique's arm. "Some of those pills you gave the doctor lady really had junk in 'em?"

"That's right." Enrique laughed, but there was no humor in the sound. "You screwed up good, didn't you, Paco? You were supposed to make sure none of the capsules that'd been messed with wound up in Doctor Phyllis's clinic."

"Shut up!" Paco shoved Enrique again. "I got to think about this."

"El Diablo'll be mad as hell when he finds out, won't he, Paco?" Enrique taunted, knowing that he was probably foolish to push Paco like this but too angry to do anything else.

"El Diablo won't ever find out," snapped Paco. "Who's goin' to tell him?" He sneered. "You?"

"Maybe," Enrique said softly. "Maybe."

"I don't think so." Paco's hand went under his jacket, came out holding a gun. On the loading dock, the other members of the gang, who had been lounging casually there, suddenly stood up, their bodies held stiff and ready for trouble.

Enrique's breath seemed to freeze in his throat. He had known that Paco was cruel and ruthless, but he hadn't expected the gang leader to pull a gun on him.

"Hey, man," Enrique said when he could speak again, "don't be doin' that. We been amigos for a long time—"

"If you were my amigo, 'Rique, you wouldn't be threatenin' to go to El Diablo."

"I was just mad! Hell, Paco, I don't even know where to find El Diablo—"

"You got it right, 'Rique."

"Huh?"

The pistol rose in Paco's hand. "You said 'Hell.' That's where you're gonna find El Diablo."

He pulled the trigger.

Enrique closed his eyes, gasped, and took a quick step backward. A couple of heartbeats passed before he realized that he wasn't dead, that Paco's gun hadn't even fired. Paco cursed and fumbled with the weapon.

Only the fact that the gun was a Saturday night special, a cheaply made, unregistered revolver, had saved Enrique's life. The pistol had misfired. Seizing the unexpected chance to escape, Enrique whirled around and dashed away down the alley.

"Get him!" shouted Paco as he pointed the gun at Enrique's fleeing back and pulled the trigger again. This time the pistol cracked wickedly, and even in the dim light, Paco and the other gang members saw Enrique stumble.

Enrique bit back the yell of pain that tried to well up his throat as a finger of pure fire lanced into his shoulder. He was running away, sure, that made sense. But his fierce pride still wouldn't let him give Paco the satisfaction of knowing that he was hit.

Rapid footsteps pounded in the alley behind him. Somewhere not far away, a dog began to bark, roused by the gunshot and Paco's shout. Enrique cast a glance over his shoulder. The whole gang was after him, and in a way that was good. Paco couldn't shoot at him again without risking that one of his men would be hit by the bullet.

A high wooden fence ran along the edge of the property where the abandoned supermarket sat, separating that property from a neighborhood of small houses. Enrique could have turned when he reached the corner of the building and tried to reach the street that ran in front of the store, but he was afraid Paco and the others would catch up to him before he could make it to the street. Instead, he lunged at the fence, leaping high to catch the top of it with both hands. His left hand slipped as pain tore through that arm and shoulder where he had been wounded, but his right clamped tightly on the wood. His feet scrambled at the smooth surface of the fence as he tried to pull himself up. The toes of his shoes found purchase, lost it, found it again. He was able to throw one leg over the top of the fence and called on all his reserves of strength to pull himself after it.

He fell over the top of the fence and tumbled to the ground on the other side.

He landed on his left shoulder, and this time he couldn't hold back the cry of agony. He rolled onto his stomach and gasped for breath, and as he did so, he heard Paco shouting on the other side of the fence.

"Get him! Climb over! Some of you go around!"

Enrique knew he had to move, and move now, if he was going to survive the next few minutes. He pushed himself onto hands and knees, then onto his feet. Breaking into a stumbling run, he started across the residential backyard where he had landed.

Lights burned in the house that stood in the yard, but no one came to the back door to see what was going on. In this neighborhood, people minded their own business, and when trouble came, they waited it out behind locked doors and steel-barred windows. In this place, predators and criminals like Paco roamed and ruled, and the honest citizens cowered in a prison of their own fear.

There was no one here Enrique could turn to for help.

Garbage cans clattered loudly as he knocked them over in the dark, and one of Paco's gang yelled, "He's over there!" Enrique felt like weeping as he stumbled on. To stop was to die, that was certain.

He made his way through several more backyards, avoiding all the obstacles he could so that he wouldn't make noise and give away his position. Luck was with him. He wound up crouching in the deep shadows next to a ramshackle shed. His wounded shoulder hurt so bad that he almost cried out as he knelt there, but he managed to keep his lips clamped tightly shut. He breathed through his nose, even though he wanted to open his mouth wide and gasp for air to fill his oxygen-starved lungs.

Maybe they wouldn't find him here. Maybe he wouldn't die tonight. Maybe . . .

Elayna Guzman stepped out the back door of the Olympia Restaurant, settled the strap of her purse more securely on her shoulder, and started walking along the alley toward the street. The clicking of her high heels on the dirty pavement echoed in the night. Her right hand was inside her purse as she walked, the fingers wrapped around the small cylinder of pepper spray. The spray wouldn't be much of a defense if someone tried to bother her, but she supposed it would be better than nothing. This was the worst part of the evening, this long walk to the bus stop, the lights of which she could already see beckoning to her.

As always when she got off work, she was tired. Waiting tables had to be one of the most exhausting jobs in the world. And in a place like the Olympia, where some of the customers belonged to a pretty rough crowd, it was even worse. Not only did she have to hustle drinks and food to the tables all night, but she had to fend off a multitude of groping hands as well, all the while wearing a smile and trying not to offend anyone. The leers, the way the men caressed her with their gazes . . . well, there was nothing she could do about that. There were worse ways for a pretty young woman to make a living. A lot worse.

Someone came out of the darkness at her.

Elayna saw the motion in the shadows and jerked back, a short scream bursting from her lips. She yanked the cylinder of pepper spray from her purse and lifted it, ready to press the button that would send the fiery stuff spraying at her attacker.

Only the man wasn't attacking her, and he wasn't a stranger, either. "Elayna," he croaked, and even though his voice was hoarse and taut with strain of some sort, she recognized it.

"Enrique!" she exclaimed. He staggered, and she dropped the pepper spray as she reached out hurriedly to catch him before he could fall. "*Dios mío!* What . . . what is wrong—?"

"Paco . . . he . . . El Diablo . . ."

She clung to him and felt him shuddering as he tried to talk. "You're hurt, 'Rique," she said. "I'll get help. I'll call 911—"

"No!" He straightened, finding the strength somewhere to steady himself. "Not 'til I . . . talk to him. . . ."

"Who, Paco?"

"Walker." Enrique's strength deserted him again, and he sagged against his sister. "Find . . . Ranger Walker. . . . Got to tell him . . . about El Diablo. . . ."

Elayna couldn't hold him up. He slipped to the ground. Elayna cried, "Enrique!" as she stumbled back a couple of steps. She held up her hands and stared at them in horror, the light from the distant bus stop revealing the dark stains there.

Her hands were covered with her brother's blood.

NINE

The George Strait song coming from the jukebox almost drowned out the ringing of Walker's cell phone. He slipped it from his pocket, flipped it open, held it to his ear, and said, "Walker."

A grim look appeared on his face as he listened to whoever was on the other end, and, after a moment, he said sharply, "Go ahead and call an ambulance. I'll meet you at the hospital."

Trivette and Alex looked at him with some alarm.

"I know what Enrique said, but if he's been shot, he needs medical attention right away. And on second thought I'll call the ambulance, Elayna. Just stay with him until it gets there."

Walker tucked the phone away as he stood up. Trivette got hurriedly to his feet, too, and said, "Enrique Guzman's been shot?"

Walker nodded curtly. "That's right. He came to the restaurant where his sister works and collapsed in the alley behind it."

"Who could have shot him?" asked Alex. She looked as concerned as the two Rangers.

"We'll find out—if he lives to talk to us," said Walker. He clapped his hat on his head and strode toward the front door of C. D.'s Place with Trivette alongside him.

Walker drove while Trivette used the radio in the pickup to contact Ranger headquarters and have an ambulance sent to the alley behind the Olympia Restaurant. The restaurant was a twenty-minute drive from C. D.'s, but the ambulance would arrive sooner than that. That was why Walker had told Elayna that he would meet her at the hospital. The important thing was getting Enrique's wound attended to as soon as possible.

Walker and Trivette pushed through the swinging doors into the corridor outside the emergency room less than half an hour later. Immediately, Walker spotted Elayna waiting next to another set of swinging doors, these leading into the ER itself. She was standing on her toes and craning her neck in an attempt to see through the small window set high in one of the doors.

"Elayna," Walker called to her.

She started and turned quickly to face the Rangers. Her features were taut with worry, and tears had left trails in the makeup on her cheeks.

"Ranger Walker," she said. "I . . . I am so glad you came."

"How's Enrique?" asked Walker.

"I don't know. They haven't told me anything since they took him in there." She cast a nervous glance over her shoulder at the entrance to the emergency room, then turned her attention back to Walker. "I hope I did the right thing by calling you. Enrique said he had to talk to you about . . . about someone called El Diablo."

Walker and Trivette exchanged a look. Walker had meant to make something happen by prodding Enrique about El Diablo and the Mexican antibiotics—but he hadn't thought that the young man might wind up getting shot.

The two Rangers and Elayna looked toward the ER doors

as they abruptly swung open. A nurse peered out and said, "Ms. Guzman?"

"That's me," Elayna said.

"You can see your brother now."

Relief shone on Elayna's face. "He . . . he is all right?"

"The doctor is waiting to talk to you, too."

The nurse stepped back to let Elayna into the ER, then moved to block the path of Walker and Trivette as they tried to follow. "We're Texas Rangers," Walker told her. "Enrique Guzman is involved in a case we're investigating."

"Well, . . . all right. But if the doctor says you go, then you're outta here, Ranger."

Walker gave the woman a tight smile and nodded his acceptance of the condition.

He and Trivette stepped into the emergency room and found Elayna talking to a tall, lanky young man with bright red hair and the harried look that most ER physicians customarily wore. He was saying, ". . . a lot of blood, so the main danger was of your brother going into shock. We've got him stabilized now, though, and we'll be sending him up to the OR in a few minutes to have that bullet removed. He should be fine, depending, of course, on what the doctors find during surgery."

"Thank you, Doctor," Elayna said. She was crying again, but this time they were tears of relief.

Walker and Trivette moved closer so that they could see past the curtains drawn around the bed where Enrique lay. He was lying on his right side, breathing shallowly. His face was pale and drawn, but his eyes were open. Walker could tell from the young man's slightly groggy expression that he had already been given something for the pain of his wound, as well as to prepare him for the imminent surgery.

The redheaded doctor glanced at Walker and Trivette and demanded, "Who are you?"

"Texas Rangers," Walker said.

"Enrique wanted to talk to them," explained Elayna. "He didn't even want me to call 911 and get him an ambulance. He just wanted to talk to Ranger Walker."

"Well, if somebody hadn't called an ambulance when they did, this young man might not have made it," the doctor said.

Walker said, "Can we ask him a few questions?"

The doctor frowned. "He'll be going up to surgery in just a couple of minutes, and I'm not sure how responsive he would be right now—"

"W-Walker . . ."

The rasping voice came from the bed. When Walker turned toward it, he saw that Enrique had lifted his hand slightly from the sheet and was trying to beckon to him to come closer.

Walker ignored the warning look the doctor gave him and stepped to the bedside. "I'm here, Enrique," he said as he leaned over to the wounded young man. "What is it you want to tell me?"

"El . . . El Diablo . . ."

Walker curbed the impatience he felt and asked gently, "What about El Diablo?"

"Paco . . . knows him . . . said the pills came . . . from Laredo. . . ."

"You mean the antibiotics that had been tampered with?"

"Y-yeah." Enrique took a deep breath and seemed to get slightly stronger for a moment. "Paco shot me 'cause I said I'd tell El Diablo about the heroin in the pills. Paco . . . screwed up."

"Do you know where I can find El Diablo?"

"No, man. I was just . . . mad . . . tryin' to get back at Paco. Stupid of me. . . ."

The doctor said, "Ranger, the orderlies are here to take Mr. Guzman up to surgery. I have to insist—"

Walker straightened. "That's all right, Doctor," he said. "Go ahead and do what you have to do."

80

The orderlies wheeled the bed itself out of the cubicle formed by the curtains and through the doors into the hallway. Walker, Trivette, Elayna, and the ER doctor watched them go. The doctor said to Elayna, "You can go up and wait in the surgical waiting room, Ms. Guzman. They'll notify you when your brother's surgery is over and he's taken to the recovery room."

"Thank you, Doctor. *Muchas gracias.*"

Walker and Trivette went into the corridor with Elayna. "Is there anything we can do for you?" Trivette asked her. "Anyone you need to notify?"

Elayna swallowed hard. "My . . . my mother. She works at Reunion Tower. She's on the night cleaning crew there."

"We can have a couple of police officers sent over there to bring her here if you'd like," offered Walker.

"*Sí,* thank you. But . . . tell them not to frighten her."

"We'll make sure the officers understand the situation," Trivette assured her.

Elayna gave them a weak but grateful smile and headed for the elevators. When she was out of earshot, Trivette went on quietly, "What *is* the situation, Walker?"

"Enrique will have to answer for his part in getting those Mexican antibiotics up here," said Walker, "but he didn't know about the heroin, either, just like Phyllis Harrison. Paco did, though. And Paco knows about El Diablo."

Trivette grunted. "Paco, huh? The leader of that gang?"

Walker nodded.

"Then I guess he's the next one we'll be paying a visit to."

"You guess right," said Walker.

Brightly colored electric lights were strung in the branches of the trees around the courtyard of the Vega Garcia hacienda, and they reflected like a rainbow off the surface of the pool. The bikini-clad beauties were gone now, chased inside by the slight chill of the night air. But Carlos was there, standing alone at the edge of the pool, hands in the pockets of his expensive designer slacks. He wore a brooding expression as he stared out over the smooth expanse of the water.

Footsteps behind him made him turn. Ramon had strolled out through the arching doors of the hacienda. He had a drink in his hand, and while he looked somewhat concerned, he didn't seem as worried as his brother.

"El Diablo will be here shortly," said Ramon. "I just spoke to him on the phone."

"Did he tell you why he wants to meet with us?" asked Carlos.

Ramon shook his head. "You know how careful he must be, especially talking on a cell phone. Almost anyone could be listening in."

Carlos spat on the carefully tended turf. "Walker!"

"No, not Walker," said Ramon. "He has no idea we are connected with El Diablo. Our people have been circumspect. They know that to be otherwise is to risk their lives."

A woman with long, honey-blond hair came out of the house and approached the Vega Garcia brothers. She wore a dark blue silk gown that left her shoulders bare, hugged the curves of her body, and brushed around her bare ankles. She smiled and asked, "Would you like a drink, don Carlos?"

He shook his head. "Not now, *chiquita*." The woman started to turn to go back into the hacienda, but Carlos stopped her by saying, "When El Diablo arrives, see that he is brought out here to us immediately."

The woman smiled sweetly. "Of course."

She went inside, and Carlos began pacing up and down beside the pool. Ramon just shook his head and sat down at one of the glass-topped tables to sip his drink. Carlos worried too much, he thought. And ever since that business with the *norteamericano*, Shrader, and that helicopter, Carlos had seemed to regard Cordell Walker with a mixture of fear, anger, and loathing, as if Walker were some sort of . . . of superhuman.

Walker was just a man, and Ramon del Vega Garcia firmly believed there was no man alive he could not out-think and outmaneuver. And if all else failed, Ramon knew that sheer ruthlessness would give him the edge.

Some twenty minutes later, the blonde emerged once again from the hacienda, and this time, El Diablo was right behind her. Ramon stood up and joined Carlos as they walked forward to greet their visitor.

El Diablo was smiling tightly. After a perfunctory hello, he said, "Everything is on schedule. My preparations are almost complete, and soon I will be taking such a large shipment of merchandise across the border that the profits will make our little cartel secure in all its future operations."

It still bothered both the Vega Garcias to hear El Diablo talk about himself as if he were an equal partner—but such was the cost of getting back into this business. Carlos nodded and said, "Good. But what about Walker?"

El Diablo waved a hand. "What about him? He will be no danger to us."

"If he becomes aware of this new shipment—" began Ramon.

"It would not even matter," El Diablo said confidently. "No one, not even the famous Walker, will be able to stop us. The merchandise will be across the border, split up, and on its way to the various distribution points before anyone even knows it is there."

"You sound sure of yourself," said Carlos.

"I *am* sure of myself. No one has ever even attempted what I, El Diablo, will soon accomplish!"

The grandiose statement made Carlos and Ramon glance at each other. El Diablo certainly had a flair for the dramatic. But if he could deliver on what he promised, no matter how he phrased it, that was all that was important.

"What do you need from us?" Ramon asked.

"Have the merchandise ready to be moved quickly when the time comes," said El Diablo. "That is all I require."

Carlos and Ramon both nodded. "It will be done," Carlos promised.

"And one other thing," said El Diablo.

Ramon spread his hands. "You have but to ask."

El Diablo turned and nodded toward the blond woman, who had moved back deferentially toward the hacienda. "I want her."

Ramon looked at the woman and snapped his fingers. "Go with El Diablo."

Instinctively, the woman had taken another step backward. The colored lights reflected from the pool onto her face, changing slightly with every ripple of the water. But that play of the light failed to conceal the sudden fear that washed across her features.

"Don Ramon, I . . . I would prefer—" she began tentatively.

"You heard El Diablo," Ramon snapped. "Go with him—now!"

The smile on El Diablo's face had widened at the young woman's reluctance to accompany him. Clearly, the fact that she was frightened of him did not bother him. In fact, if anything it made him want her that much more.

She turned and appealed to the older brother. "Don Carlos . . . ?"

He shook his head mercilessly. "You heard don Ramon and El Diablo. Go."

El Diablo stepped over to her and took hold of her bare arm in a steely grip, his fingers digging painfully into her flesh. "Do not worry, *querida*. You will enjoy it."

He started toward the hacienda, tugging the blonde with him. She threw one final despairing glance over her shoulder at the Vega Garcias, but if either of the brothers felt any pity for her, they did not show it. El Diablo disappeared into the house with her.

"At least he does not kill them, like Shrader did," said Carlos.

Ramon shrugged. "Even if he did, we could deal with

it. Her loss would be a small price to pay if he can succeed in what he has promised. There are always more beautiful women in the world."

"I do not know what to make of a man such as that," Carlos said with a sigh. "From one of the best families in all of Mexico, with all that culture and education and wealth, and look at what he has become."

Somewhere in the hacienda, a short, pained cry sounded.

"You make of him exactly what he has become to us," Ramon said. "A tool . . . a tool to bring us back to our rightful place in the world."

"And when that has been accomplished?"

Ramon picked up what was left of his drink from the table and drained the glass. He lowered it, licked his lips, and said, "Then we will have no more need of the great El Diablo, will we?"

Slowly, Carlos began to nod, and for the first time tonight, a smile spread across his face.

TEN

Even in the parking lot of the nightclub, the *Tejano* music coming from inside the building was loud. Walker and Trivette got out of the pickup and started toward the club. Several couples were leaving, and they looked curiously at the two Rangers as they passed. It wasn't unheard of for whites or blacks to patronize this dance club, but it was unusual.

The bouncer on duty just inside the front door was almost as broad as he was tall. Bare, muscular arms like small tree trunks were crossed over his chest. He wore a T-shirt with the sleeves cut off, a fringed and beaded vest, and jeans. He moved slightly as Walker and Trivette entered, not enough to block their way completely but sufficient to ensure that they paid attention to his presence.

"We're looking for a man named Paco," Walker said politely to him.

"We don't want no trouble in here," replied the bouncer, still standing there with his arms crossed.

Trivette said, "Neither do we. We just need to talk to Paco."

"I don't allow no fighting."

"We're not here to fight," Walker assured him—although he knew quite well that was what it might come down to when he and Trivette attempted to take Paco into custody.

The bouncer didn't believe them for a second, but he knew the law when he saw it. Given the Western shirts and jeans and the Stetsons sported by Walker and Trivette, he made an educated guess and said, "Texas Rangers?"

Walker nodded.

The bouncer stood aside and angled his head toward the dance floor. "I don't know if Paco's still here or not. He came in earlier, but there's a back door."

"No one watches it?" asked Walker.

"There's a guy to keep track of who comes in. I don't know how well he watches the ones going out."

"Thanks," said Walker as he and Trivette moved into the interior of the club.

The music was much louder in here, almost an assault on the eardrums. The garish lighting was inconsistent, leaving several shadowy areas in the big main room. A dance floor, which was packed at the moment, took up the center of the room. A U-shaped bar was on one side, and the rest of the floor space was dotted with small tables, most of them occupied. Walker and Trivette moved through the press of people, aware of the stares they were getting. Some of the expressions were merely curious, while others were openly hostile. The Rangers' keen eyes searched for a glimpse of Paco or one of the other gang members who had been at the apartment complex that afternoon.

Instinct warned Walker before his senses did. But then he caught a glimpse of sudden movement from the corner of his eye, saw someone at the bar being shoved aside as a tall, muscular figure headed abruptly for the rear exit. Walker swung in that direction and called, "Paco! Hold it!"

His commanding voice cut cleanly through the clamor of the music. The fleeing figure's head jerked around, and even in the dim light Walker recognized Paco's sullenly handsome features. He started moving quickly toward the bar, with Trivette right behind him.

Paco's left arm shot out and shoved aside a young woman in a short dress. His right hand went behind his back and plucked a small pistol from the waistband of his jeans. The young woman's date yelled, "Hey!" and lunged forward to grab Paco's arm, but Paco chopped at him with the pistol, slashing it across his face. The young man grunted in pain as the gun's sight ripped a gash in his cheek. He stumbled backward, clapping a hand to the bleeding wound as his girlfriend screamed.

"Gun!" Walker said sharply to alert Trivette. Then he shouted, *"Everybody down!"*

Immediately, the club was chaos. People shouted questions or screamed in fear, punctuated by the pounding beat of the music. The throng on the dance floor became a lunging, seething mob as everyone tried to get to safety at once. The bouncer at the front door, plus another man from the back of the club, tried to breast the tide of out-of-control humanity to reach Walker, Trivette, and Paco, but they were held back by the churning sea of arms and legs.

Walker and Trivette tried to shoulder their way past the human obstacles, too, but it wasn't until Paco began shooting that their path started to clear. As shots cracked wickedly from the pistol, people flung themselves to the floor. Walker hurdled over a couple of them and drew his own pistol, but there were still too many people scurrying around madly for him to risk a shot. He saw spurts of orange flame winking from the muzzle of Paco's gun as he threw himself forward and down.

Walker somersaulted, covering most of the distance between Paco and himself as the gang leader's bullets whined over him. As Walker came up from the roll, he thrust his foot out, driving the heel of his boot into Paco's belly. The kick doubled Paco over and sent him stumbling backward.

Paco wasn't alone in the club. Several of his followers,

the same young men who had been at the apartment complex that afternoon, leapt to his defense. One of them grabbed Trivette's shoulder, only to receive a short, powerful right hook for his trouble. A couple more closed in on Trivette, and he slugged it out with them for a long moment, dealing as much punishment as he received.

Walker leveled his gun at Paco and snapped, "Drop it!" but he was still reluctant to fire if Paco didn't obey. He didn't want to risk killing the young man. There was too much Paco could tell them about El Diablo, but he couldn't spill a thing if he were dead.

Paco stumbled against the bar, caught his balance, and started to jerk the pistol up again. Walker sprang forward, striking with his own gun. The barrel cracked across the wrist of Paco's gun hand. Paco howled in pain, and the Saturday night special slipped from his fingers.

Walker jabbed a left into Paco's face. Paco sagged against the bar. That gave Walker a chance to slide his gun back in its clip, then he grabbed Paco by the shoulders. He whirled the young man around, caught hold of his right wrist, and forced it up into the middle of his back. It was an old-fashioned technique, but it had been around for so long because it worked. Walker knew a dozen ways to break out of that hold, had he been on the other end of it—but Paco didn't.

Meanwhile, Trivette still had his hands full with the other gang members. One of them was stretched senseless on the floor, but another had managed to pin Trivette's arms behind him while a third stood in front of the Ranger and sank punches into his midsection.

Walker saw what was happening and shoved Paco in that direction, intending to take a hand in the fight if he could. Before he could get there, however, the bouncer from the front door finally reached the spot and clamped his huge hands on the neck of the man who was dealing out the beating to Trivette. The man gasped for air and flailed his arms and legs as the bouncer literally lifted him off the floor by his throat.

Trivette broke away from the man who was holding him and spun around, putting all his strength into a right-left combination that smashed into the man's jaw and jerked his head from side to side. The man fell backward, knocking over a couple of bar stools as he crumpled.

The bouncer shook the man he was holding by the throat, like a dog shaking a rat, then threw him aside. Turning angrily to Walker, he said, "I thought you said you didn't want no trouble, man!"

"I didn't," Walker said as he tightened his grip on Paco. "But we don't always get what we want, do we?"

The bouncer jerked a thumb at the door. "Get outta here. I got no fondness for Paco and his boys, but it don't look good, you know, a couple of Rangers comin' in here and hasslin' the customers."

Walker prodded Paco toward the exit. Trivette followed, picking up both of their hats on the way, along with the pistol Paco had dropped.

Paco was cursing loudly as Walker shoved him out into the parking lot. "I'll kill you for this, man!" he threatened. "Nobody does this to me!"

"I just did," said Walker. "And I'll do worse if you don't cooperate."

"You got to read me my rights!"

They had reached the pickup. Walker let go of Paco's wrist, grabbed his shoulder, spun him around, and pushed him up against the door of the vehicle. "You know all about your rights, don't you?" Walker said tightly. "What about the rights of Manuel Rodriguez?"

"Who . . . ? Wha . . . ?"

"The little boy who nearly died because of the heroin El Diablo smuggled into the country in what was supposed to be antibiotic capsules. Or what about Enrique Guzman? Did you read him his rights before you shot him?"

Paco shook his head stubbornly, but Walker could see

the fear in his eyes. "I didn't shoot nobody!"

"Enrique will testify differently," said Trivette. "And you'll go to prison for attempted murder as well as drug smuggling."

Paco looked back and forth from Walker's face to Trivette's, noting the grim expression that both of the Rangers wore as they crowded him against the pickup. Red and blue lights suddenly washed over the parking lot as a couple of Dallas police cruisers turned in from the street with sirens blaring, summoned by reports of the shooting inside.

"Are we talkin' about a deal?" Paco asked hesitantly.

"No deals," snapped Walker. "But the only way you can do your case any good at all is to cooperate with us."

"And we want to know about El Diablo," added Trivette.

Paco swallowed hard. "I . . . I don't know much. I never met him."

"Enrique seemed to think you were working for El Diablo."

"Well, I guess I am, but I still never saw him! All I know is he works out of Nuevo Laredo. He got the stuff across the border and sent it up here in those pills, and then I was supposed to take out all the pills that had been loaded with junk before I gave the rest to 'Rique to give to that lady doctor. That's the truth, I swear it!"

"But you made a mistake and didn't get all the capsules you were supposed to," said Walker.

"Yeah, I guess so," Paco said miserably. "Or else they screwed up down in Laredo and marked the stuff wrong. I don't know, man."

"There's got to be more than that," Walker insisted. "Something that will lead us to El Diablo."

The pickup was surrounded by uniformed officers from the police cruisers by now. The last shreds of Paco's pride and arrogance vanished as he looked around at the cops, then at the implacable Rangers in front of him. He wasn't getting out of this. No way.

"Cabeza de Oro," he said.

Walker blinked. "What?"

"Cabeza de Oro," repeated Paco. "I don't know what it means, man, but I heard that it has something to do with El Diablo. Well, I do know what it means—Head of Gold—but I don't know what it has to do with El Diablo, understand?" He was practically babbling by now.

"That's all you can tell us?" asked Trivette.

"That's all I know, man. I swear."

Walker grasped Paco's arm and propelled him toward the waiting officers. "Book him for attempted homicide, resisting arrest, and suspicion of narcotics trafficking."

"And be sure to read him his rights," Trivette added wryly. "He's picky about that."

When Paco had been handcuffed and placed in the back of one of the patrol cars, Walker took his hat from Trivette and brushed some of the dust from it before he put it back on. "Cabeza de Oro," he mused.

"Like Paco said, it translates to Head of Gold. But what does *that* mean?"

Walker shook his head. "I don't know. But I've got a hunch where we may be able to find the answer."

"Laredo?" guessed Trivette.

Walker nodded. "Laredo."

ELEVEN

Elayna Guzman stood up when she saw Walker, Trivette, and Alex coming down the hospital corridor toward her. A middle-aged woman had been sitting beside her on the waiting room chairs, and Elayna put a hand on her shoulder. "Mama," she said as the others walked up, "this is Ranger Walker and Ranger Trivette." She looked curiously at Alex.

"I'm Assistant District Attorney Alex Cahill, Ms. Guzman," Alex explained.

Elayna's mother looked up at them. "You are here to arrest my son?" she asked.

Walker smiled and shook his head. "No, the main reason we stopped by was just to see how Enrique was doing."

"The doctors say he will be all right," Elayna said. "We have thanked God for that."

Mrs. Guzman said, "You are not going to arrest Enrique?" She seemed unable to believe it.

"The district attorney has decided not to press charges against him for delivering those antibiotics to Mrs. Harrison," said Alex. "Even though under the law the drugs were illegal without a valid prescription, Ranger Walker suggested that there were mitigating circumstances."

"But he doesn't need to do it again," added Walker.

"He will not, I promise you this," vowed Mrs. Guzman. She and her daughter both looked exhausted, a result of the all-night vigil they had stood here at the hospital.

Trivette said, "We were hoping we could talk to Enrique for a few minutes."

"He is down the hall, in the Intensive Care Unit," Elayna said.

Walker nodded his thanks and led the others to the nurses' station to clear their visit to ICU. A few minutes later, after receiving a warning from the doctor on duty not to tire Enrique too much, they were ushered in to the cubicle where he lay on a hospital bed, his shoulder heavily bandaged, an IV in his arm, and an oxygen tube clipped to his nose. He looked up at his three visitors groggily and asked the same question his mother and sister had asked. "Am I under arrest?"

"Not this time," Walker said, "but you're going to have to be more careful in the future, Enrique."

"Yeah," said Trivette, "no more playing doctor."

"I . . . I didn't know nothin' about that heroin."

Walker nodded. "We know. That was Paco's doing, just as you thought."

"Then Doctor Phyllis . . . she won't have to . . . go to jail?"

"Probably not," said Alex. "She will have to face charges of possession of dangerous drugs without a proper prescription, but we're going to recommend a suspended sentence."

"Pretty lady," murmured Enrique. "Who're you?"

"Alex Cahill. I'm an assistant DA. And I can tell you that you're very lucky not to be under arrest, Enrique."

"I know." He seemed to get a little stronger, and there was a hint of anger in his voice as he asked, "Did you find Paco?"

"He's behind bars," said Walker.

"Did he . . . tell you about El Diablo?"

"What little he actually knew." Walker frowned slightly. "Have you ever heard of something or some place called Cabeza de Oro, Enrique?"

"Head of Gold," the young man mused. After a moment, he shook his head. "I don't remember ever hearin' that before."

"It has something to do with El Diablo. That was really all Paco could tell us, that and the fact that El Diablo operates out of Laredo, just like you said."

"I . . . I wish there was more I could do to help you."

"There is," Walker said. "When you get out of here, steer clear of the gangs this time."

"Count on it, . . . Ranger."

Phyllis Harrison was at the small, rented house that had served as her clinic when Walker and Trivette stopped there a little later after dropping Alex at her office. She summoned up a weary smile as she greeted them.

"I was released on bond," she went on. "Don't worry, I didn't bust out of jail."

"I didn't think you did," Walker assured her, returning the smile. Then he grew more solemn and continued, "You nearly got into some really bad trouble, Mrs. Harrison."

"I know," she said with a sigh. "But I didn't mean any harm. I was just trying to help people." She shook her head. "That's not an excuse for breaking the law, though, is it?"

"You must know plenty of doctors," said Trivette. "Why didn't you get one of them to write a prescription for the antibiotics?"

"In the kind of quantities I was buying? Any physician would have known something was wrong. This was something that *I* wanted to do. I don't expect you to understand, but it was important to me that I do this on my own."

"Except you weren't really on your own," Walker

pointed out. "Enrique Guzman was involved, too, and he wound up getting shot because of it."

Phyllis's eyes widened. "Shot!" she repeated. "Enrique? Oh, my God! Is he all right?"

"He will be," Trivette told her. "He pointed us toward the person who was responsible for the heroin being in those capsules, too."

"You can't arrest him," Phyllis said emphatically. "He was just trying to help me. I'm to blame, not him—"

"He's not going to be arrested," said Walker.

Phyllis closed her eyes for a moment. "Thank God for that. I . . . I've been so lucky that I haven't caused any more harm than I already did."

"We checked on the Rodriguez boy while we were at the hospital," Walker said. "The doctors still don't know if he's going to make it."

Phyllis looked down at the floor. "I . . . I wish there was something I could do . . . to make up for . . . for what I've done. . . ."

"Cabeza de Oro."

She lifted her eyes to meet Walker's level gaze. "What?"

"You've had contacts among the Hispanic gangs. Does the name Cabeza de Oro mean anything to you?"

"Head of Gold," Phyllis translated the expression, just as Paco and Enrique had earlier. She frowned in thought, then shook her head. "I don't believe I've ever heard that phrase before."

"Well, it was a long shot," admitted Walker. "It has something to do with the man responsible for sending the heroin across the border in those antibiotic capsules."

"I hope you find him, whoever and wherever he is."

"We intend to," Walker promised. "In the meantime, you know that you're going to have to close this place down."

"Yes, I know." Phyllis looked around the waiting room with a wistful expression on her face. "I really did some good here, you know. I may have gone about it the wrong way, but I truly helped some people."

"I'm sure you did," Walker said gently.

He and Trivette left a moment later. "Where to now?" asked Trivette.

Walker considered, then said, "We've squared everything away here. I think it's time we head south."

The small Department of Public Safety airplane angled down toward Laredo International Airport late that afternoon. To the east was the shimmering blue surface of Lake Casa Blanca, surrounded by the monte, the flat, scrubcovered lowlands that made up the principal terrain of the Rio Grande Valley. To the southwest of the airport, clearly visible from the windows, were the twin cities of Laredo and Nuevo Laredo, straddling the Rio Grande itself. Though El Paso and Ciudad Juárez, at the western tip of Texas, were larger cities, Laredo and Nuevo Laredo formed the two halves of the busiest crossing point on the entire United States–Mexico border. More legal immigrants flowed back and forth across the border here than anywhere else, and the import-export traffic in goods was also extremely heavy.

It was no wonder, thought Walker as he gazed out the window of the plane, that no one had ever noticed a few cases of Mexican antibiotics being brought across the river.

After some phone calls to the Ranger office in Laredo to let their fellow officers know they were coming, Walker and Trivette had debated driving down but had opted to fly instead to save time. Captain Hector Lopez, the head of the local office, had promised to have a rental vehicle waiting for Walker and Trivette at the airport. Knowing Walker's fondness for pickups, he had said that he would try to rustle up one, but he wasn't able to guarantee that.

"I hope Captain Lopez doesn't feel like we're intruding on his territory," Trivette said as the pilot lined the plane up for its landing.

"When he heard that we might have a lead to El Diablo," said Walker, "he promised to welcome us with open arms."

The landing gear touched down and the plane rolled smoothly to a stop. Walker and Trivette thanked the DPS pilot, then climbed out. A stocky man in black jeans, white shirt, black string tie, and white Stetson was waiting for them on the tarmac. He extended a hand with a grin and greeted Walker warmly. "Good to see you again, Cordell," he said.

"And it's good to see you, too, Hector. What's it been, five years?"

"Six," said Hector Lopez. He turned to Walker's partner. "And you must be Jimmy Trivette. I saw you play in the Super Bowl. That was some catch you made down there on the five-yard line. Dallas couldn't have kicked the winning field goal without it."

"I was lucky," Trivette said modestly as he shook hands with Lopez. Then he broke into a big grin and added, "And incredibly talented, too, of course."

"Of course," Walker said dryly.

Lopez chuckled, then grew more serious as he led them toward the pickup parked nearby. It was a different make and model than Walker usually drove, but it was a full-size job with a powerful engine, and Walker was satisfied.

"Now, what's all this about El Diablo?" Lopez asked solemnly.

"First, why don't you tell us what you know about him?" suggested Walker.

Lopez agreed. When they were all in the pickup heading toward downtown Laredo, he said, "We first started hearing about El Diablo six months ago. It sounded . . . well, you know, silly at first, somebody calling himself El Diablo. Then we realized that he took it seriously, and so did the members of the local underworld. They were as frightened of him as if he were the Devil himself. I've heard rumors that he killed two or three men who dared to cross him."

"Other drug smugglers?" asked Walker. He was behind the wheel, guiding the pickup expertly through the heavy traffic on the state highway.

Lopez nodded. "That's right. El Diablo didn't want any competition. Our informants told us that at first he was content just to smuggle a few drugs across the river. Getting his feet wet, I guess you could say."

"That didn't satisfy him for long, though, did it?"

"Not hardly. We got a few tips that he was expanding his operation . . . but then all the tips dried up."

"Do you know why?" asked Trivette.

"Probably because two of our informants wound up floating facedown in the river," Lopez said grimly. "They'd been shot in the back of the head."

"Executed," said Walker. "And El Diablo got the credit for the murders."

"Of course. Now everyone is afraid to talk to us."

Walker steered the pickup onto Interstate 35, which would take them the rest of the way downtown. He said, "When I called earlier, I asked you about Cabeza de Oro. Have you been able to come up with anything on it?"

Lopez shook his head. "I'm afraid not. I thought it might be a nightclub, but there are no clubs or any other businesses in Laredo or Nuevo Laredo by that name."

"What if it's a person's name?" said Trivette. "There was that famous explorer, Cabeza de Vaca."

"It's possible, but again, I haven't been able to turn up anyone with that name in the area. And I've checked with everybody from the utility companies to the Social Security Administration on this side of the river. It's a little harder to get information about Mexican nationals, but I've got somebody working on that, too. Speaking of that, I've asked a friend of mine to meet us at the office. I guess you could say he's my opposite number from the Mexican government—"

Walker jerked the wheel to the side and jammed on the brakes, sending the pickup into a controlled skid. Lopez was thrown against the passenger door. He let out a surprised curse in Spanish.

A car rocketed past the pickup. Gunfire sprayed from the muzzle of an automatic weapon that was poking its ugly snout through the rear passenger window. The slugs chewed up the asphalt in front of the pickup Walker was driving. The car's brake lights flared momentarily, then winked off as the driver began to accelerate instead.

"I saw him coming in the mirror," Walker said as he brought the careening pickup under control and tromped down on the accelerator. The vehicle leaped forward. "I thought he was just driving like a bat out of hell at first, but then I saw something stick out that rear window."

"*Dios mío!*" said Lopez. "If you hadn't acted so quickly, Cordell, they would have shot us full of holes."

The car carrying the gunmen was moving at an even greater pace now. Walker's fast actions—and faster thinking—had ruined the assassination attempt before it even got started good. Now the would-be killers were just trying to get away from their erstwhile targets.

Lopez drew the service revolver that was holstered at his hip and leaned out the open window of the pickup. He started to aim at the fleeing car, then cursed and pulled his head back into the pickup. "Too much traffic on the road," he said. "I can't risk shooting."

Walker nodded his agreement and pressed down harder on the pickup's accelerator. It was up to him now to catch the car carrying the shooter.

Up ahead, just past downtown Laredo, was the Rio Grande itself. Interstate 35 ended at International Bridge #2, which carried most of the vehicle traffic over the river. International Bridge #1, Walker recalled from previous visits to the border town, was a few blocks to the west and handled most of the pedestrian crossings. Neither bridge presented a good option to the fugitives, since they would both be clogged with traffic.

Not surprisingly, the fleeing car veered suddenly off the interstate. Brakes screeched as its driver narrowly avoided several cars on the frontage road. The car made a speeding right-hand turn onto one of the side streets, coming up dangerously on two wheels for a second before settling back down with a thump. Walker followed at a slightly slower speed, torn between the need to keep the suspects in sight and his concern for the other drivers on the road. He swerved around several vehicles that had pulled over to avoid being struck by the gunmen's car.

"He's turning left!" Trivette said as they sped past the railroad station. The fugitives were pinning themselves in. The Rio Grande made a sharp turn northward, just west of the city, so that it blocked any routes that headed south or west.

Someone in the fleeing car must have figured that out, because it made another hairpin turn and headed east again, into the heart of downtown. Walker was less than a block behind when he made the same turn.

Suddenly, the car veered again, this time into a large open-air market. People screamed and leaped desperately out of the way as it bounced over a low curb and plowed through a wooden booth belonging to a tamale vendor. The vendor barely threw himself out of the path of the speeding car. Tamales, sauce, melted cheese, and scraps of wood flew high in the air from the impact.

The rear end of the car slewed violently from side to side for a moment before the driver brought it back under control. The vehicle lunged forward across the flagstone walkways of the market as shoppers and vendors scrambled to safety. Pushcarts full of brightly colored clothing exploded into kindling and scraps of fabric as the car slammed them aside.

Walker skidded the pickup to a halt at the curb. He and Trivette and Lopez leaped from the cab and sprinted through the chaos of the market in pursuit of the car. No way would Walker put all those people at risk by trying to drive through the crowd as the fugitives had done.

The car sideswiped a solidly built stall full of serapes and sombreros. The roof of the stall collapsed on top of the car. The vehicle spun as the driver, no doubt blinded by the serape that had wound up draped over most of the windshield, looked for a way out.

He found instead one of the palm trees that dotted the walkways of the market. The car slammed head-on into the tree, coming to a violent halt as the front grille crumpled. Steam shot into the air from the ruptured radiator. The doors popped open and three men piled out of the wrecked vehicle.

A hundred yards away, Walker yelled, "Hold it! Texas Rangers!"

Two of the men were carrying handguns, while the third brandished the automatic weapon that he had fired earlier at the pickup. He swept the barrel toward the onrushing lawmen and squeezed off a burst that made Walker and his companions dive for cover behind some of the market's stalls. The man kept turning and firing, the gun chattering and bucking in his hand. The line of slugs was tracking inexorably toward a knot of terrified tourists, among them several children.

Walker didn't have time for anything fancy. He lined the sights of his pistol on the gunman and squeezed off two fast shots. Both bullets drilled into the man's chest and flung him backward. His finger was still on the trigger as he fell, but the last burst went harmlessly into the sky. He flopped loosely onto the pavement.

His two buddies were still running, pausing only occasionally to throw some shots behind them. They reached the far side of the market and plunged into the crowds that regularly thronged the sidewalks of Laredo. Walker and Trivette ran after them, losing sight of the men but still able to track them by the shouts and screams that sounded as startled pedestrians caught sight of the guns. Lopez stayed behind in the market to check on the gunman Walker had downed.

After a few moments, Walker and Trivette realized that not only could they no longer see the men they were chasing, but they didn't hear any new shouts of surprise and fear. The men had probably tucked their weapons away out of sight and perhaps ducked into an alley or one of the many small shops that lined the street. Walker and Trivette slowed to a stop and exchanged a grim look. "We'll never find them in this crowd," Trivette said.

"We've got to try," replied Walker.

For the next fifteen minutes, they did just that, checking in every business they came to, but finally they were forced to admit that their quarry had given them the slip. They headed back to the market and found Lopez talking to several officers from the local police force who had arrived in response to the reports of shooting. The body of the gunman was still lying on the flagstones, but someone had covered it up with a canvas tarp.

"Is he dead?" Walker asked Lopez. He nodded toward the gunman.

"Yeah." Lopez knelt beside the body and pulled back the tarp, revealing a rough-hewn, pain-contorted face. "Ever see him before?"

Walker and Trivette studied the dead man's features for a moment, then shook their heads. "Nope," said Trivette. "Is he a local?"

"Probably," replied Lopez. "No ID on him, which isn't that unusual. Somebody probably gave him and his amigos a handful of pesos and pointed them at me, just like pointing a gun."

"You think you were the target?" Walker asked.

"A Texas Ranger makes enemies wherever he goes, but especially in a border town," Lopez said with a shrug. "I'm pretty well known to the criminal element around here, and it's no secret they'd like to see me dead."

Trivette looked at Walker. "Were you thinking that maybe they were after us?"

"I don't see how," Lopez said before Walker could answer. "I've kept your arrival quiet."

"But someone could have found out," said Walker. He nodded again at the dead man, whose face was now covered once more with the tarp. "And this guy was part of the welcoming committee."

Lopez grunted. "Some welcome. You're going to think Laredo's not a friendly place."

"We didn't come here to make friends," said Walker. "We came here to find one man. El Diablo."

TWELVE

Walker, Trivette, and Lopez gave brief statements to the Laredo police officers who had responded to the violence in the market, then left the officers to finish the mopping up. The cops would know where to find them later if they needed more information about the deadly incident.

The license plates on the wrecked car that the gunmen had used had already been run through the computer. The car was stolen—no surprise there. The police were going to check the fingerprints of the dead man and promised to get in touch with the Rangers as soon as they had the results.

The local Ranger office was in an old building on San Augustin Plaza, an area of downtown Laredo which had been restored to the elegance of its late nineteenth-century origins. Across the plaza stood the impressive building known as El Mercado, once a public market. Part of the building was still used for that purpose, but it also housed Laredo's city hall and administrative offices.

Trivette looked around at the flagstone plaza dotted with palm trees and beds of brightly blooming flowers, surrounded by brick and adobe buildings with red tile roofs, and asked, "How do you ever get any work done around here? I'd feel like taking a siesta all the time."

"You learn how to pace yourself," Lopez assured him.

The building that housed the Ranger offices was graceful old Spanish architecture on the outside but modern and functional on the inside. Lopez ushered his visitors into an office that was heavy on the chrome and tinted glass. Central air conditioning hummed softly. What was a pleasant late spring in northern Texas was already hot and humid early summer in the Rio Grande Valley.

A man was sitting in a chair in front of Lopez's desk. He stood up as the Rangers came in and turned to welcome them with a smile. "Hector," he said as he shook hands with Lopez. "Good to see you again."

"And you, Jorge," replied Lopez. He hung his Stetson on a hook on the wall, then went behind the desk and waved a hand at Walker and Trivette. "Rangers Cordell Walker and James Trivette," he said by way of introduction, "this is Jorge Alvarez, the man I spoke of earlier."

Alvarez was a handsome man around forty, wearing a well-cut, expensive suit. His grip was firm as he shook hands with Walker, who sensed considerable strength in the man.

"Jorge is on detached duty from the Mexican State Police," explained Lopez. "He heads up the antidrug task force that we've formed with law enforcement officers from both sides of the border."

Walker said, "Sounds like a challenging job."

Alvarez shrugged. "We do what we can. Unfortunately, it's a little like fighting a forest fire with a garden hose."

"Drug smuggling is a big problem all along the border, I'd imagine," said Trivette.

"The biggest," agreed Alvarez. "We work with the Mexican authorities, the U.S. Border Patrol, the DEA, and you Rangers, and still we can't do much more than make a dent in the drug traffic."

"Sooner or later we'll do more than that," Walker asserted confidently. "This is a war we can't afford to lose."

Alvarez nodded. "That's right."

"And we're going to start with El Diablo," said Walker.

"Sit down, all of you," said Lopez. "Jorge, we had a little trouble on the way here from the airport."

Alvarez frowned. "Trouble? What sort of trouble?"

"Someone tried to kill us."

Lopez's simple statement caused Alvarez's eyebrows to lift in surprise. "What?" he exclaimed.

"Some gunmen came after us on the highway," Walker said. "We turned the tables on them and chased them to a public market. They wrecked their car but still tried to shoot it out."

"What happened?" Alvarez asked anxiously.

"One of the shooters was killed," Lopez said. "The other two got away, unfortunately."

Alvarez shook his head, as if dismayed that such a thing could happen. "Do you think it was just a random shooting?" he asked. "Such things happen from time to time."

"No, it was deliberate," Walker answered without hesitation. "We don't have any proof of that, but I'm convinced of it."

"The guys seemed like they knew who they were after, all right," put in Trivette.

Alvarez looked at Lopez. "You were the target, Hector?"

"That's what I thought at first," said Lopez. "But Cordell thinks they might have been after him and Ranger Trivette."

"El Diablo," Alvarez breathed.

Walker leaned forward in his chair. "Why do you say that?"

"The poor people of the border say he has . . . powers. He is said to know everything, to see everything."

"You don't believe that, do you?" asked Trivette.

Alvarez shrugged. "Our informants wound up dead, and we protected their identities scrupulously."

"He knew we were coming, all right," said Walker, "but it wasn't because he has any sort of mystical abilities. He was tipped off, or the information leaked some other way." Walker looked across the desk at Lopez. "Who did you tell about our conversation earlier today?"

There was a flicker of irritation in Lopez's dark eyes. "Only my second-in-command, Lieutenant Thompson, and my secretary." He nodded toward Alvarez. "And Jorge here."

"And I told no one," Alvarez added without being asked.

"Did the two of you talk by phone?"

"That's right," said Lopez.

"Our lines are secure," said Alvarez.

"You're certain of that?" asked Trivette.

"We have our offices and all communications equipment swept every few weeks by electronics experts," Lopez explained. "The people we're up against, this so-called El Diablo and his ilk, can afford to use high-tech tactics against us, so we have to use them, too."

"And the same is true of my office," said Alvarez. "We've found bugs in the phones before, but they're clean now."

"In that case, we have to look at the other two people who knew Trivette and I were on our way down here," said Walker.

Lopez shook his head emphatically. "I'd trust Sam Thompson with my life," he said. "We've been Rangers together for years."

"I know Sam," Walker said with a nod, "and it doesn't seem likely to me that he'd sell us out to El Diablo, either. But who knows what pressure might have been brought to bear on him?"

"I trust Sam," Lopez insisted stubbornly. "No matter what."

Trivette said, "Then what about the secretary?"

"It's hard for me to believe that Gloria isn't trustworthy," Lopez said with a frown. "She's worked here for almost two years, and you know that civilian employees are subject to an extensive background investigation before the Department will hire them."

"You might want to have a talk with her anyway, Hector," suggested Alvarez. "If Walker's right about what happened to you being a deliberate hit, then *somebody* told El Diablo they were coming."

Lopez looked uncomfortable, but he finally nodded. "All right. But I just don't believe that Gloria would turn traitor like that."

"In the meantime," said Walker, "we still have to carry on with the job that brought us here." He turned to the head of the task force. "Señor Alvarez, have you ever heard of something called Cabeza de Oro?"

"Head of Gold," mused Alvarez, automatically translating the phrase as had everyone else Walker had asked about it. "Hector mentioned that to me earlier. I've been trying to think, but I haven't come up with a thing, Ranger Walker."

"What about the authorities in Mexico?"

"I've already faxed a request for information to my superiors in Mexico City," Alvarez said with a nod. "So far I haven't heard back from them."

"Well," said Trivette, "other than knowing that El Diablo was aware of our plans, we seem to be at a dead end."

"Not necessarily," said Alvarez. "I have something in mind."

Walker nodded. "Go on."

Alvarez leaned forward in his chair, clasping his hands together earnestly in front of him. "As I said, our sources have pretty much dried up since those two informants were murdered, but we still get tips from time to time. One of them was about a place called the Red Rooster."

Lopez frowned and said, "I've heard of it. A cantina, isn't it? Pretty rough place."

Alvarez nodded. "That's right. It's on this side of the

river, so I checked it out with the Laredo PD. It doesn't have a reputation for drug-related activities, but it is known to be a hangout for cockfighters.''

''What does that have to do with El Diablo?'' asked Trivette.

''We know very little about the man,'' replied Alvarez, ''but we have heard that he enjoys betting on cockfights. I thought perhaps if we paid a visit to the place, we might get a line on him that way.''

''I hadn't heard that about him. But those boys aren't going to talk to a couple of Rangers and a Mexican cop,'' Lopez said with a shake of his head.

''No, they won't,'' agreed Alvarez, ''but they might talk to some high rollers with plenty of money to bet.''

Walker smiled tightly. ''You know, señor Alvarez, I believe I'm beginning to like the way you think. . . .''

The Red Rooster was a cinder-block building on a scrubby lot on the outskirts of Laredo. Extending behind the building was a long, shedlike wooden structure with no windows and a roof of corrugated tin. Beyond the shed, the flat, scrub-covered monte ran for half a mile to the Rio Grande. There were no other businesses along the road within a quarter mile of the Red Rooster.

Cars, pickups, and sport utility vehicles crowded the gravel parking lot, even though the hour was barely past dusk and a strip of red from the sun still shone along the western horizon. Walker, Trivette, and Alvarez climbed out of the rented pickup that Walker had parked on the edge of the lot. Hector Lopez was too well known around Laredo to risk taking part in this undercover operation, but the other three men hoped to be able to blend in with the crowd here at the cantina.

Tejano music blasted from inside, clearly audible in the parking lot. People were coming and going from the place, mostly men. Alvarez took the lead as he and the Rangers approached the door. The Mexican official had traded his elegant business suit and Italian shoes for boots, jeans, and a denim jacket over a work shirt. Walker and Trivette were dressed in a similar fashion, a little rougher than their usual garb.

Walker was reminded of the club in Dallas where he and Trivette had caught up to Paco the night before. The Red Rooster was an even tougher place, however. The customers were mostly Hispanic, and they turned hard, suspicious faces toward the newcomers. Walker spotted a few gringos in the crowd, but Trivette appeared to be the only black man.

A plain hardwood bar ran the length of the right-hand wall. Dark booths lined the left-hand wall, and the floor between was cluttered with tables. There was no bandstand; the blaring music came from a jukebox. In the left rear corner of the room, past the booths, was a tiny dance floor about the size of a postage stamp. Well, maybe a little bigger than that, Walker thought dryly. People didn't come to the Red Rooster to dance. They came to drink and maybe find a woman.

And to bet on the cockfights. Couldn't forget about that.

In the center of the rear wall was a door. Two men stood casually beside it, but Walker suspected they weren't really casual at all. They were guarding the entrance to that shed-like building in the back. The door looked thick and solid, and Walker wondered if it had a steel core.

The air was thick with smoke. Walker smelled both tobacco and the sickly-sweet odor of marijuana. Despite his dislike of the stuff, Walker was prepared to ignore it. He and Trivette and Alvarez were after something much bigger and more dangerous than a few pot smokers.

Alvarez led the way to the bar. He ordered three tequilas from a surly, bullet-headed man in a tight tank top that showed off bulging muscles. When the bartender brought the drinks and slapped them down on the hardwood, Alvarez dropped a twenty dollar bill beside the glasses. "Horacio around tonight?" he asked.

The twenty disappeared. "You know Horacio?" growled the bartender.

"Never met the *hombre*," Alvarez answered honestly. "But I know some friends of some friends of his. They told me to visit the Red Rooster and ask for him if I wanted some excitement."

The bartender sneered. "Find your own *putas*, man," he said. "I ain't no pimp."

Alvarez shook his head. "That's not the kind of excitement we're looking for." He glanced over at Walker and Trivette. "Is it, boys?"

"We're more interested in wagering," said Trivette.

Walker inclined his head toward the door in the rear wall. "Back there, unless I miss my guess."

The bartender scowled at them. "Nobody goes back there unless Horacio vouches for them. Not for twenty dollars."

"How about a hundred?" Walker asked bluntly.

"My life's worth more than a hundred."

Alvarez reached inside his denim jacket and partially withdrew a tightly sealed plastic packet. The plastic was transparent, and the white powder inside was plainly visible. "What about this?" he asked. "Will that buy us a ticket?"

Walker and Trivette kept their faces carefully impassive, even though both Rangers were surprised by Alvarez's gambit. He hadn't told them anything about having drugs on him. Yet it wasn't a total surprise. Alvarez was, after all, the head of an antidrug task force, with access to plenty of dope that had been confiscated in various raids. And finding El Diablo might fall into the category of a case where the ends justified the means.

Maybe. Walker was still troubled. But for the time being, he was willing to play along with Alvarez.

"Put that stuff up, man!" the bartender hissed, a worried frown on his face.

"It's yours if you put in a word for us and get us back

there,'' said Alvarez, jerking his head toward the door as he put the package back in his jacket.

The bartender licked his lips, clearly tempted by the prospect of getting his hands on several thousand dollars' worth of heroin. Finally he nodded. ''All right. But that better be good stuff.''

''The best,'' Alvarez assured him.

The bartender reached underneath the bar, and Walker wondered if he was pushing some sort of signal button. He must have, because one of the guards left the door and started across the room toward them.

''Horacio's back there,'' said the bartender. ''You better hope you were tellin' the truth about knowin' friends of his.''

''Gracias.'' Alvarez started to turn away with Walker and Trivette, but the bartender stopped him by leaning over the bar and placing a hand on his arm.

''Why don't I hold that jacket for you?'' the bartender suggested.

''Yeah, I almost forgot.'' Alvarez shrugged out of the jacket and passed it across the bar, the packet of dope concealed inside it. ''I'll get it back when I leave, right?''

''Sure, man. I'll take good care of it for you.''

The guard from the door had come up to join them. ''Come on,'' he said harshly.

Walker, Trivette, and Alvarez followed the man across the room. The other guard opened the door slightly and stepped back. Alvarez took the lead again, stepping through first into the shed.

Walker and Trivette followed, and the heavy door closed behind them with a thud.

THIRTEEN

The first things Walker became aware of were bright lights and the smell of blood.

And a loud, animalistic noise that he recognized as the yelling of frenzied bettors.

A match was going on as he and Trivette and Alvarez entered the shed. People were lined up three and four deep around a long, rectangular pit that had been dug in the center of the space. A waist-high wooden wall circled the pit, and Walker hoped it was as sturdy as it looked. The way the crowd was leaning against it, the wall might be in danger of collapsing and dumping some of the spectators into the pit. None of them seemed worried about that possibility, however. All their attention was concentrated on the two birds trying to kill each other on the blood-spattered sand.

A tall, lean man stood at the head of the pit, his arms crossed over his chest and a satisfied look on his face. Alvarez turned to Walker and Trivette and said over the clamor of the crowd, "That's Horacio. He owns this place."

Walker nodded. He and Trivette and Alvarez moved

closer. Through an occasional gap in the crowd, Walker caught glimpses of the birds in the pit. Their colorful plumage was made even brighter by the blood that stained the feathers, blood drawn by the razor-sharp spurs each bird wore on his claws.

Walker's guts tightened, but despite the revulsion he felt at this barbaric spectacle, he kept an interested expression on his face. He and his companions worked their way around the pit toward the spot where Horacio stood watching with pride.

The tall man's eyes flicked toward them, and he frowned slightly. All the other spectators were probably regulars here at the Red Rooster, so Horacio would notice any newcomers. And he would be curious about them as well.

"Gentlemen," he said as they came up to him, raising his voice enough so that he could be heard over the shouting. "Welcome to the Red Rooster."

His voice told Walker something surprising. Despite his name and his swarthy complexion, Horacio was not Hispanic. And as Walker looked at him, something clicked in the back of his brain. He recognized this man.

In the early days of the Texas Rangers, many of the men who wore the circle star carried with them a book of photographs of wanted men. That would have been too cumbersome in this day and age, but Walker had a mental file of his own, and in it were tucked away the descriptions of dozens of criminals wanted for various felonies. He was looking directly at one of those criminals now, in this shabby, border town dive.

Horace Wilkins was the man's name, alias Harry Williams, alias Harvey Winthrop, a.k.a. Horace the Horse, probably because of his long face. He had gotten his start working as a legbreaker for a loan shark in Odessa, and anyone tough enough to deal with oil field roughnecks was tough indeed. He had moved on down to San Antonio and set up shop as a fence, then eventually headed to Houston, where he had moved up to white-collar crime such as insurance fraud. After that, Horace Wilkins had dropped out of sight, taking with him a long rap sheet that included a couple of convictions for assault and an eighteen-month stay in the penitentiary in Huntsville.

Now he was running a cockfighting operation here in Laredo, a definite step down from his brush with a more genteel brand of crime in Houston. A man's true nature usually wins out in the end, Walker mused as Horace's history flashed through his brain in a matter of seconds.

"You must be Horacio," said Alvarez. He didn't offer to shake hands.

"That's right." Horace craned his neck to look past Alvarez, and he winced slightly as one of the birds scored a particularly bloody point. "Do I know you?" he asked, turning his attention back to the newcomers.

"Only through a friend of a friend. You know Willie Sanchez?"

"What if I do?" Horace asked coolly.

"Well, so does my friend. And Willie told him about the little . . . exhibitions . . . you stage here."

"Willie does spread the word for me sometimes," admitted Horace, his tension easing a little. "I'm afraid the betting is closed on this match, though."

"We don't mind waiting for the next one," Walker said.

"And you are . . . ?"

"A friend of his." Walker inclined his head toward Alvarez.

Horace looked at Trivette. "And I suppose you're friendly, too."

"Very," said Trivette. "I'm also looking for some excitement I can bet on."

"Well, you've come to the right place." Horace unfolded his arms and gestured toward the pit.

One of the birds was on its last legs. It staggered backward under the slashing attack of the other rooster. The polished steel blades of the spurs flashed in the glow of the fluorescent lights that hung in a long row down the center of the shed. With a loud squawk and a flapping of wings, the stronger bird lashed out once again at the weaker one, and blood spurted into the air, accompanied by an outburst of even louder shouting. The wounded bird toppled over and flopped grotesquely on the sand for a few moments before lying still.

"Too bad," Horace said, not sounding too broken up about the rooster's death. "He was a good bird. But not as good as Hellion."

"That's the winner?" asked Trivette.

Horace nodded. "That's right."

One of the men crowding around the pit opened a narrow gate in the wall and jumped down onto the sand. With a sorrowful look on his face, he picked up the dead rooster. Another man hopped down into the arena and rounded up the victor, grinning hugely as he held up the bird to the cheers of the spectators. The owner of the defeated rooster shot him a vicious glare behind his back.

Horace applauded the winner politely, then turned back to Walker, Trivette, and Alvarez. "Since you gentlemen are new to our little circle, could I offer you a drink?" he asked. He gestured toward a small bar set up along the wall of the shed. "First one's on the house."

"Thanks," said Alvarez. "Lead the way."

Horace took them over to the bar, which was doing a booming business between matches. He looked at them and arched an eyebrow inquisitively, and Walker said, "Just beer for me, thanks."

"Me, too," echoed Trivette, and Alvarez nodded to make it three.

Horace held up three fingers to the bartender, then chuckled. "You obviously want to have a clear head when the betting starts on the next fight."

"I try never to muddle my mind when money's involved," Walker told him. Which was certainly true.

Someone came up to Horace and drew him away, whispering in his ear. Trivette took advantage of the opportunity to lean close to Walker and say in a low voice, "This is sick, Walker. How can people enjoy this?"

"There have always been people with a taste for blood, Trivette," replied Walker, his words pitched equally low. "We'll have to put up with it for a while, though, if we want Horace to trust us."

Trivette nodded his understanding.

Walker turned to Alvarez and said, "When are you going to ask him about the man we're looking for?" He didn't want to mention El Diablo's name until the right moment came.

"We'd better wait until after the next match has started," Alvarez said. "By that time, maybe he'll trust us a little."

Walker doubted that. Knowing what he did about Horace Wilkins, he figured it was unlikely the man would ever really trust anybody. Alvarez clearly had no idea who "Horacio" really was, and Walker didn't want to go into it here and now.

A slight commotion drew Walker's attention, and he looked over to see the owner of the rooster that had been defeated in the previous match. He was carrying a burlap bag, and from the stains on it, Walker assumed the dead bird was inside. But it was the young boy beside the man who really caught Walker's attention. The boy, who Walker hadn't noticed in here earlier, was crying. Tears cut tracks in the dust on his cheeks. The man tried to comfort him by putting a hand on his shoulder, but the boy said something in angry Spanish and knocked the man's hand away.

Father and son, Walker speculated. And the boy had probably raised that rooster, the rooster whose blood was now soaking through that burlap bag.

Finding El Diablo was more important, but Walker vowed that if there was any way he could manage it, he was going to see this cockfighting operation closed down, too.

Horace rejoined the three lawmen as they sipped their

beers. "Almost ready to get started again," he said. "If you'd care to place some bets . . ."

"We'll take a look at the birds first," Alvarez said coolly.

Two men had climbed down into the pit, each of them carrying a hooded rooster. The birds were beautiful in a sleek, deadly way.

Horace supplied the birds' names and pedigrees as their owners readied them for the match. Alvarez nodded and placed a five hundred dollar bet on one of the roosters. Trivette followed his lead, but Walker bet a thousand on the other bird. It was all confiscated drug money, so none of them worried much about winning or losing. All around them, other bets were being shouted out among the spectators. Someone in the crowd, some employee of Horace's, had to be keeping track of the wagers, but Walker couldn't spot whoever it was.

The hoods were removed and the deadly match got underway. The roosters circled, clucking and preening, then leaped to the attack. The volume of noise from the spectators around the pit grew louder with each slash and thrust of the spurs.

Walker tried to get into the spirit of the thing, knowing that he had to pretend to care about the bet he had riding on the outcome, but he kept seeing the tear-streaked face of the boy who had lost a feathered friend.

Near the end of the match, as one of the birds was clearly tiring and on the verge of defeat, perhaps even death, Alvarez leaned over to Wilkins and said, "This is quite a match. I'm sure if El Diablo were here, he would enjoy it."

That was a risk, since none of them really knew what El Diablo looked like. He might already be here, perhaps even directly across from them on the other side of the pit. But Horace merely smiled and asked, "So you know El Diablo, too, eh?"

"We know of him," Alvarez answered, an honest reply as far as it went. "We'd like to meet him."

"Then you are different from most," said Horace. "Most men don't want to meet El Diablo. It's said he carries death with him."

"I'm more interested in the money he and his associates make."

Horace gave Alvarez a penetrating stare. "You want to meet El Diablo?" he finally asked after a long moment of silence on his part. The shed's interior was still noisy, though, as the cockfight continued.

"I think we can do him some good," said Alvarez. "And I know he can help us."

"It could perhaps be arranged—" Horace began.

That was as far as he got when a burst of shrill, angry Spanish curses rose above the clamor. Walker stiffened as his brain automatically translated the words and he realized that one of the owners of the birds currently in the pit had just accused the other of cheating.

Walker knew an accusation like that could lead to only one thing.

Trouble.

In the next couple of seconds, as screams broke out and the crowd began to eddy and swirl violently, Walker knew that trouble had indeed come to the Red Rooster.

FOURTEEN

The brawl spread quickly through the entire shed. Fists flew, men shouted angrily, and some pushed toward the single exit, wanting to get out, while others tried to get to the center of the action.

With men crowded all around him, Walker's martial arts skills weren't much use to him. They required room to move, something that was in short supply in this chaos. He saw a fist coming at his face, ducked under the blow, and threw a short, powerful punch of his own that thudded into the solar plexus of his attacker. That man staggered back, but another instantly took his place.

Walker felt someone at his back, and then Trivette called, "I've got this side, Walker!"

Satisfied that he and Trivette were fighting back to back, Walker continued lashing out at the circle of madly flailing combatants. He wondered what had happened to Alvarez when this riot broke out, but there was no time to check on the Mexican cop. Alvarez would just have to fend for himself for the time being.

So far during the brawl, Walker hadn't seen the flicker of steel, and he was glad of that. If everyone was willing to stick to fists, maybe nobody would get killed. If knives or guns came into play, however, it would be a whole different story.

Walker blocked a punch, sent a short jab into the face of the man who had thrown it. The man's head rocked back, and he stumbled to the side. At Walker's back, Trivette disposed of another opponent with a wicked right cross.

Suddenly there was a cracking noise, followed by a loud crash and frenzied squawking. The wall around the pit had broken, just as Walker had thought it might earlier in the evening, and several of the fighting men had been dumped onto the sand right on top of the roosters. The birds reacted as any animal will when threatened: they struck out in self-defense, slashing at the stunned men with the razor-sharp spurs. One of the men shrieked as a blade swiped across his face and laid his cheek open to the bone. Blood instantly turned his face into a crimson mask.

Other men got bad cuts on their hands as they tried to ward off the roosters' attacks. The carnage in the pit sort of took the steam out of the brawl around it. The owners of the roosters tried to get to their birds and corral them, while others leapt to the assistance of the wounded men.

Still back to back, Walker and Trivette stood with their fists poised in case anyone else jumped them, but the fighting was rapidly winding down now. Walker glanced around, looking for Alvarez and Horace Wilkins.

He didn't spot either of them, but he did see the man sidling closer to Trivette, hand held low along his hip. Suddenly that hand came up and flashed toward Trivette, and light winked from the blade that it held.

Walker slammed an elbow into Trivette's back, not hard enough to injure him but with sufficient force to knock him out of the way of the knife attack. Continuing the same motion, Walker spun around. The press of people around him had thinned out somewhat, so he was able to bring his right leg up in a kick that connected with the knife wielder's wrist. The heel of Walker's boot cracked against bone and sent the knife spinning out of suddenly nerveless fingers. The man staggered back, clutching his broken wrist to his body and howling in pain.

"Watch it, Walker!"

The warning came from Trivette. Instinctively, Walker crouched. As he did so, an empty whiskey bottle being swung like a club whistled over his head. Walker whirled and hooked a punch into the midsection of the man who had just tried to brain him. The man's breath, laden with the fumes of the raw whiskey that had been in the now-empty bottle, puffed out into Walker's face. Walker brought his left up and sent a sharp back fist blow into the man's face.

The rush of feet behind him alerted him, and he kicked out with his right foot, aiming instinctively. His heel sunk into the belly of the man charging him and sent the man flying backward.

One man grabbed Trivette from behind, wrapping his arms around the deceptively slender Ranger. As another man tried to close in from the front, Trivette lifted both feet and crashed them into the second man's chest. The reaction to that impact sent the man holding Trivette staggering back a few steps. Trivette broke his hold, whirled, and brought both hands down in vicious chops against the sides of the man's neck. The man folded up and fell to the ground.

Trivette backed up, just as Walker was doing the same thing. Their backs bumped together, and once again they were ready to take on all comers. From the way several men were ringing them, it was obvious that Walker and Trivette were targets. This whole brawl might have been set up to get to them, but it had taken some ugly, unexpected turns with the damage handed out by the maddened roosters.

And where in blazes were Alvarez and Horace Wilkins? Even though he and Trivette were in a bad fix, Walker hoped no serious harm had befallen the Mexican cop.

"Walker, this doesn't look very good," Trivette said

over his shoulder. "They're ganging up on us."

"Yeah," said Walker.

Before he could go on, the sound of sirens split the night. The wailing was close by, and instead of closing in on Walker and Trivette, the hardcases surrounding them were suddenly looking back and forth at each other nervously. A second later, one of them broke for the exit, and that started an exodus. All the men pounded out through the cantina, and Walker heard tires squealing in the parking lot as they fled. In a matter of heartbeats, he and Trivette were left standing there, ready to defend themselves against an empty room.

"Well, what do you know?" said Trivette. "I guess if they were really after us, whoever paid them didn't give them enough to make them risk waiting around for the cops."

So Trivette had come to the same conclusion, thought Walker. This had been a setup of some sort.

"Did you see Alvarez after the brawl started?"

Trivette shook his head. "Not really. He and Horacio were waltzing around, but then I lost track of them."

"Alvarez was fighting with Horacio?" Walker frowned.

"Yeah."

"Come on. Let's see if we can find them."

The two Rangers stalked out of the shed. The front room of the Red Rooster was deserted now, just like the back. And the sirens were fading away instead of coming closer.

Trivette laughed. "They weren't even coming here," he said. "Those guys cut and ran for no reason."

"You get what you pay for," said Walker, "and those were just cheap thugs."

He and Trivette stepped out of the building into the parking lot, moving quickly through the doorway so that they wouldn't be silhouetted against the light inside for more than a split second. There were several vehicles still parked on the lot, including the rented pickup in which Walker, Trivette, and Alvarez had arrived.

"Walker!"

The low-voiced call made the Rangers stiffen. They were reaching for the guns hidden under their jackets when a man came out from behind one of the parked cars. "Damn, I'm glad to see you!" Alvarez went on. "I was afraid you'd gotten hurt in that brawl."

"You all right?" Walker asked the Mexican cop.

Alvarez nodded. He was close enough to them now so that Walker could see the bruises and the streaks of blood on his face. "I'm fine," said Alvarez. "Horacio took off, and I went after him. I think that son of a bitch knew who we were all along! That brawl was nothing but a setup. I saw him give a high-sign to somebody just before it started."

"I thought the same thing," Walker said. "What happened to Horacio?"

Alvarez jerked a thumb at the truck. "He's over there, out cold. He put up a fight, but I finally took him down."

"What about those sirens?" asked Trivette.

"Lucky break for us," Alvarez answered with a grin. "Some fire trucks went by. If that hadn't stampeded Horacio's goons . . . well, we might have been in trouble."

"Come on," said Walker. "I want to have a talk with Horacio." He was still keeping his knowledge of the man's true identity to himself. It might be a useful card to play during the interrogation of Horace Wilkins. *Someone* had tipped off the cantina owner about who Walker, Trivette, and Alvarez really were. Walker had the first faint glimmerings of an idea who that someone might have been, but he wanted his theory confirmed.

Alvarez led them around the rear end of the truck. Walker saw a dark shape sprawled on the ground next to the vehicle. Alvarez said, "I didn't have any cuffs with me, of course, so I used his belt to tie his hands behind his back."

"He must still be unconscious," said Trivette. "He's not moving."

Walker leaned over and grasped Horace's shoulder. He

rolled the man onto his back. As he did so, Horace's head fell loosely to the side. Walker frowned and rested a couple of fingers on the side of Horace's neck.

After a moment, Walker straightened and said grimly, "He's not unconscious. He's dead."

"Dead!" Alvarez exploded, sounding shocked. "But . . . he can't be. He was all right when I tied him up."

Walker checked the passenger door of the truck. It was unlocked, and when he opened it, the dome light came on and spilled illumination out onto the ground, and onto the face of Horace Wilkins as well. The light was bright enough to show the ugly dent in Horace's temple. Trickles of blood had seeped from the cantina owner's ears and nose.

"Fractured skull," Walker said.

"I didn't hit him that hard," snapped Alvarez. "But he bounced off the truck when he went down. That must have been when it happened." He slammed his open palm against the roof of the truck in frustration. "Damn it! I was counting on asking him some questions."

"So was I," said Walker, "but he's not going to be telling us anything now."

"So you're convinced this fellow Wilkins knew who you were all along?" asked Hector Lopez as the Rangers and Alvarez gathered in Lopez's office later that night. Walker had explained about recognizing "Horacio" as the long-time criminal Horace Wilkins.

Walker nodded. "It looked that way to me."

"And me," added Trivette.

"We were set up," Alvarez said. "I'm sure of it."

"Then that means there's a leak somewhere in this office," said Lopez, "and we have to find it."

Walker asked, "Did you tell your secretary or Lieutenant Thompson about our plans?"

Lopez shook his head. "No one knew where you were going but the four of us." He leaned back suddenly, his eyes widening. "Hey, you don't think that *I*—"

"Of course not," Alvarez said quickly. "Nobody's accusing you of anything, Hector. We all know you too well for that."

"But if it wasn't any of us," said Trivette, "then who tipped off Wilkins?"

"I think maybe you'd better have the room swept for bugs again, Hector," Alvarez suggested.

Lopez slapped his palm down on the desk. "Damn it! When a man can't say what he wants in his own office without his enemies hearing it—"

"Have that attended to as soon as you can, Hector," Walker said. "In the meantime, we'll make our plans elsewhere."

Lopez scraped his chair back. "Good idea. Come on."

A few minutes later, the four men were strolling along Zaragosa Street, next to the San Augustin plaza. Though the hour was fairly late, there were still tourists and other pedestrians in the area. Even if El Diablo's men were tracking them with parabolic mikes or other high-tech surveillance equipment, the street noises would probably be enough to muffle and distort the conversation among the lawmen.

"I think the key is still Cabeza de Oro, whatever that is," said Walker.

"Maybe there'll be some information on it from Mexico City at my office in the morning," said Alvarez.

"Be careful what you say there," Walker told him. "If El Diablo has bugged Hector's office, he could have done the same to yours."

"I know," Alvarez said with a nod. "Don't worry; I'll play everything close to the vest."

Trivette asked, "In the meantime, what do we do?"

"About the only thing we can do right now," said Walker. "Get some rest tonight and start over again in the morning."

"You think we'll ever find El Diablo?" asked Lopez,

sounding discouraged, which was not common for him.

"I'm sure we will," said Walker. "In fact, after everything that happened tonight, I think we're closer to El Diablo than ever before."

FIFTEEN

The sun was barely up when the tour bus pulled out of the large garage on the edge of the city and headed for downtown Laredo. Its powerful engine rumbled loudly, and its air brakes hissed every time it came to a stop. It was painted in a bright red, green, and white pattern that was reminiscent of the Mexican national flag. Cheerful mariachi music came from speakers mounted on its roof. Everything about the long, heavy vehicle said fun and excitement. Later this morning, after the bus had taken on a full load of passengers from the downtown hotels, it would cross International Bridge #2 and carry the American tourists into Nuevo Laredo for a day of shopping and sightseeing. The tour company promised the passengers a day they would never forget.

In this case, the claim was certainly right.

Walker heard the telephone ringing and rolled over in bed. He and Trivette were staying in a small hotel not far from San Augustin Plaza and Ranger headquarters. He reached for the phone on the bedside table. "Walker."

"I've got it! I know what Cabeza de Oro means."

The excited voice belonged to Jorge Alvarez. Walker sat up in bed, instantly wide awake. "What is it?"

"A landmark," said Alvarez. "A hill about fifteen miles south of Nuevo Laredo. Evidently there's some sort of big rock on top of it, and when the sun hits it just right, it shines like gold."

"Head of Gold," Walker mused. "Could be. How did you find out about it?"

"There was a fax waiting for me at the task force office when I got here this morning. Someone in Mexico City turned up the reference on an old topographical map used by the *Rurales* a hundred years ago."

Walker glanced at the clock that was next to the phone. Its digital read-out said 6:37. "You're at work early."

"Couldn't sleep," said Alvarez. "I kept thinking about how El Diablo was making monkeys of us."

Walker grunted, then said, "This sounds like a good lead. We should check it out."

"I'll come by there and pick up you and Trivette in, what, thirty minutes or so?"

Walker chuckled dryly. "Better make it an hour. Trivette's not that easy to wake up in the morning." He paused, then added, "I take it jurisdiction won't be a problem, since we'll have to cross the border."

"Don't worry about that," Alvarez assured him. "As head of the antidrug task force, I'll be all the jurisdiction you'll need."

"See you in an hour, then."

"Right." Alvarez hung up.

Walker sat there for a moment, staring at the phone and frowning deeply in thought.

Then he replaced the receiver on the cradle, swung his legs out of bed, and started getting dressed. A few minutes later, he was knocking on the door of the adjoining room, where Trivette was sleeping soundly. Walker smiled faintly as he heard a groan from the other side of the door.

Trivette would wake up quickly enough when he heard what Walker had to tell him.

Alvarez picked them up in a jeep. Trivette, who was alert now after several cups of coffee, looked dubiously at the vehicle, which appeared to be of World War II vintage.

"Where'd you get that?" he asked. "Anzio?"

Alvarez grinned. "It's not quite that old, Ranger. But my government has had to learn how to operate more frugally. Military surplus comes in handy for that."

Walker opened the door and stepped into the jeep. "I don't care what it looks like, as long as it gets us to Cabeza de Oro."

"It'll get us there," said Alvarez. When Trivette had climbed into the back seat, he sent the jeep into traffic and headed for International Bridge #2.

Cars and buses were already backed up in both directions at the bridge, waiting to cross the border. Alvarez seemed to grow impatient as he waited his turn, and after several minutes of sitting beside a brightly colored bus full of tourists, he jerked on the wheel and sent the jeep into a lane that was blocked off at the moment by garish orange plastic cones. A couple of the cones went spinning, knocked out of the way by the jeep's wheels, but Alvarez didn't look back.

His credentials got them past the U.S. Customs agents on duty at the American end of the bridge. The guards seemed a bit annoyed at the way Alvarez had jumped the line, but they got over that when they saw his badge and the silver star set in a silver circle that was pinned to Walker's shirt.

The Mexican guards at the southern end of the bridge were even more accommodating. All Alvarez had to do was hold up his badge, and they waved the jeep on through the checkpoint. Once the border was behind them, Alvarez gave a somewhat sheepish grin and said, "I hate to pull rank like that, but I'm anxious to get down to Cabeza de Oro and see what we can find out."

"Do you think it's El Diablo's headquarters?" Trivette asked from the back seat.

"It could be," said Alvarez. "It's in a fairly isolated area, even though it's not really that far from Nuevo Laredo. There are some big ranchos in the vicinity."

"Do you know who owns the land where this hill sits?" asked Walker.

Alvarez shook his head. "Not yet. My people in Mexico City were still researching that for me. I wouldn't be surprised, though, if El Diablo turned out to be some rich *hacendado* who's decided that drug smuggling is even more profitable than ranching."

"Maybe we should have some backup," Trivette suggested, "since we don't know what we're going to run into down here."

Alvarez gestured toward a radio mounted under the dashboard of the jeep. "I can call in for help any time I need to."

"Speaking of calling," said Walker, "are you sure no one was listening in on that call to our hotel this morning?"

"Positive. The phones in my office are clear. I checked them myself."

Walker nodded.

Alvarez drove south from Nuevo Laredo, past the large circular track where horse races and dog races were held, past the bull ring, past the small airport. So far they had traveled on the highway, but not long after passing the airport, Alvarez swung the jeep to the left, turning onto a road that was narrow but paved. "The roads will get pretty rough before we reach our destination," he told Walker and Trivette. "That's another reason I brought the jeep."

The edge of the city was a sharply defined border. Once the buildings stopped, the open landscape took over, and it looked much as it must have looked a hundred years earlier. The terrain was flat for the most part, with only an occasional hill, and was covered with a mixture of grasslands and scrubby mesquite trees, broken up by stretches of rocky outcroppings. In the distance, a few rugged-looking mesas rose, and a dark blue line on the western horizon marked the northern reaches of the Sierra Madre Oriental mountain range.

A couple of miles after leaving the highway, Alvarez turned south again, and this time the jeep bounced into the ruts of a dirt road. "This will take us to Cabeza de Oro," he said.

Trivette glanced behind them at the plume of dust rising from the path. "If El Diablo has a lookout posted, he's liable to see that dust and know we're coming."

Walker had already thought the same thing. But Alvarez just shrugged. "There's no other way out there," he said. "We'll just have to chance it."

Walker's gaze moved constantly, checking out the landscape around them, so he was the first one who seemed to notice that they were no longer alone in the vast, empty terrain. "We've got company," he said as he nodded toward a long, shallow ridge a couple hundred yards to the right of the road.

Alvarez looked in that direction, too, and exclaimed, "Damn!" A pickup was bouncing along the ridge, keeping pace with the jeep.

"I warned you about that dust," said Trivette, drawing an angry glance from the Mexican cop.

Alvarez put his attention back on the road, however, instead of letting his glare linger on Trivette. "That pickup might not have anything to do with El Diablo," he said, but the hollow ring in his voice was evidence that he didn't really believe what he was saying. "It could belong to some rancher."

"Then what about that one?" said Walker, pointing to the left this time.

"Holy . . ." Trivette breathed as he looked where Walker indicated and saw the second pickup. Trivette leaned forward and spoke to Alvarez. "You'd better turn around while you can, otherwise they're liable to box us in."

"And give up finding out what Cabeza de Oro means?"

"It means a trap," Walker said calmly. "Look."

Ahead of them, about a mile down the dirt road, another cloud of dust rose into the already hot morning air. A vehicle was coming toward them, and from the looks of the dust, it was barreling along at a pretty good clip, too.

Alvarez cursed and jammed on the brakes. The jeep rocked to a stop, its engine dying. Still cursing, Alvarez turned the key. The engine ground noisily but didn't catch.

"Uh-oh," Trivette said softly.

Walker opened the door of the jeep. "Come on."

"Wait a minute," said Alvarez. "Maybe I can get it started."

"Not in the next five minutes. It's flooded." Walker gestured toward the approaching dust cloud. "And whoever that is will be here by then. We'd better get off the road while we still can."

"Sounds like a good idea to me," said Trivette as he climbed quickly out of the jeep.

"Wait," Alvarez said again. "I don't know—"

"Stay here if you want, Alvarez," said Walker. "Trivette and I are going to see if we can give them the slip."

Alvarez muttered under his breath, but he gave up trying to start the jeep and got out. "All right," he said. "Whatever you think is best, Walker."

Trivette looked into the jeep. "You don't happen to have any extra weapons in there, do you? Maybe a bazooka or two?"

Alvarez shook his head. "Not so much as a slingshot."

"We'll take our chances with what we've got," Walker said curtly. "Let's go."

He broke into a trot, heading off the road toward the west. The ground was more rugged in that direction, and the pursuers might not be able to follow them as easily in the vehicles. Trivette and Alvarez fell in behind him.

Their low-heeled boots weren't really made for running, but the three lawmen did the best they could. Though this was Alvarez's country, Walker took the lead. As he ran, he glanced back toward the road. The vehicle that had been approaching them from the front was in sight now. It was an old, low-slung station wagon, barreling along at the base of the dust cloud its wheels were kicking up. The two pickups that had been flanking them had driven on for a short distance before their drivers realized that the jeep had come to a stop. Now the pickups had turned around and were racing back in the direction they had come from.

And there was a fourth dust cloud to be seen now, too. Someone had been following the jeep, and now that vehicle was coming closer in a hurry.

Walker squinted at that fourth plume of dust. He had a pretty good idea who was responsible for it, and he certainly hoped his hunch was correct.

The three lawmen reached the first of a series of arroyos that slashed through the landscape like giant claw marks. Walker pointed and said, "Down there!" The sides of the gully were steep, but he and Trivette and Alvarez were able to slide down them. The bed, which had been washed out by flash floods over the years, was flat and sandy and only about ten feet wide. No one would be able to get down here in a vehicle.

"These gullies are like a maze," Trivette said as he trotted alongside Walker. "We might be able to dodge them down here for a while."

Alvarez was already panting a little from the exertion. "Looks like I should have . . . arranged for some backup after all," he said between puffs.

"They haven't caught us yet," Walker said grimly.

The arroyo ran in a generally north-south orientation, and Walker and his companions were heading north, away from the mysterious Cabeza de Oro. That bothered Walker more than anything else. He had hoped to find out what significance that landmark had before they ran into trouble. But

139

under the circumstances, trouble had indeed been inevitable.

El Diablo had seen to that.

After a few minutes, Walker held up a hand to bring the little group to a stop. He listened intently. He heard the growl of engines in the distance. Then, a loud snapping and popping sound that carried well over the empty landscape.

Gunfire.

Alvarez looked up in surprise. "What . . . ? That sounds like shooting!"

"It is," said Walker. "Somebody's putting up a fight."

"But . . . I don't understand. Those men . . . they had to be after us. Who else is out here for them to be shooting at?"

"Stay here," said Walker. "I'll try to take a look."

He went to the side of the gully, found footholds and handholds on the steep bank. In a matter of moments, he had pulled himself to the top, so that he could peer out cautiously. Before he did so, he took his Stetson off and dropped it down to the waiting Trivette. No point in advertising their presence any more than he had to.

Edging his head above the level of the ground, Walker looked toward the distant sound of gunshots. So much dust hung in the air that he had a difficult time making out anything. But then, as the wind shifted and grew slightly stronger, he was able to see both the station wagon and one of the pickups, most likely the one that had closed in from the east. They were stopped in the road, each vehicle canted at an angle so that they completely blocked the trail. In front of them, some fifty yards away, another vehicle was stopped, this one a late-model sedan. Figures crouching behind the station wagon and the pickup fired toward the sedan. Walker was convinced they were El Diablo's men. Someone was behind the sedan, using it for cover as he returned the fire.

Walker's lips drew back in a grimace. As far as he could

tell, there was only one man behind the sedan. Walker had expected to see more than that.

One man couldn't hope to hold out for very long against the superior numbers of El Diablo's forces. That became even more obvious a moment later when one of the gunmen reached inside the station wagon and brought out a long, thick tube of some sort. Trivette had been making a grim joke earlier when he asked Alvarez about bazookas, but this was the real thing. That was a rocket launcher those men were readying.

Walker wished he could cry out a warning, but there was no chance that the man behind the sedan would hear it. All Walker could do was watch the deadly drama unfold.

"What is it?" Trivette called softly from below. "What do you see, Walker?"

"Trouble," replied Walker. "Bad trouble."

One of El Diablo's men thrust the ugly-looking tube over the hood of the station wagon, and smoke and flame suddenly geysered from it. With a loud *whump!* that seemed to shake the ground even as far away as the arroyo, the rocket slammed into the sedan and exploded. The car's gas tank followed suit a split second later, shaking the ground again and sending a fireball into the air. Walker saw a figure stumble away from the blazing wreckage. The man was on fire, flames licking at his clothes and skin. He staggered out into the open, and El Diablo's men fired again. The bullets made the burning figure jerk and sway in a grotesque dance for a second, then the man toppled over.

Walker looked down at the dirt in front of him, closed his eyes, drew a deep breath. He would avenge the brutal killing he had just witnessed.

He just hoped that wasn't an empty vow. A chance to settle the score, that was all he wanted. . . .

"What the devil was that explosion?" Trivette asked anxiously from the bottom of the arroyo.

Walker released his handholds and slid back down.

141

"We're on our own now," he said. "There won't be any more help."

Alvarez shook his head. "I don't understand."

"Neither do I." Walker just looked at the Mexican cop for a second, then jerked his head. "Come on."

They hurried along the bottom of the gully again. The narrow slash in the ground began to twist and turn. Walker wasn't sure how far north it ran. The pickup that had been to their west might still be over there somewhere, looking for a way past the natural barrier of the series of arroyos. That wasn't the case, however, as Walker discovered when he and Trivette and Alvarez reached another of the sharp bends in the gully. The sound of a nearby engine made all three of them jerk to a stop. A second later, the engine died away, to be replaced by the slamming of doors and the angry voices of men.

"Spread out!" someone shouted in Spanish. "They're probably down in one of these arroyos! Find them!"

Walker took his hat, but he held on to it this time as he peered carefully around the bend. Up ahead about fifty yards, an old wooden bridge crossed the gully. The pickup was parked on it, and four men had gotten out of the vehicle. All of them held automatic weapons. They slid down the banks, and two started to the north while the other two headed south, straight toward Walker and his companions.

Walker ducked back from the bend and clapped his hat on. His hand went to the gun at his hip. "Time to make a stand," he said.

"I don't think so." The unmistakable metallic clicking of a pistol's hammer being drawn back sounded. "Keep your hands away from those guns."

Walker's head turned, slowly and deliberately. He saw Jorge Alvarez, head of the joint Mexican-American anti-drug task force, backing away from him and Trivette. Alvarez had a small revolver in his hand, and the weapon was leveled at the two Texas Rangers. Alvarez went on, "I don't want to kill you yet, but I will if I have to."

A faint smile curved Walker's lips, but his eyes were cold and hard as he said, "You took long enough to slither out into the open . . . El Diablo."

SIXTEEN

Frank Dailey, his wife, Karen, their eight-year-old son, Chad, and six-year-old daughter, Elizabeth, all boarded the tour bus in front of their hotel. The bus was already crowded, but the Daileys found seats near the back.

Chad was surly. "I don't want to go wander around some ol' Mexican market," he muttered. "I don't like shopping. I want to go to the bullfights."

"Your mother doesn't want to see a lot of bloodshed, son," Frank told him. "You'll see, you'll have fun. Hey, maybe I'll buy you one of those silver rings with the head of a snake carved on it."

Chad looked up with a grin. "Yeah, that wouldn't be so bad. But I still think this is going to be a boring day."

If Alvarez was surprised at Walker's comment, he didn't show it. His face was as hard and impassive as the stone of the arroyo wall. But he couldn't resist asking, "How long have you known, Walker?"

"I wasn't sure until right now," Walker replied. "And I was hoping I was wrong."

Alvarez's eyes flicked over toward Trivette. "What

about you? Were you smart enough to figure it out, too?''

"The simple answers are usually the best, Alvarez," said Trivette. "Walker and I trust each other, and he vouched for Hector Lopez. But neither of us knew you until we got to Laredo. It was easier to believe that you might be the leak instead of somebody in Lopez's office. And that business at the Red Rooster last night clinched it. None of our suspects from Ranger headquarters even knew where we were going. But you did. It was your idea.''

"And there was no bug in Hector's office," Walker put in. "We've just been stringing you along, Alvarez, trying to find out what your plan was.''

Alvarez sneered. "Then why isn't the cavalry coming down on us right now? What happened to your backup, Walker? Did that explosion a while ago have something to do with that?''

Walker's jaw tightened as he said, "Hector didn't want to believe you could be El Diablo. I told him to bring plenty of men with him, but he came alone. I guess he was hoping we were wrong about you, Alvarez.''

"What made you do it?" asked Trivette. "Why did you sell out? Are you even really a cop?''

"Oh, I'm a policeman, all right . . . but I have my reasons for everything I've done. You'd never understand them, though." Alvarez gestured curtly with the gun. "Move on around that bend so that my men can see you. It's time to put an end to this foolishness.''

"Yeah," said Walker softly, "it is.''

He burst into action with blinding speed. Only a fool would charge right at a cocked and leveled gun, so Walker threw himself to the side, but as he did so, the toe of his boot kicked up a fist-sized rock from the bed of the gully and sent it flying toward Alvarez. Alvarez jerked the pistol toward the rock and fired instinctively.

Trivette had launched himself the other way, opposite from Walker. He went down, rolled, came up with his gun in hand. He snapped a shot at Alvarez, missing but coming close enough to make Alvarez scramble for cover.

At the same time, shouts came from the men who were searching the arroyo. Alerted by the gunshots, they would be here in a matter of seconds.

Walker didn't waste time. Alvarez's reaction to Trivette's shot had given him a second's respite. Walker used that time to set himself and throw a punch. His fist crashed into Alvarez's jaw and sent the traitor stumbling back against the wall of the arroyo. Walker leaped up and kicked out as Alvarez bounced off the steep slope. His foot thudded into Alvarez's chest and sent him sprawling.

Meanwhile, Trivette whirled around to meet the new threat. He was ready as El Diablo's men came pounding around the bend. Trivette's first bullet slammed one of them back as if the man had run into a wall. His second one missed but kicked up dust at the feet of the other man. The man ducked back around the bend, triggering a wild burst of fire from the automatic pistol in his hand as he did so.

Alvarez tried to get up, but Walker was there to meet him with a hard fist. The blow knocked Alvarez flat on the ground. Walker bent over him and plucked the pistol from Alvarez's limp fingers, then turned to Trivette and called, "Come on! We'll find a better place to make a stand!"

Trivette turned and started to run, following Walker, but as he passed Alvarez, the turncoat came to his senses enough to suddenly lunge out and grab Trivette's ankle. Trivette yelped in surprise as he fell, landing hard on the bed of the arroyo.

Walker heard Trivette's shout and turned back to see what had happened. Trivette was trying to get up, but the fall had knocked the wind out of him and left him half stunned. Alvarez tackled him and began struggling with him.

And Alvarez's men were running toward them again. The other two had joined the one who had survived the exchange of lead with Trivette. They couldn't fire for fear of hitting Alvarez, but they were ready to take a hand in the fight.

Walker met them head-on.

For a couple of frenzied minutes, the Texas Ranger seemed to be everywhere, leaping and spinning and kicking and striking out with his fists. Two of Alvarez's men went flying, knocked off their feet by Walker's flashing blows. Walker had fought multiple opponents on numerous occasions. It took speed, strength, and utter concentration. While his hands were full dealing with Alvarez's men, he couldn't pay any attention to what was happening with Trivette and Alvarez.

Alvarez had recovered quickly, and he fought with skill and intensity. He grappled with Trivette and wound up atop the Ranger, his hands locked around Trivette's throat. Gasping for the air that Alvarez's brutal grip denied him, Trivette kicked out desperately, bringing his right leg up and hooking his ankle around Alvarez's shoulder. He arched his back and thrust as hard as he could with his leg, breaking Alvarez's hold. Trivette rolled to the side, gagging and gulping air down his tortured windpipe.

A second later, Alvarez came down hard on top of him once again, this time driving his knees into Trivette's back and lacing his fingers together under the Ranger's chin. He jerked up.

"Walker!"

The shout made Walker pause as he crouched, ready to launch another attack. One of Alvarez's men still faced him, and the other two were climbing back to their feet.

"I'll kill him, Walker! I mean it! I'll snap his neck!"

Walker's eyes flicked toward Alvarez. He saw the treacherous Mexican cop pinning Trivette to the ground. All it would take was a quick wrench of Alvarez's arms to break Trivette's neck. Trivette was only half conscious, his eyes rolling back in his head.

"Give it up," hissed Alvarez, "or Trivette dies."

If Alvarez had his way, Trivette would eventually die anyway, Walker knew, but where there was life, there was hope. Walker straightened from his crouch, lowered his arms, opened his fists.

"All right, Alvarez," he said. "You've got us. Now, what are you going to do with us?"

Alvarez's face twisted in a savage grin. "Just what I said I was going to do. I'm taking you to Cabeza de Oro."

The tour bus's first stop after crossing the bridge into Nuevo Laredo was one of the large open-air markets so popular in towns all along the border. With a hiss of air brakes, the bus drew up at the curb, and the driver opened the doors. He stood up and turned around to face his passengers, a fresh-faced young man who looked as if he should have been in college. His uniform was clean and neatly pressed, and his teeth shone white as a smile spread across his face.

"Señores, Señoras, y Señoritas," he said, "you may now shop and explore to your heart's content here in Nuevo Laredo. The merchants here welcome you. The bus will return here to pick you up at one o'clock this afternoon. Until then, *buenos dias!"*

Chattering excitedly among themselves, the passengers began to file off the bus. Many of them were carrying maps of Nuevo Laredo supplied by their hotel and the tour company. This was an unguided excursion, meaning that they were free to go wherever they chose. The only thing these tourists had to do was be back here at the *mercado* at one o'clock, so that they could catch the bus back to the American side of the Rio Grande.

Two young men who got off the bus stumbled a little and squinted at the bright sunshine. "Whose idea was it for us to come on this tour, man?" asked one of them. He was tall, rather gangly and loose-limbed, and had long brown hair.

His companion, who was shorter and stockier, said, "I think it was yours."

"I'm trying to remember . . . how many bottles of tequila did we drink last night?"

The other young man grinned. "I don't know. How many worms do you remember eating?"

"Tequila doesn't have a worm at the bottom of the bottle. That's pulque, man."

The second young tourist's grin widened. "Who said anything about the worms being at the bottom of a bottle?"

The first young man just shook his head and set off into the *mercado* at a slightly unsteady pace. His companion followed. Both of them had gotten drunk in a popular tourist nightspot the previous evening, and signing up for today's excursion had seemed like a good idea at the time.

Now, though, in the depth of a miserable hangover, the first young man thought that he would be lucky if he could just make it through the day without his head exploding. Right about now, it felt as if bombs were already going off inside his skull.

Well, if nothing else, he told himself, this outing should be pretty peaceful.

Walker and Trivette were prodded at gunpoint out of the arroyo and into the back of the pickup that had stopped on the rickety old bridge. The body of the man who had been shot by Trivette was thrown into the back with them. Two of the surviving men rode with them as well, covering them with automatic pistols, while the third man drove. Jorge Alvarez—El Diablo—rode up front with the driver.

The truck bounced over the rough road that was little more than a pair of ruts. A few hundred yards from the arroyo, it joined the trail Walker, Trivette, and Alvarez had been on earlier, which was a little better but not much, and the driver swung south. Through the rear window of the pickup, Walker noticed that Alvarez was talking to someone on a cellular phone, but he couldn't hear what the treacherous cop was saying.

In a matter of moments, the station wagon and the other pickup came into view. Nearby, the burned-out hulk of the destroyed sedan was still smoldering in places. A few tendrils of black smoke twisted into the clear blue sky above it.

A few feet from the blown-up sedan, the burned, bullet-riddled body of Ranger Hector Lopez still lay, mute testimony to the savageness of El Diablo's men.

The driver of the pickup carrying Walker and the others skirted around the body and came to a stop not far from the old station wagon. Alvarez and the driver got out, and Alvarez motioned with the gun he held for Walker and Trivette to climb out of the back of the pickup.

"I had planned on taking you to Cabeza de Oro myself," said Alvarez as Walker and Trivette hopped down from the bed of the pickup, "but I have a pressing engagement back in Nuevo Laredo. So I'm going to turn you over to Sanger here. He'll take good care of you."

One of the men from the station wagon gave the Rangers an ugly grin. He was a tall, burly Anglo with lank, fair hair on a balding, sunburned skull. "Get on over here, you two," he ordered as he pointed a heavy caliber pistol at Walker and Trivette.

"We'll be seeing you again, Alvarez," Walker said quietly and solemnly.

Alvarez shook his head. "I don't think so. This is nearly the end of the line for you, Walker. I've already called my partners and let them know that you'll be coming to Cabeza de Oro. They're anxious to see you two again."

That statement threw Walker for a loop, but he was careful to keep his surprise from showing. With his face still impassive, he said, "Who are your partners, and what do they have to do with Trivette and me?"

"They have an old score to settle, especially with you, Walker," Alvarez said with a smile. "You may remember them . . . Carlos and Ramon del Vega Garcia."

This time Walker couldn't keep his expression from showing some of the reaction he felt, and Trivette looked shocked. "I thought they were still in prison," exclaimed Trivette.

"They're free—and I'm sure they have plans for the two of you." Alvarez waved a hand at the landscape surrounding them. "All this is part of their rancho, you know. And there's a cave at the base of Cabeza de Oro that the vaqueros who ride for the Vega Garcia family have used for a hundred years or more as shelter. Don Carlos and don Ramon are putting it to better use these days, though.''

"As a drug warehouse?" guessed Walker.

"You'll see soon enough," Alvarez replied. He jerked the pistol in his hand. "Enough stalling. Get in the station wagon."

Surrounded as they were, outnumbered and outgunned, Walker and Trivette had no choice but to comply. The man called Sanger, who seemed to be Alvarez's second-in-command, gave Walker a rough shove as Walker got into the rear seat of the station wagon. Trivette followed, and the door slammed shut. Sanger and another gunman got into the front seat, Sanger sliding behind the wheel. Two more gunmen climbed into the back of the vehicle, sitting cross-legged on the flat bed so that they could cover the Rangers with their guns.

Alvarez got into one of the pickups with another man and drove off to the north, toward Nuevo Laredo. Walker wondered what the "pressing engagement" was that would make Alvarez give up taking them on to their destination himself. It probably had something to do with the business Alvarez was in with the Vega Garcia brothers . . . the business of dealing in heroin, dealing in death.

Sanger backed and turned the station wagon until it was pointed south, then he pressed down on the accelerator. The other pickup followed. Both vehicles bounced along the rutted trail, kicking up dust behind them, and in a matter of moments had vanished, leaving the vast, rugged landscape empty behind them.

Except for the body of the gallant Texas Ranger who had met his fate here.

The Ranger who would be avenged, if Cordell Walker had anything to say about it. . . .

SEVENTEEN

Once the red, green, and white tour bus was empty of passengers, the driver closed the doors and put it back in gear. He wheeled the bus expertly through the crowded streets of Nuevo Laredo, soon leaving behind the central district where the tourists congregated. He drove to a large, corrugated steel building on the east side of town, which, judging from its massive roll-up doors, was either a garage or a warehouse of some sort. The driver brought the bus to a stop in front of the big doors and sat there for a moment with the vehicle's engine idling. The street was deserted.

The driver tapped the horn once, knowing he was already being observed by hidden cameras that relayed a picture of the bus into the building. A moment later, with a rumble that was audible over the sound of the bus's engine, the huge doors began to roll slowly upward.

With a smile on his face, the driver took his foot off the brake, shifted back into gear, and drove forward as soon as the doors were high enough. When the bus was inside, the doors reversed themselves and started descending. In a matter of moments, the bus had vanished as if it had never been there.

About a half an hour after Walker and Trivette had been prodded into the station wagon, an upthrust of rocky ground became visible up ahead through the vehicle's grimy windshield. It was a rugged hill, made to appear even more prominent by the overall flatness of the surrounding landscape. Roughly cone-shaped, the hill was crowned by a large boulder. Judging by the distances involved, Walker estimated that the rock had to be at least as big as a normal-sized house.

And it shone like gold in the glow of the late morning sun.

"Cabeza de Oro," Walker said quietly, as much to himself as to any of the other people in the station wagon.

"That's right," said Sanger, twisting his head so that Walker could see the smirk on his face. "You can see how the place got its name."

"That rock looks like gold, all right," said Trivette. "How in the world did it get up there?"

"Beats the hell outta me," Sanger said. "I've heard stories about how the farmers down here used to think it was really gold. When they climbed up there, though, they found out it was just a big ugly rock. It wasn't going to make anybody rich." He laughed harshly. "What we've got stashed down in that cave, though . . . that's a different story."

The other gunmen joined in the laughter. Walker and Trivette just exchanged a grim glance. They had found the source of the heroin El Diablo was smuggling across the border, and they had discovered as well that Carlos and Ramon del Vega Garcia were involved in the operation. Walker had hoped that after he'd helped put the Vega Garcia cartel out of business several years earlier he had seen the last of the drug-dealing brothers. Obviously, that was not going to be the case.

He had suspected Jorge Alvarez of being connected with El Diablo almost from the first time he had met the man. Alvarez had known that Hector Lopez was bringing Walker and Trivette to Ranger headquarters for a meeting; Alvarez was the most likely one to have set up that first attempt on their lives.

Like Lopez, Walker and Trivette had been reluctant to believe that a fellow law enforcement officer could be playing such a crooked game, so they had deliberately cooperated with Alvarez's suggestions, giving the man enough rope to see if he would hang himself. The riot at the Red Rooster had been designed to get rid of the Rangers from Dallas, too, and when that had failed as well, Alvarez had played his strongest card: his knowledge of Cabeza de Oro.

There had been no fax from Mexico City, Walker would have been willing to bet on that. The whole thing had been a trap, and by the time Walker and Trivette had walked into it, they had both begun to suspect that Alvarez might well be El Diablo himself. When Alvarez had pulled a gun on them, Walker's verbal thrust had confirmed the suspicion.

So they had found out what they wanted to know, but at the cost of a good man's life—and perhaps their own lives as well. Walker and Trivette had been in some bad spots before in their careers, but now they were being taken directly into the stronghold of two of their worst enemies.

The Vega Garcias would probably take great pleasure in having both Rangers tortured to death.

Now that the station wagon was closer to the hill, Walker could see the dark opening at the base of the slope. That would be the cave Alvarez had mentioned. Sanger veered off the road onto a smaller path that snaked across the arid terrain toward the hill. He drove straight to the cave, and as the station wagon approached, Walker could see that the opening was about forty feet wide and perhaps fifteen feet high. Electric lights were burning inside the cave, no doubt powered by a generator. They revealed a large chamber with an arching ceiling that rose to a height of approximately thirty feet once they were past the mouth of the cave. In several places around the room, long wooden crates were stacked in tall piles. Three deuce-and-a-half trucks with tarp-covered beds were parked in the rear of the cave. Half a dozen tents had been erected as well.

More than anything else, the place reminded Walker of a military encampment.

Sanger brought the station wagon to a stop and killed the motor. He got out, as did his companion in the front seat. The two gunmen in the back slid out through the station wagon's raised rear gate. All of them managed to keep their guns pointing at Walker and Trivette as they got out.

"All right, now you two," ordered Sanger. One of the other men stepped closer to the vehicle and threw open the rear door on the driver's side before hurriedly stepping back out of the line of fire.

Walker had considered trying to kick the door at the man, but he hadn't had a chance. All he and Trivette could do was climb out of the station wagon, still under the menacing snouts of the automatic weapons.

Sanger grinned. "Welcome to Cabeza de Oro, gents. Sorry your stay won't be a very pleasant one. Don Carlos and don Ramon ought to be here pretty soon, and I'm sure they've got some ... entertainment ... in mind for you boys."

Walker didn't doubt that. The Vega Garcias were probably both drooling over the prospect of taking their revenge on him and Trivette.

In the meantime, though, Walker looked around the cave, his keen eyes taking in every detail. After a moment, he said, "Let me see if I've got this straight. The drugs come up from Central and South America, and the Vega Garcias store them here until El Diablo arranges to have them smuggled across the border."

"Sure," Sanger said with a shrug. "Go ahead and pump me for information, Ranger. It's not going to do you any good."

Walker nodded toward the stacks of wooden boxes. "Some of those crates look like the right size to have heroin packed in them. But some of them don't. What else has Alvarez got stashed away in here?''

Sanger glanced at one of the other men, then shrugged again. "Hell, what's it going to hurt? Keep those two covered." He stalked over to one of the crates which had been taken down from its stack and placed on the hard-packed dirt floor of the cave. Its lid was already loose, and Sanger bent down to raise it.

Walker and Trivette both saw the sleek, deadly, cylindrical shapes inside. "Rocket launchers," said Trivette.

"Just like the one you used to blow up Hector Lopez's car," Walker added grimly.

"Call it a field test," Sanger said. "Had to make sure these babies work before we sell them."

"Is this El Diablo's idea?" asked Walker. "Branching out into arms dealing as well as drugs?"

"El Diablo's a smart man. If there's money to be made, he'll find a way to do it."

"Do the Vega Garcias know about this?" asked Trivette.

"Not yet," said Sanger. "But they won't complain when they find out how much Alvarez is going to get for these weapons from the guerillas down in southern Mexico. Some of the payment will be in cash, the rest in merchandise."

"So it all fits together like the pieces of an ugly puzzle."

"That's right, Walker. And it's a puzzle that's going to make us all rich men. Isn't that right, boys?"

Grunts of assent came from the other gunmen.

Walker changed the subject by asking, "How far is it to the Vega Garcia hacienda?"

"About twenty miles. They ought to be here any minute."

That was what worried Walker. Carlos and Ramon would undoubtedly have more gunmen with them when they arrived. The odds against Walker and Trivette were already high enough. The addition of more men would make them impossible to overcome. What that meant was simple.

If he and Trivette were going to have a chance to get away, Walker knew, it was going to have to come soon.

Very soon.

The limousine was made for traveling on smooth highways, not over such rough terrain. Even its superb suspension was not enough to cope with the washboard surface of the dirt road. The car bounced and jolted, and so did its occupants.

Carlos and Ramon del Vega Garcia barely noticed the discomfort, however. They were too excited about what was waiting for them at their destination to care about how they got there.

Finally . . . *finally!* . . . the score with Walker would be settled.

The call had come from El Diablo about forty-five minutes earlier. "They fell into my trap, just as I expected them to," El Diablo had said. "Sanger will take them to Cabeza de Oro."

Ramon was the one who had taken the call, and he had exclaimed, "No, here! Have them brought here to the hacienda!"

El Diablo had just laughed. "No, I want them to see our stronghold for themselves. They worked so hard to find it, you know."

Such defiance grated on Ramon's nerves, and he thought once again about how glad he would be when he and Carlos no longer needed El Diablo. Then the man would be properly rewarded for his arrogance and disrespect.

But for the time being, they had to play along with him. "All right," Ramon had said. "Carlos and I will be there as soon as possible."

Carlos had been standing by, about to go mad with impatience as he waited to find out from his brother what El Diablo was saying. When Ramon explained, Carlos had been equally angry at the high-handedness of the man. However, he shared Ramon's feeling that revenge on El Diablo would have to wait.

A much greater need for vengeance on Cordell Walker cried out to them at the moment.

They had called together four of their men, who were now following the limousine in a jeep. The limo's driver manipulated the wheel skillfully, but it was impossible to avoid all the ruts and potholes in the old, unpaved road that led across the Vega Garcia rancho to the ancient, mysterious landmark known as Cabeza de Oro.

In the lavish rear seat of the luxury automobile, Carlos said softly, "Walker must die very slowly."

Ramon nodded. "And painfully."

Carlos turned to his brother and asked, "What about El Diablo? Why did he not bring Walker to Cabeza de Oro himself?"

"The operation in Nuevo Laredo," Ramon answered curtly. "El Diablo wants to supervise it personally."

Carlos leaned back against the thickly padded seat. "Fifty million dollars," he mused. "A nice sum."

Ramon smiled tightly. "And once we have it, we will never have to look back again, my brother."

"And we will no longer need El Diablo," said Carlos, returning the smile.

Ramon reached for the small bar built into the back of the limo. "We should drink to that . . . to the death of El Diablo."

Carlos nodded and said, "And to the death of Walker as well. . . ."

EIGHTEEN

A car pulled up in front of the large garage on the outskirts of Nuevo Laredo. The driver honked the horn, impatient to get inside and make sure that everything was going according to plan. The morning had been a busy one, but the day was far from over.

The doors of the garage began to lift, and in the car he had picked up after dropping off the jeep he had been using earlier, Jorge Alvarez drove inside.

He was smiling with anticipation. After today, the name of El Diablo would be even more widely known—and feared—than it was now, because no one had ever attempted anything as daring as what he was about to do.

No one.

With a rumble and a rattle, the doors descended behind him as he brought the car to a stop. Even with the midday light from outside cut off, it was still very bright inside the garage. There was a single, high-ceilinged room inside the sheet metal building, and powerful fluorescent lights dangled from the ceiling. The red, green, and white tourist bus was parked in the center of the vast space. All around it bustled men in the grease-stained coveralls of mechanics.

Metal panels had been removed from both sides of the bus, as well as the underside and the roof, and they lay helter-skelter on the floor around the vehicle, which looked almost mutilated in its current state. With the metal panels removed, shallow storage spaces were revealed. Into those spaces were being packed bag after clear plastic bag of white powder.

A young man wearing the uniform of a bus driver came hurrying up to Alvarez with an eager smile on his face. "El Diablo!" he said. "Welcome!"

"Any trouble here, Jaime?" asked Alvarez.

"No, sir. Everything is going exactly as you planned." Jaime glanced at the watch on his wrist. "In a little more than an hour, I will take the bus back to the *mercado* to pick up the gringo tourists. Then it will carry them—and its real cargo—back across the border."

Alvarez clapped a hand on the young man's shoulder. "Excellent work, Jaime . . . but there is one slight change in the plan."

A frown of concern appeared on Jaime's face. "A change?"

"That's right. *I* will drive the bus back into Texas."

"But, El Diablo . . . have I done something to displease you?"

Alvarez shook his head. "Of course not. Call it . . . vanity on my part." He looked with pride at the bus. "When the largest shipment of heroin ever to cross the Rio Grande enters Texas . . . I will be at the wheel!"

"I knew this trip was going to suck," Chad Dailey muttered under his breath as he followed his parents and sister through the market. All they had done since they had gotten here was look at a bunch of stupid stuff and argue with the Mexican merchants who were selling it. Chad's dad seemed to be having a great time, though. He liked to haggle, as he called it.

He hadn't bought Chad one of those cool snake rings,

though. They had been too expensive, even after the haggling. Instead, Chad had a totally dorky straw sombrero perched on his head. His dad had said that Chad could wear it to school when they got back home so everybody would know he had been to Mexico.

Yeah, right, Chad had thought. Might as well wear a sign saying *Beat Me Up*.

Still, it was a little cool actually being in another country. But the streets were dirty, and everybody was talking in Spanish so Chad couldn't understand them, and he had felt vaguely nervous ever since he and his family had gotten off the bus.

He would be glad, he decided, when he was back in the good ol' U.S. of A., as his dad called it, where nothing could happen to them.

Sanger's confidence had led him to be boastful so far, thought Walker. Maybe he could coax a little more information out of the man in the little time he had left.

Walker gestured toward the crates of heroin. "The thing I don't understand," he said, "is how Alvarez intends to get all this dope across the border. He's been moving a little at a time in shipments of contraband antibiotics, but at that rate, what he's got stored here would take years to smuggle across."

Sanger laughed. "You really don't know much, do you, Walker?"

"Why don't you enlighten me?"

"Sure." Sanger slapped a palm down on one of the crates. "There's as much heroin in Nuevo Laredo right now just waiting to go across as there is in this cave. And it's going across today."

"That's crazy!" said Trivette. "There's no way Alvarez can get that much junk past the border guards."

"Sure there is. He's going to drive it across, and the guards will just wave him on with a smile."

Walker began to have an idea where this conversation was leading.

Sanger chuckled and continued his gloating. "What goes back and forth across the border more than anything else?"

"Tourists," said Walker.

"That's right. And later on today, a whole busload of tourists are going to return to Laredo from a trip across the border. The bus will drop them off at their hotel—"

"Then go somewhere private so that the heroin can be removed from the hidden compartments built into the bus," Walker guessed.

Sanger nodded in mock appreciation. "Say, you *are* pretty sharp, Ranger. I can see why El Diablo and the Vega Garcia brothers want to get rid of you. But that's not the only thing special about that bus—"

He stopped short as he glanced toward the mouth of the cave, and Walker's teeth almost grated together in frustration as Sanger walked over to the opening instead of continuing. "Look," Sanger said as he pointed out across the monte. "See that dust, Walker? That'll be don Carlos and don Ramon, coming to say hello."

Walker looked and saw the plume of dust in the distance. He estimated it was still several miles away. A vehicle couldn't travel very fast on the rough ranch roads. He and Trivette might have five minutes before the Vega Garcias got here, six or seven minutes at the outside. They had already been luckier than they had any right to be.

Now it was time to manufacture a little more luck.

Sanger was perhaps a dozen paces away. The other three men were deeper in the cave, about fifteen feet behind Walker and Trivette. They were still holding their guns ready, but Sanger, in his casual confidence, had lowered his weapon.

The station wagon was parked to the right of the Texas Rangers. Trivette was the closest to it, close enough so that one good leap would carry him behind it and give him a little cover from the guns of the three guards. Walker looked at Trivette, then looked meaningfully at the station wagon, hoping Trivette would understand. Walker thought he saw his friend and partner give a minuscule nod, but he couldn't be sure.

Either way, Walker had to make his move now. Otherwise, he and Trivette would die for sure. At least this way, they would have a fighting chance.

Walker suddenly strode forward toward Sanger. "I don't see any dust," he said.

"Right there, damn it—" began Sanger, jabbing a finger toward the distant cloud. He half-turned toward Walker, and a look of alarm appeared on his face as he realized that the Ranger was closer to him than he'd been before.

One of the other men shouted for Walker to stop, but just as Walker had hoped, the guards held their fire, because the way they were arranged now, a burst aimed at Walker might tear through his body and hit Sanger, too.

Sanger started to jerk his pistol up, and Walker moved with blinding speed. "Now, Trivette!" he shouted as he launched a flying kick that flashed up and connected with Sanger's wrist, knocking the gun into the air.

At the same instant, Trivette went into a rolling dive that carried him behind the ancient station wagon. The guards risked a shot at him, the roar of the guns filling the cave, but the slugs splattered on the stony floor where Trivette had been an instant earlier. Trivette came up in a crouch, safe for the moment behind the station wagon . . . but in a matter of seconds, the guards would rush around the old vehicle and have clear shots at him again.

Walker used the momentum of his kick to carry him on into Sanger. His fist lashed out and connected with the man's jaw. Walker pivoted smoothly in another efficient continuation of his move.

What he did next required all of the hand-eye coordination he had developed over years of hard work and dedicated practice. Moving so fast that everything else seemed to be in slow motion, he reached out and plucked Sanger's falling gun from midair. His fingers wrapped around the butt of the pistol, and his index finger found the trigger. Walker dropped to one knee and fired, aiming at the man who was about to run around the station wagon to blast Trivette. The bullet caught the guard in the chest and flipped him backward. Before he even hit the ground, Walker had shifted his aim and squeezed off a second shot. This one lanced into the shoulder of another guard and sent him spinning off his feet with a howl of pain.

Before Walker could fire again, Sanger tackled him from behind, roaring in fury. He fell on Walker like an avalanche, and both men went down.

The first man Walker had shot had dropped his gun, and it had gone skittering across the floor of the cave and slid underneath the station wagon. Trivette flung himself full-length on the ground and reached desperately for the weapon as the third man tried to run around the station wagon. Trivette grabbed the automatic pistol and angled the barrel toward the running feet of the third guard. He squeezed the trigger. With a horrible racket, the gun belched out a burst of lead that stitched across both of the man's ankles. He shrieked in pain and tumbled off his feet.

The way Sanger was lying on top of him, the pistol was pinned underneath Walker, so it wasn't going to do him any good. Sanger was trying to get an arm looped around Walker's throat. Walker had barely gotten his free hand in the way, and he was holding off the choking grip as best he could. Sanger caught hold of Walker's hair and yanked Walker's head up. Walker knew what the man intended: he was going to drive Walker's face down against the rocky ground.

Walker let go of the gun and brought his right arm up as hard as he could, driving the elbow into Sanger's mid-section. Sanger grunted in pain, and his grip loosened enough so that Walker was able to tear his head free. Walker slapped his right hand against the ground, and with the slight leverage it gave him was able to heave himself up.

Throwing his feet and legs into the maneuver, he suddenly flipped himself over, which threw Sanger underneath him. Sanger's head struck the ground hard, stunning him, and Walker broke completely free of him. Walker rolled and came up on his feet. Sanger did the same thing.

The gun was lying on the ground between them.

Sanger ignored it. "I'll beat you to death with my bare hands!" he roared, then with a bull-like bellow, he charged at Walker.

Trivette hurried around the station wagon and kicked the guns away from the fallen guards, covering them as he did so. The man Walker had shot appeared to be dead, and the other two were wounded badly enough to be out of the fight. Trivette turned toward Walker and Sanger in time to see Sanger's charge. Trivette's hands tightened on the automatic pistol. He wanted to fire, but he knew that Walker was too close to Sanger. Walker would have to finish this fight himself.

Sanger tried to get his hands around Walker's throat, but Walker wasn't there anymore. Instead the Ranger had slipped deftly aside. He threw a punch that clipped Sanger's jaw as Sanger stumbled past him. Sanger recovered quickly and swung a backhand that Walker couldn't quite avoid. The blow staggered him, but Walker absorbed the punishment and kept his feet. He blocked another punch and hammered his fist into Sanger's body. In the back of Walker's mind, seconds were ticking away, and each one of them brought the Vega Garcias closer to Cabeza de Oro. It was time to finish this fight.

Walker leaped up, his right leg sweeping out in a spinning back kick that packed an incredible amount of power. Just as Sanger started forward again, the kick landed squarely on his jaw, breaking it. He dropped like a stone, crashing onto the floor of the cave, out cold.

Walker landed lightly. He was breathing a little hard. Sanger had been a formidable opponent. A glance out the mouth of the cave told Walker that the cloud of dust marking the progress of the Vega Garcias had covered about half of the distance from where he had first seen it.

Three minutes left. Maybe four.

"You all right?" Walker asked Trivette.

"Yeah."

"Get those wounded men outside the cave," Walker said as he bent to catch hold of Sanger's unconscious body. He started dragging the man toward the mouth of the cave.

Trivette looked puzzled, but he did as Walker said. Both of the wounded men had passed out, so it wasn't too difficult for Trivette to haul them out of the cave one by one.

"Over there," said Walker, indicating a little hollow to one side of the opening where he had deposited Sanger. Trivette left the first man there and hustled back for the second one. The other man, the one Walker had shot, was dead. Trivette had already checked for a pulse and confirmed that.

While Trivette was getting the last of the injured men out of the cave, Walker climbed into the station wagon. The keys were still in the ignition. He started the engine and backed the old vehicle out into the sunlight. Another glance at the plume of dust.

Two minutes. Surely no more than that.

Walker would have liked to get Sanger and the other two men farther away from the cave, but they would just have to take their chances. He ran back into the cave, leaving the station wagon running, and picked up one of the crates. Trivette was already climbing into the passenger seat of the vehicle while Walker shoved the crate into the back.

Behind the wheel again, Walker tromped down on the accelerator and sent the station wagon spurting across the sandy ground. He ignored the road and took out across country instead. Dust spiraled up behind the station wagon. The Vega Garcias had to be able to see it, but they had no way of knowing what was going on. All they could do was hurry on to Cabeza de Oro.

When the station wagon had covered several hundred

yards, Walker slammed on the brakes. He threw the door open and ran to the back of the vehicle. Trivette joined him there, and they yanked the lid off the crate Walker had placed in the back.

Walker reached into it and brought out one of the rocket launchers. Trivette picked up one of the shells that were also packed into the crate.

Walker settled the thing on his shoulder. He had used similar weapons in Vietnam and in other circumstances since then.

"Company coming," said Trivette.

Walker looked toward Cabeza de Oro and saw that the cloud of dust had split into two. One of them was continuing on toward the hill, but the other was angling across the monte toward Walker and Trivette. Walker squinted slightly and made out the jeep that was causing the dust.

"Better take care of them first," he said.

"You're ready to go," said Trivette.

Walker sighted in the rocket launcher, his thumb resting lightly on the button that would activate it. When he was satisfied with his aim, he held his breath and pressed the button. With a *whump!* and a *whoosh!* the rocket erupted from the launcher and arced out over the arid landscape. It slammed into the ground and detonated about ten feet in front of the racing jeep. The force of the fiery explosion sent the jeep spiraling into the air as the men who had been in it leaped for their lives.

Walker tossed the launcher aside. These were the disposable type that burned out and had to be discarded after one firing.

Lucky for them they had a whole crate full of the things, Walker thought as a grim smile flitted across his face.

In the limousine, Carlos and Ramon saw the explosion that sent the jeep flying into the air. "What—!" Carlos exclaimed. They had seen someone leaving Cabeza de Oro and had used the radio in the limo to send their men in the jeep to check it out, and now someone was setting off explosions!

"Something is wrong!" Ramon said unnecessarily.

"Driver, stop!" barked Carlos. The limo rocked to a halt, and the brothers leaped out.

They were about a hundred yards from the base of Cabeza de Oro. Carlos and Ramon both saw a couple of men stumbling away from the hill, half-carrying, half-dragging another man between them. One of them was Sanger, the man El Diablo had left in charge of this place.

"Come on," Carlos said. He started forward to meet Sanger and the other two men, Ramon at his side. The limo driver trailed behind them.

They were halfway between the limo and Cabeza de Oro when the luxurious vehicle was engulfed in a ball of fire.

The shock wave from the explosion threw Carlos and Ramon off their feet. The other men tumbled to the ground, too. The Vega Garcias turned shocked expressions back toward their limo, which was now blazing furiously.

"Walker!" shouted Sanger, his voice thick and almost incoherent. "Ish tha' damned Walker! He got rockets—"

Then, riding a tail of flame, another of the deadly missiles came whistling over the sandy, brush-covered ground.

This one disappeared into the mouth of the cave.

Sanger screamed, threw his hands over his head, and buried his face against the ground.

Under the circumstances, Carlos and Ramon thought the smart thing to do was to go along with him.

The world exploded.

"I guess that's what they mean when they talk about all hell breaking loose," Trivette said as he and Walker stood and watched the towering column of flame and smoke and debris that had been Cabeza de Oro. The rocket had set off the rest of the munitions stored inside the cave, destroying them along with millions of dollars' worth of heroin. That was a good day's work, all by itself.

But Walker tossed the burned-out rocket launcher aside and said, "Let's go. We've got to get back to Laredo and catch up to Alvarez."

He and Trivette piled back into the station wagon, and Walker sent it bouncing over the open ground toward the north. He was acutely aware that the Vega Garcias were back there, and it was difficult to leave them behind.

But El Diablo was up ahead, with enough heroin hidden on that tour bus to cause untold misery if it reached the other side of the border and disappeared into the distribution network.

The Vega Garcias would just have to wait until another day, Walker told himself. . . .

NINETEEN

In the *mercado* in Nuevo Laredo, the young man who was hung over from too much tequila the night before had found a vendor's booth that sold bottled water. Figuring that was safe, he bought two bottles and sat down at a small, umbrella-shaded table on a patio just outside the main entrance of the market. He opened one of the bottles and sipped from it while he held the cold plastic surface of the other bottle against his forehead. That helped to ease the pounding in his skull . . . but only a little.

His friend came out of the market a few minutes later, wearing a wide-brimmed, high-crowned sombrero and a brightly colored serape decorated with intricate beadwork. "Hey," he said, "I look like a *bandido,* don't I? 'We don' need no steenkin' badges!' " He seemed oblivious to the stares of disapproval directed at him by the Mexican nationals on the patio.

"Oh, that's good," said the hungover young man. "Get us killed, why don't you?" He groaned. "It couldn't hurt any worse than my head already does."

His friend slapped him on the back. "Lighten up, man. It won't be long now until that bus gets here, and then we can head back to the hotel. There's nothing wrong with you that a little hair of the dog won't fix.''

Instead of finishing the rest of the water that was in the opened bottle, the young man upended it instead and poured it over his head. As the cold liquid dripped down his face, he blinked and looked toward the street, hoping to see the red, green, and white tourist bus.

It couldn't get here soon enough to suit him.

Carlos and Ramon del Vega Garcia climbed shakily to their feet and stumbled over to Sanger and the other two men who had come from the cave. Debris from the explosion was still pelting down around them. Something was wrong with Sanger's jaw; it was twisted to one side and seemed to hang unnaturally. The other men were injured as well. One of them had a large bloodstain on the shoulder of his shirt, while the third man, the one who had been unable to walk, was bleeding from both ankles.

''What happened here?'' Carlos practically screamed. ''You were supposed to hold Walker! El Diablo said you captured him!''

''Got 'way,'' mumbled Sanger through his broken jaw. He waved a hand disgustedly at the ruins of what had been the stronghold in the base of Cabeza de Oro. ''Blow all up.''

''We can see that, you damned fool,'' grated Ramon. He pointed at a column of dust to the north that was gradually dwindling. ''And there he goes now! How could you let such a thing happen?''

''Don' know. Thought we . . . ha' 'em both.'' Sanger winced and put a hand to his jaw. ''Gotta get . . . to doctor. . . .''

Ramon plucked a small pistol from behind his belt at the small of his back, brought it around in front of him, lifted it, and shot Sanger. A red-rimmed black hole appeared in the center of Sanger's forehead as he jerked from the impact of the bullet. His eyes went wide and looked more surprised than anything else, and then he toppled over backward.

The other two men looked startled, but they didn't say or do anything. They were probably too scared to move.

"All gone," Carlos practically moaned as he stared at what was left of Cabeza de Oro. The blast had dislodged the huge rock that had crowned the hill for unknowable centuries, and it had rolled down to come to a stop at the base of the hill. The cave had collapsed in on itself, taking half the hillside with it, so that a large gaping valley now ran up the slope. The devastation was incredible.

"Millions of dollars' worth of drugs," Carlos went on, sounding like a man caught in the grip of a nightmare. "All gone now. What will we do?"

"There is still the shipment El Diablo will take across the border today," said Ramon as he put his left hand on his brother's shoulder and squeezed hard. Ramon's right hand still held the pistol with which he had killed Sanger. "We will survive, Carlos."

Carlos turned a hurt, befuddled expression toward Ramon. "But . . . but Walker will try to stop El Diablo. He will ruin everything—"

"No," Ramon said stubbornly. "You know how El Diablo explained the plan to us. Even if Walker gets back to Laredo in time to interfere, he will be unable to stop the operation. El Diablo will see to that." Ramon's lip curled in anger and the thirst for vengeance on Walker. "The Texas Ranger will have a big surprise waiting for him. . . ."

Walker had been driving north for about five miles when the station wagon suddenly coughed, lurched ahead a few more yards, then died.

"What's wrong?" asked Trivette as he leaned forward anxiously.

Walker glanced at the instrument panel, checking the gauges for engine temperature, oil pressure, voltage from the alternator . . . and fuel. He sighed when he saw that one.

175

"We're out of gas."

"Blast it!" Trivette slammed an open hand against the dashboard. "I thought there was enough to get us back to Laredo."

"The tank was half full when we left the cave," Walker said as he opened the door beside him. He stepped out of the vehicle, walked to the back on that side, and knelt to look underneath the station wagon. Almost right away, he saw the hole in the gas tank. It was big enough that he could have stuck his little finger in it.

He straightened as Trivette came around the station wagon from the other side. "Bullet hole in the tank," said Walker. "One of the bullets those men fired at you in the cave must have ricocheted up into the tank. We're lucky it didn't blow up."

"Yeah. Lucky." Trivette didn't bother trying to hide the bitterness in his voice. "Now what do we do?"

Walker pointed toward the north. "Laredo's that way. We walk."

"What about the Vega Garcias?"

"We took out both their vehicles with rockets. They can't catch up to us on foot."

"And we can't get to Laredo in time to stop Alvarez, either."

"We've got to try," said Walker. "Come on."

He set off toward the north, walking at a good pace, not too fast and not too slow. After a moment, Trivette sighed and said, "Wait for me." He hurried to catch up to Walker and fell in beside him. "What if one of the Vega Garcias has a cell phone in his pocket and calls for help?"

"That's a chance we'll just have to take," said Walker.

"We should have brought the chopper in the first place," Ramon said as he punched numbers into the phone in his hand. Luckily, being tossed around during the explosions didn't seem to have hurt its circuitry. The connection went through, and Ramon heard ringing on the other end, back at the hacienda.

"I don't like helicopters," said Carlos. "I haven't ever since . . . well, what happened with Dragonfly."

"That was Shrader's fault," snapped Ramon. "He underestimated Walker. Answer, damn it!"

A voice spoke in his ear.

Ramon rattled off instructions in Spanish to the startled servant who had answered the phone in the Vega Garcia hacienda. Within minutes, he knew, the helicopter would be rolled out of its hanger and would lift off from the private airstrip behind the massive ranch house. It could reach this site in less than a quarter of an hour.

Then Walker would regret interfering in the affairs of the Vega Garcia cartel. Ramon would find the Ranger and kill him personally. It would be his finger on the trigger of the machine gun that would blow Walker to hell.

There was a slight smile on Ramon's lips as he snapped the phone closed and tucked it away in his pocket. He was lost in the bloodthirsty fantasy that filled his mind. . . .

Jorge Alvarez tugged down the driver's cap on his head. "How do I look?" he asked.

"Fine, El Diablo," replied Jaime.

The uniform jacket was a little tight on Alvarez's shoulders, which were slightly broader than Jaime's. But it was not tight enough to constrict his movements, and the pants fit all right, too. If any of the tourists noticed that a different man was driving the bus after they were picked up at the market, they would probably just assume that the tour company had made the change for some reason.

Air-powered wrenches whined as the plates that had been removed earlier were reattached to the bus. The coverall-clad men worked quickly and efficiently. In a few more minutes, no one would be able to look at the bus and tell that fifty million dollars' worth of heroin was concealed within its chassis.

Just as no one could look at it and guess the other modifications that had been made to it over the past few weeks, ever since El Diablo had put this plan into motion.

Alvarez looked at his wristwatch. Twelve-thirty. The bus would be ready to roll in a matter of minutes, and he would arrive back at the market in it precisely at one o'clock. Everything was on schedule.

And in less than an hour, the bus would be in a similar garage on the Texas side of the border, where the process would be reversed and the heroin would be unloaded. The drugs would leave that garage in dozens of cars and small trucks, all bearing legitimate Texas license plates, driven by men who had been cautioned not to break any traffic laws and attract the attention of the police. In less than thirty-six hours, the heroin would be fully into the distribution network, spread out all over Texas and the Southwest.

And El Diablo would be a richer, more powerful man than ever before.

The Texas Rangers had been fools to think they could stop him.

The shifting sand under their feet made for difficult walking, and the boots worn by Walker and Trivette didn't help, either. They trudged on anyway. Both men wished their hats hadn't been lost in the fight back at Cabeza de Oro as the sun climbed directly overhead and beat down on them mercilessly. Sweat covered their faces and darkened their shirts.

"Man, what I wouldn't give for a tall, cold beer back at C. D.'s Place right about now," said Trivette.

"You're just torturing yourself," Walker told him.

"No, really, I've heard that if you think about something hard enough, you can get some of the benefits from it." Trivette closed his eyes. "I'm thinking about that cold, cold bottle, so cold that ice is dripping off of it, and I'm lifting it to my mouth, and now I'm tilting it up and drinking and the beer is so cold and—''

Trivette tripped on a rock and almost fell headlong. He would have fallen if Walker had not reached out and grabbed his arm to steady him.

"Visualizing something is fine," Walker said, "but it pays to keep your eyes open while you're doing it."

"Yeah, I guess so," admitted Trivette. Suddenly, he stiffened and said, "Walker . . ."

"I see them," Walker said softly.

Up ahead, something was moving. The figures came closer and resolved themselves into half a dozen men on horseback. In more than an hour of walking, these men were the first sign of human life Walker and Trivette had seen. The first sign of any life, in fact, except for a few lizards and birds.

"Do you think they've spotted us?" asked Trivette.

The riders were coming straight toward the two men on foot. Walker nodded and said, "I think there's a pretty good chance of it."

"What do we do?"

"We wait and see what *they* do."

The Rangers stood where they were. It was pointless to try to hide now. Besides, the scrub brush of the monte offered only pitiful concealment.

Within minutes, the riders pounded up, keeping their horses at a fast trot. They spread out in a semicircle around Walker and Trivette before drawing rein and bringing their mounts to a halt. Walker and Trivette waited, hands at their sides, not making any sort of threatening moves.

The men were all Mexicans, hard-faced individuals whose features were shaded by Stetsons with rolled brims. They were all armed, too. Four of the men carried modern rifles. Another sported a double-barreled shotgun, while the sixth and final man was holding what appeared to be an antique Winchester. Walker would have been willing to bet that despite its age, the rifle was in good working order.

Trivette licked his lips and asked quietly, "What do you think, Walker? Are they bandits? More drug smugglers?"

"I don't know."

Abruptly, the man holding the Winchester heeled his horse into motion, walking it forward a few steps toward the Rangers. He brought the rifle to his shoulder and fired.

TWENTY

Walker didn't flinch as smoke and flame geysered from the muzzle of the Winchester. He had already realized that the man wielding the weapon was not aiming at him or Trivette. Instead, the man fired past them, into the brush.

Then he rode around them and reached down beneath a scrubby mesquite tree with the barrel of the rifle. He hooked it underneath the limp body of a snake, which he lifted and displayed proudly. The snake was as thick around as a man's arm and nearly six feet long. A score of rattles adorned the tail end of its body.

The rifleman's companions called out congratulations to him in Spanish. He tossed the snake off into the brush and wheeled his horse, rode back to face Walker and Trivette. A broad grin was on his face.

"You gringos are lucky," he said in English. "That big fella was sleeping in the heat of the day. You walked within five feet of him."

"Not that we don't appreciate it," said Walker, "but we were already past the snake. You didn't have to shoot it."

The man shrugged. "If you kill a snake today, you don't have to kill the same one tomorrow."

Walker couldn't argue with the logic of that statement. Besides, he was too busy thinking about something he had just realized. There was something familiar about this man. But why would Walker be acquainted with someone riding across the wilds of Mexico like this?

It seemed that Walker wasn't the only one who was puzzled. The man with the Winchester had begun to frown as he looked at Walker, and after a moment, he said in a disbelieving voice, "It cannot be . . . but it is. You are señor Walker, the Texas Ranger, no?"

Walker nodded. "That's right. Have we met?"

"No, not really." The man swung down from his saddle, still gripping the rifle, and began to come toward Walker. "But I know you. I have seen you before."

Walker tensed. This man could be any one of a number of Mexican criminals he had arrested in the past. From the intent look on the man's face, Walker had certainly made an impression on him. Walker was ready in case the man tried to attack him—although with the odds against them, it was unlikely he and Trivette could put up much of a fight.

But the man had something else in mind besides a fight. He handed the Winchester to a stunned Trivette, then threw his arms around Walker and began slapping him on the back. "Señor Walker, it is good to see you again! You don't know me, but I was at the Halifax labor camp a few years ago when you and Jesse Rodriguez were there. I was one of the slaves brought there by El Coyote. But you freed us! You freed us, and you defeated El Coyote and all his men. I will never forget that day!"

Walker grinned and relaxed. The job this man was talking about had been a harrowing one, but at the same time, the case had been one of the most satisfying Walker had known. With the help of the Mexican cop Jesse Rodriguez, he had broken up a vicious ring of smugglers that had been bringing illegal immigrants across the border from Mexico. The men had gone into slave labor camps, and the women had been turned into unwilling prostitutes. Taking down El Coyote had been one of the highlights of Walker's career.

"Call me Chama," the man went on.

"I'm glad to meet you, Chama," said Walker. "What are you and your friends doing here?" Walker was still going to proceed cautiously. Just because Chama had been a hapless victim of El Coyote a few years earlier didn't mean the man hadn't returned to Mexico and become a drug smuggler or some other sort of criminal. If that was the case, Walker and Trivette could still be in trouble, because Chama knew they were Texas Rangers.

Chama laughed. "Seems like we ought to be asking you that question, señor Walker. We are more at home here than you, no?" Without giving Walker a chance to answer, Chama went on, "We are mustangers. Our camp is a couple of miles north of here."

"Mustangers?" repeated Trivette. "You mean you catch wild horses?"

"That's right."

"I didn't know there were any of them left," said Walker.

"*Sí,*" Chama said with a nod. "Not as many as there used to be, but still enough to make it worth our while."

"Do you have a jeep or any sort of vehicle there?" asked Walker. "It's very important that Trivette and I get back to Laredo as soon as possible."

"*Sí,* there is a jeep. Come on, a couple of us can ride double—"

The throbbing sound of an engine made Chama stop in midsentence. He looked past Walker and Trivette, who turned to gaze off to the south.

Coming toward them, and coming fast as it flew only a short distance off the ground, was a helicopter.

"The Vega Garcias," said Trivette.

"More than likely," said Walker. He turned to Chama. "I'm afraid we may have gotten you and your amigos into more trouble than you bargained for, Chama."

• • •

Carlos had regained some of his strength after being shaken so badly by the destruction of Cabeza de Oro. He was sitting behind Ramon, who occupied the seat next to the chopper's pilot. Ramon had already taken the small but deadly machine gun from the storage compartment in the back of the helicopter's cabin and fastened it to the mounts on the frame of the open door. He was feeding a belt of ammunition into it now.

Carlos leaned forward and raised his voice to be heard above the noise of the engine and the beating of the chopper's blades. "Is that them?" he shouted. Wind came in the open door and buffeted both Carlos and Ramon, twisting their hair crazily askew.

"I think so!" Ramon shouted back. He locked the lever on the machine gun into firing position and curled his hands around the grips. His finger found the trigger.

"But who are those men on horseback?"

"Who cares?" asked Ramon. "If they're with Walker and Trivette, they die, too!"

The helicopter was rapidly closing the distance between itself and the small group of men on the ground. "Tell your friends to spread out," Walker said hurriedly to Chama. "There's about to be shooting!"

Chama turned and shouted to the other mustangers, who immediately wheeled their horses and kicked them into a gallop. They scattered in all directions, and Walker was glad to see it. The Vega Garcias' fight was with him and Trivette, not with these innocent mustangers.

One of the men didn't run, though. He spurred his horse toward Walker, Trivette, and Chama instead. As he came closer, Walker saw that he was the one with the shotgun, an older man with a face like leather.

"Come on," Chama said as he grabbed the reins of his mount. "You can ride double with my papa and me."

"We'll slow you down," protested Walker.

"You saved my life in that labor camp without even knowing me, señor Walker. I will not leave you behind."

There was no time to argue. Chama swung up into the saddle, and Walker sprang onto the back of the horse behind him. While Walker was doing that, Trivette took the hand extended by the older man, who was evidently Chama's father, and climbed up behind him. Chama and his father spurred the horses into motion and galloped side by side toward the north.

It was impossible to outrun a helicopter on horseback. Walker knew that. But these rangy mustangs could turn on a dime, which was something the chopper couldn't do. Walker heard a racket even louder than the pounding of the horses' hooves, and he glanced back over his shoulder to see dirt being kicked into the air and brush being shredded by the spray of bullets coming from a machine gun mounted on the helicopter. The track of the slugs was coming steadily closer to the riders as the gunner got the range.

Chama shouted in Spanish and veered his horse sharply to the left. His father went to the right. The machine gun fire hosed harmlessly between them, and then the helicopter shot past overhead. It started to bank for another pass at them.

"Give me your rifle," Walker said to Chama.

The Mexican reined in and handed the Winchester back to Walker. Walker worked the lever to jack a cartridge into the chamber, then brought the weapon up. The stock settled comfortably against his shoulder. He sighted in on the turning helicopter and began firing as fast as he could work the lever. A booming sound from off to the right told him that either Trivette or Chama's father had opened up with the shotgun as well, but that was more of a gesture of defiance than anything else. At that range, the buckshot wouldn't ever reach the chopper.

But the slugs from the Winchester were a different story. Walker saw a starburst of cracks appear on the thick glass canopy of the helicopter where one of the bullets had hit it. It didn't appear that the bullet had penetrated, though. He kept firing, hoping for a luckier shot.

Ramon flinched and screamed a curse as the bullet slammed into the canopy. The glass was too thick for the slug to come through, but the spiderweb effect of the cracks certainly made visibility more tricky. "Stay with them!" Ramon shouted at the pilot.

"This is crazy!" Carlos yelled from the back seat. "A man on a horse can't shoot down a helicopter with an old rifle!"

Only Walker would try such a thing, thought Carlos. Sweat popped out on his forehead, only to be dried immediately by the blast of hot air coming in through the open door. But more beads of sweat replaced the ones that dried. Carlos's throat was squeezing shut, and he realized suddenly that in their thirst for vengeance on Walker, he and Ramon might well die themselves. . . .

Walker slid off the horse, still holding the Winchester. "I'll draw their fire!" he called to Chama. "Get out of here!"

"No! I stay with you, señor Walker—"

Walker didn't give the man any more time to argue. He slapped the rump of Chama's horse and shouted as loud as he could. The horse bolted, carrying Chama with it. Walker went the other direction, hoping that the onrushing helicopter would follow him.

It did. The machine gun opened up again, and again Walker watched the deadly track of bullets crawling toward him.

He took a deep breath and fired more slowly this time, trying to place his shots where they would do the most good. He slammed another bullet into the windshield of the low-flying chopper, but again it didn't penetrate. That glass had to be armored—which was no less than he would expect from the Vega Garcias. Walker lowered his sights a little and aimed for the helicopter's undercarriage, squeezing off a couple of shots before he had to fling himself desperately to the side to avoid the machine gun fire.

The hail of slugs chewed up the ground beside him as he rolled quickly away from them. Then the chopper was past again, and Walker could imagine the frustration on the part of the man who was using the machine gun. Windows of opportunity opened and closed quickly when one was firing from a fast-moving aircraft.

Walker came up on his knees and lifted the Winchester to his shoulder once more. He had lost track of how many shots he had fired, but he hoped there were a few more in the rifle's magazine. The chopper had slowed to make another turn, and Walker had time to pour three more slugs into its undercarriage. He was rewarded this time by a sudden burst of flame.

"We're hit!" The pilot sounded frightened as he shouted the warning to Carlos and Ramon.

Ramon slammed his hand against the door jamb. "I don't care! I want Walker! Turn around!"

"No!" Carlos shouted. This had gone on long enough. Carlos's instincts were screaming that they had tempted fate almost too far. "Go back to the hacienda!"

Ramon twisted around in the front seat. "Damn it, I want Walker—"

"Another day." Carlos gripped the seat so that his brother would not see how badly his hands were shaking. "We will kill him another day, Ramon."

"We're losing one of our engines," the pilot said. "I can probably still limp back to the hacienda. . . ."

"Do it," ordered Carlos.

Ramon's teeth ground together in rage and frustration, but after a moment he nodded curtly as well. "Go back," he said. He slumped against his seat, the picture of utter defeat.

Carlos swallowed hard. All their hopes were now riding on El Diablo.

But at least, with any luck, they would live.

And sooner or later, Walker's luck would run out.

That would be a sweet day indeed.

Trivette let out a triumphant whoop as he and Chama's father rode up to Walker. "They turned tail and ran!" he said excitedly. "Man, that was some shooting, Walker."

Walker smiled tightly and handed the Winchester to Chama, who had gotten control of his horse and ridden back to join him. "It's hard to miss with such a fine gun," he said.

In the distance, he saw the other mustangers regrouping and riding back toward them. The helicopter, listing to one side, had almost vanished now as it flew off to the south. The immediate threat was over.

But El Diablo was still on the loose, and there was still that tour bus with millions of dollars' worth of heroin hidden on it. Heroin that, unless it was stopped, would eventually find its way into the veins of thousands of users.

Maybe some of those users would be kids, trying the junk for the first time on a dare. And some of them would probably die. . . .

"I hate to impose any more on your hospitality, Chama," said Walker, "but Trivette and I have to get to Laredo. Fast."

Before the deaths kept piling up. . . .

TWENTY-ONE

Karen Dailey's feet hurt, the kids were tired and cranky, and even her husband seemed less enthusiastic now that they had wandered through the market for several hours. Frank loved to haggle—that probably came from being a salesman himself, Karen had thought on more than one occasion—but enough was enough. She wanted to stretch out on the king-size bed in their nice, air-conditioned hotel room, put her feet up, and order something from room service. This touristy stuff was overrated . . . but room service *was* nice.

"When can we go back to the hotel?" asked Elizabeth, a slight whine creeping into her voice.

Karen glanced at her watch. "Soon, kiddo. The bus ought to be back here to pick us up in about fifteen minutes."

"Good," Chad said. "There's a movie on the hotel TV I want to watch this afternoon."

"Hey," said Frank, "we're in Mexico. A foreign country. A totally different culture. We shouldn't be thinking about things like watching movies on TV."

Karen and the kids just exchanged a look and trudged

on behind Frank as he spotted yet another vendor's stall packed full of brightly colored jewelry, clothing, and souvenirs.

Jorge Alvarez drove the bus out of the garage and glanced in the big side mirror to see the door sliding back down behind him. The workers who had concealed the packets of heroin in the bus would clean the place up, then leave. No evidence would remain to indicate what had happened here today.

The bus itself looked perfectly normal. Without a thorough inspection, no one could tell that it carried such a lucrative cargo. And that inspection would not come about, because the border guards were used to seeing such vehicles go back and forth across the international bridge. This bus was owned by a legitimate tour company, and until several weeks earlier, there had been nothing unusual about it.

Then, through the efforts of the company's chief mechanic, whose son was one of the men who worked for El Diablo, the bus was made available for some secret, after-hours modifications at the deserted garage. The spaces where the heroin was stashed had been created, and other changes had been put in place as well. Everything had been the idea of El Diablo, so it was only appropriate that he was at the wheel as the bus began the first of what he hoped would be many of these special runs.

And with each successful operation, El Diablo would gain more power. The Vega Garcias had given him the opportunity, but soon Alvarez would no longer need them. Soon, the entire cartel would be his. His days as a civil servant, a cog in a vast, corrupt, incompetent machine, would be at an end.

Power . . . was there anything better in the entire world? Not to the man known as El Diablo.

The two young men were sitting on a bench on the sidewalk, in front of the spot where the bus had parked at the curb that morning. The aspirin he had been gulping all morning was finally starting to put a dent in the headache of the one who was hung over. As someone else sat down beside him, he looked over and vaguely recognized a man who had been on the bus when it came over from Laredo. The young man nodded. "Hey, man, how you doin'?" he asked.

"Fine," the newcomer responded rather curtly. He was an Anglo, with a pale face and very dark hair that made his features look even more washed out. He looked a little like a vampire, thought the young man. But that was impossible because, after all, it was broad daylight.

There was something else odd about the man. It was a warm day, almost hot, in fact, but he was wearing a jacket. A lightweight windbreaker, true, but it was still a jacket, and the young man thought that was a little strange.

Then the man shifted a little on the bench, and the young tourist beside him caught a glimpse of something underneath that windbreaker. It looked like . . . nah, it couldn't have been, the young man told himself . . . but it had sure looked like the butt of a gun in some sort of shoulder holster.

The young man stood up and said to his sombrero- and serape-wearing friend, "Come on, I want to go back in the market for a minute before the bus shows up."

"Why, man? I thought you were tired of this place. You've been bitchin' about coming over here all morning."

"Let's just say I want to take a last look around, because I ain't ever coming back."

The truth was, if that dude did have a gun, the young man wanted to be as far away from him as possible.

And he sure as hell wasn't going to sit next to him on the bus going back to Laredo.

The mustangers' camp was primitive, just a few tents clustered around a ring of rocks where the ashes of a small fire were heaped. But parked to one side was a jeep, and it was a sight to make Walker's heart glad.

Chama took a set of keys from a pocket in his jeans and handed them down to Walker as soon as the Ranger had slid off the back of the horse. "Take the jeep with our blessing, señor Walker."

"We'll leave it parked somewhere close to the bridge in Nuevo Laredo," Walker promised.

Chama nodded. "A couple of us will ride in later and pick it up."

Walker reached up to shake hands with the mustanger. "You've done more than save our lives, Chama," he said. "You may have helped save dozens of lives today."

"De nada," said Chama with a grin. "The debt I owe to you, señor Walker, I can never pay back. But this is a good start."

Trivette shook hands with Chama's father, then hurried over to join Walker. "We'd better get moving," he said. "Alvarez has a big lead on us already. He's probably been back in Nuevo Laredo for a while by now."

Walker nodded as he climbed into the jeep and slid behind the wheel. "That's right. But as long as we can get word to the customs agents to stop that bus when it tries to cross the border, it should be all right."

The jeep's engine cranked a little reluctantly, then burst into life with a roar. Walker and Trivette waved at Chama and the other mustangers as Walker tromped the gas and sent the jeep leaping ahead. He drove north, cutting across country according to the directions Chama had given him, the vehicle's rugged suspension allowing it to bounce over any obstacles. Walker was too busy wrestling with the steering to look at his watch.

But if he had checked the time, he would have seen that it was ten minutes until one o'clock.

"Finally," Karen Dailey said as the bus pulled up to the curb with a hiss of air brakes. She had insisted that they come out here to wait for it. Quite a few of the other tourists were already on hand, as well. Most of them were chattering happily. The group had enjoyed its excursion across the border.

The bus doors opened. Karen looked inside at the driver, a handsome man in his thirties who was wearing sunglasses. He wasn't the same driver as the one who had brought them across that morning, she realized.

That thought flitted across her mind and then was gone. She was busy herding the children—and her husband—on board the brightly colored vehicle.

Alvarez had noticed the dark-haired man waiting on the bench as soon as he drove up. A feeling of satisfaction went through him. Another part of the plan was working. The dark-haired man was one of his. Alvarez opened the doors so that the passengers could begin boarding, and as the dark-haired man climbed up the three steps into the bus, his eyes met those of El Diablo for an instant. Alvarez gave a tiny nod, and the man moved on to find a seat. Five more of El Diablo's men would be scattered through the bus, pretending to be tourists, just in case there was any trouble during the run across the border. All of them were Anglos, of course, but Alvarez didn't mind working with gringos.

Greed knew no nationality.

"Let's sit back there, man."

"All the way in the back? It'll take us forever to get off when we get back to the hotel."

"I don't care. I'm sitting *back there*."

"Okay, okay, whatever you say. *'La cucaracha, la cucaracha. . . .'"*

Walker and Trivette hit the dirt road Alvarez had taken earlier, when they had been driving down to Cabeza de Oro. Chama had said they would find it without any trouble, and the prediction had proven to be true. Walker pressed down a little harder on the accelerator, even though driving on the unpaved road wasn't that much smoother than cutting across country.

"When did Sanger say that bus was supposed to go back across the border?" asked Trivette, raising his voice to be heard over the roar of the wind in the open vehicle.

"Sometime early this afternoon," Walker replied.

"It's almost one o'clock."

Walker nodded grimly. He and Trivette would be cutting it close, even if they made it back to Nuevo Laredo in time to alert the border guards.

"I'm driving straight to the bridge," Walker said. "The local police are probably trustworthy, but since Alvarez is one of them . . ."

"Yeah," said Trivette. "It makes more sense to warn U.S. Customs. They can stop all the tourist buses and search them."

Dust boiled up behind the jeep as Walker continued to push it at breakneck speed. Through the grimy windshield, he spotted more traffic moving up ahead and realized they were coming to the paved highway that ran south out of Nuevo Laredo. A few moments later, the jeep skidded onto the asphalt as Walker sent it careening through a right-hand turn onto the highway.

Within minutes, the big arena where bullfights were held came into view. Walker saw the buildings of the border towns on the horizon. Traffic on the highway was fairly light, and he was grateful for that. He was able to swing out into the other lane and pass the vehicles he came up behind without taking too many chances.

Unfortunately, when he and Trivette reached Nuevo Laredo itself, the streets were more crowded. Walker's jaw tightened in frustration as he had to slow down considerably. He sent the jeep darting through every opening in the traffic he could find, but his progress was much slower now.

"Come on, come on," muttered Trivette as he leaned

forward, one hand gripping the rim of the windshield.

Walker turned to the right around the bus station onto a street that paralleled the Rio Grande. Off to his left, he could see International Bridge #1, the pedestrian walkway. International Bridge #2 was the one that tour buses would use, and it was still several blocks ahead.

Walker saw the line of cars and trucks at the bridge before he reached it. The line was over a block long. Walker's eyes scanned the group of vehicles, looking for a tour bus, but he didn't see any.

Spotting an open space at the curb, Walker suddenly swung the wheel over and brought the jeep to a stop. "We can get there faster on foot now," he said as he hurriedly got out of the jeep.

Trivette hopped out of the vehicle, too, and joined Walker on the sidewalk. They broke into a run as they headed for the bridge. They had to swerve around knots of people on the sidewalk, and startled questions began to be shouted after them in Spanish.

Small wooden guard booths flanked the traffic lanes at this end of the bridge. One of them on the left served double duty; the guard there monitored both incoming automotive traffic and any pedestrians who wanted to use the narrow walkway. Walker heard an angry shout from the man as he and Trivette dashed past the booth. Walker turned his head and called back, "We're Texas Rangers!" He didn't know if the guard heard him or not, or if the man believed him if he had heard. There was no time to worry about such formalities now.

The bridge arched up and over the Rio Grande, the banks of which were lined on both sides with a high chain-link fence topped by barbed wire. On the U.S. end, a long, metal, shedlike building stretched all the way from one side of the road to the other, with openings for cars to drive through. Agents of the U.S. Customs Service were stationed here, and Walker knew that overall they did a very good job. In fact, right now several uniformed officers were already gathering in the pedestrian walkway, no doubt in response to a telephoned warning from their opposite numbers at the other end of the bridge that a couple of crazy men were coming in their direction.

Walker and Trivette slowed to a trot as they approached the customs agents. One of the officers called out, "Hold it, you two!"

Walker came to a stop and pointed to the badge pinned to his sweat-stained shirt. "Texas Rangers," he said. "I'm Walker, this is Trivette. You can check us out with the Laredo office if you want, but right now it's important we talk to your commander."

The customs agents recognized the silver star on a silver circle. The one who had challenged Walker and Trivette asked, "What's wrong, Rangers?"

"Have any tour buses come through here since noon?" asked Trivette.

The officer looked at the other customs agents with a frown, then turned back to Walker and Trivette. "Just one," he said. "Most of them cross back over later in the day."

"Stop and hold any that come across until you hear from us," said Walker. "What about the one that already crossed? We'll need a description."

"Well," said the customs officer, turning and pointing up Interstate 35, which began only a few yards away, "as a matter of fact, there it goes now."

Walker and Trivette peered past the man and saw the bus, which was already several blocks away and building up speed.

It was painted in bright shades of red, green, and white, just like the Mexican flag.

TWENTY-TWO

Alvarez knew he was grinning. He couldn't help it.

The Rio Grande was behind him. The bus had crossed the border successfully, just as he had planned. The U.S. customs agents had taken one look at the brightly painted vehicle with its seats full of tired but happy American tourists and given it only a cursory examination.

There had been a little more to it than a simple wavethrough: Alvarez had had to stop and open the door so that an agent could step up into the bus and address the passengers. But the officer hadn't done anything other than ask the group at large if they were all American citizens, which they had answered with nods and a few called-out affirmatives. Then he had rattled off by rote a list of prohibited and/or regulated items and asked if anyone had purchased any of them while in Mexico. Once everyone had said no, the customs agent had stepped back off the bus and motioned for Alvarez to pull ahead. Alvarez had smiled and nodded his thanks.

Now it was almost over. Ten minutes to reach the hotel and drop off the passengers, another ten or fifteen minutes to reach the garage on this side of the river where the work of uncovering and unloading the heroin would begin.

A half hour, roughly, to more wealth and power than most men ever dreamed of.

But Jorge Alvarez—El Diablo—dreamed big.

"We've got to have that bus stopped and searched," Walker said urgently to the group of U.S. customs agents clustered around him and Trivette. They had gone into one of the offices in the shedlike building to listen to the Rangers' story. Walker and Trivette had filled them in as quickly as possible, and the skepticism on the faces of the federal agents had turned into grudging acceptance.

"It might not be the right bus," added Trivette, "but we can't take that chance. Since it's the only one that's gone through since noon, we have to make sure."

One of the customs men nodded. "And we'll stop and search all the other buses in the meantime."

Walker picked up a phone and said, "I'll call Ranger headquarters. They can alert the Laredo police and have that bus stopped."

Trivette said, "If that bus is the right one, Walker, El Diablo probably has some of his men planted on it. The patrolmen who check it out need to be careful."

Walker's face was taut with worry as he nodded and began to punch numbers into the phone. "That's right," he said. "Alvarez and his men are too close to success to surrender without a fight."

"And that bus is full of innocent American tourists, too," Trivette said softly.

Walker's voice was almost a whisper as he said, "I know."

Officer Robert Gallegos was working alone today, because the shift was shorthanded due to some illnesses. Normally he would have had a partner with him in the patrol car, and usually it would have been Officer Andy Simms. But Simms was sick at home with the mumps, of all things. A kids' disease. But Gallegos had heard that mumps could be pretty serious when adults got it, especially adult males. The illness made a fella's *cojones* swell up and hurt like blazes. At least, that was what Gallegos had always heard. He'd had the mumps when he was seven, thank God.

He'd have to rib Andy a little about it when he got back to work, Gallegos decided.

He was driving north on the service road along Interstate 35, just before the exit for Clark Road and Park Street. As he slowed to yield to the traffic coming off the freeway, he glanced over and saw the tourist bus taking the exit.

It was at that moment that his cruiser's radio crackled with the bulletin requesting all units to be on the lookout for a red, green, and white tourist bus. If spotted, the bus was to be stopped and everyone detained until the officers could call it in and get some backup. Gallegos's eyes widened in surprise as he realized he was looking at the very bus that the dispatcher was talking about.

His surprise deepened as he heard the code numbers indicating that possible danger was involved, to approach the bus with caution.

Gallegos's cruiser was directly behind the bus now. He leaned forward slightly as he studied the passengers through the windshield of his car and the rear window of the bus. The two back seats were occupied by a couple of young men, one sprawled in each seat. One had long brown hair and glasses; the other wore a sombrero he had no doubt purchased in Nuevo Laredo and was grinning broadly. They didn't look the least bit dangerous.

But Gallegos took the warning seriously anyway. As the bus reached the intersection and turned left on Park Street, under the freeway overpass, Gallegos reached over with his right hand to snag the microphone hanging on the dash. He used his left to wheel the cruiser after the bus and keyed the mike with his right.

He identified his unit and said, "I've spotted the bus

from that bulletin that just came over. It's headed west on Park Street, crossing I-35.''

Acknowledgement came back from the dispatcher. Gallegos hung up the mike and pushed the cruiser a little closer to the bus. He swung slightly to the left and hit the switch for the flashing lights on top of his car, then gave a short burst with the siren. The driver of the bus couldn't have failed to miss either of them.

But the bus kept going instead of pulling over.

Gallegos frowned and turned the siren on again, letting it blast out for a few seconds longer this time. Still, the bus didn't even slow down.

Gallegos swung out to pass. He would pull even with the bus, he decided, and motion for the driver to pull over.

If that didn't work, the guy was really going to be in trouble.

Alvarez's teeth practically ground together in rage and frustration. So close, so damned close! Another five minutes and the gringo tourists would have been off the bus! He would have been on his way to the garage to finish the operation.

But now . . . now some stupid cop was right behind him, trying to get him to stop.

Alvarez drew in a deep breath and told himself to calm down. It wouldn't do for a man such as El Diablo to panic. There was no way the police could know what else this bus was carrying besides American tourists. That cop had to be stopping him for some other reason. Maybe a brake light was burned out or something. The bus was supposed to be in perfect repair, but such things happened.

He should have pulled over immediately and cooperated as much as possible, Alvarez realized. Now his refusal to do so was likely to make the cop suspicious. Alvarez hesitated, his brain racing as he tried to figure out what to do. A glance in the big side mirror told him that the police cruiser was pulling out to pass him. It sped up and drew even with the bus.

Someone behind Alvarez screamed.

His eyes jerked to the inside mirror, and he saw the man he had noticed earlier, the one with such dark hair and such pale skin. The man was on his feet with a gun in his hand. Alvarez cried, ''No!'' as the man lunged past a couple of shrieking passengers to get to a window on the left side of the bus. He jerked the window up and thrust the barrel of the automatic pistol out. Flame burst from the muzzle of the weapon as lead stitched across the police car.

All over the bus now, El Diablo's men were on their feet, guns coming out, voices raised in shouts. ''Shut up! Shut up!'' one of them yelled at the passengers. ''Everybody stay in your seat!''

All wrong, Alvarez thought fleetingly as he tromped down hard on the gas pedal and sent the bus spurting forward with an ungainly burst of speed. This wasn't the way things were supposed to be. It had all gone wrong.

The police car, its passenger side windows blown out by the automatic weapon fire, slewed crazily away to the left, cutting across oncoming traffic and leaping onto the sidewalk to slam into the front of a building. On the street, cars rear-ended each other. The wail of horns and the crash of steel against steel filled the air.

Alvarez drove on, speeding past the hotel where he was supposed to have left the tourists.

Now, after everything that had happened, there was nothing else he could do.

With his right arm clamped across his midsection in an attempt to hold himself together, Officer Gallegos used his left hand to try to open the car door beside him. The impact of the crash had sprung the door and jammed it, and it refused to open. Gallegos tried to blink away some of the blood that had run into his eyes from a long, ragged gash on his forehead sustained in the wreck. He knew he was hit, but he wasn't sure how bad the wound was. He peered through a red haze out of the shattered windshield, across the crumpled hood of the police cruiser. He wondered if the car was on fire.

Despite the pain it caused him, he threw his whole body against the door, and this time it gave a little. He was about to try again when a figure suddenly loomed outside the wrecked vehicle. The man wrenched at the door, heaving hard on it. With a squeal of tortured metal, the door slowly came open. Gallegos's rescuer, a tall young man with red hair sticking out in tufts from underneath a baseball cap, reached inside the cruiser and caught hold of him.

"Hang on, Officer," the young man said as he slid Gallegos from the glass-littered seat onto the sidewalk. "Somebody already called 911."

Gallegos looked back into the car. "M-my radio . . . ," he gasped.

The young man reached past him and grabbed the hand-held unit lying on the seat. Gallegos took it from him with a bloodstained hand and thumbed the transmit button. "Officer down, officer down," he said. "Sh-shots fired. Need help . . . now. . . ."

The radio slipped from his fingers, and Gallegos couldn't find the strength to pick it up again. In fact, even keeping his eyes open was too exhausting. He had to rest. . . .

Darkness took him, and the sounds of chaos that had surrounded him faded away to nothing.

Alvarez spun the wheel of the bus, taking a hard right onto Santa Maria Avenue. He pressed down hard on the accelerator again and jerked the bus around a slow-moving pickup. Buses weren't designed for weaving in and out of traffic, Alvarez knew, but he had no choice. Now that everything had gone to hell, all he could do was try to salvage as much as he could from the situation.

He had to get back to the interstate. Once he was on the

freeway again, the bus's other special modifications could come into play.

If only the gunman hadn't lost his head when that cop came up alongside them. El Diablo expected better than that from all of his men.

"What now?"

Alvarez glanced up. The dark-haired man who had started the shooting was standing beside him. With an effort, Alvarez controlled the rage that welled up inside him.

"You fool," he said coldly. "Why did you open fire?"

"That cop was about to stop us. You saw him."

"He didn't know what we're carrying. He couldn't have."

"Don Carlos and don Ramon gave me my orders. Nothing's going to happen to our cargo."

Alvarez's lips pulled back from his teeth. That had been the wrong thing for the man to say. With his left hand still on the steering wheel, Alvarez reached underneath the uniform jacket and pulled out a small automatic. He jammed the short barrel into the belly of the dark-haired man and pulled the trigger three times, fast.

The man jerked over, bending nearly double as the slugs tore through his body. He dropped the gun he was holding and gave a loud grunt, then folded up and collapsed down the three steps leading to the bus's front door. His shirt was already sodden with blood.

Alvarez put the pistol in the pocket of his jacket and reached for the door lever. He pulled it toward him, opening the doors. The dead man tumbled out and hit the street, bouncing a couple of times before coming to a stop in a limp tangle of arms and legs.

Alvarez closed the door and then looked up into the mirror. He saw the other gunmen watching him with shocked expressions on their faces. Perhaps they had learned something from what they had just seen.

No one ruined El Diablo's plans and went unpunished.

• • •

"We've got it!" said Trivette, cupping a hand over the phone's mouthpiece. "Laredo PD reports shots fired from that tourist bus when one of their officers tried to pull it over. The bus driver kept going. You think it could be Alvarez himself?"

"I hope so," Walker said. He turned to the customs agents. "There are Rangers on the way here, but Trivette and I can't wait. Can we borrow a vehicle?"

"Sure. I'll come with you," one of the agents volunteered. "Let's go."

The three men hurried outside, and the agent led Walker and Trivette to a late-model sedan with government plates parked nearby. They piled in, the agent getting behind the wheel.

"Where did the police say the incident took place?" the agent asked Trivette as he started the car.

"On Park Street, west of I-35."

The agent nodded. "I know where that is." He put the car in gear and sent it out into the traffic, reaching out the window to clamp a magnetic flashing light to the roof as he did so. "Name's O'Donnell, by the way. Do you think your guy is going to keep running?"

"What else can he do?" asked Trivette.

"How's he going to get away in a *bus*? The cops'll be all over him in a few minutes, and he sure can't outrun anybody in something like that."

"Maybe he's not planning on outrunning anybody," Walker said.

O'Donnell glanced over at him. "What do you mean?"

"He's got hostages," Walker pointed out. "A whole bus full of them. And if it's El Diablo ... he won't give up without a fight."

This chase, Walker thought bleakly, might just turn into a bloodbath unless they were very, very lucky. . . .

TWENTY-THREE

Frank Dailey's heart was hammering so hard inside his chest that it felt as if it were going to tear right out through his body. He had one arm around Karen, holding her tightly against him, and the other around Elizabeth. Both of them were crying, Karen silently with tears running down her face, Elizabeth with the loud sobs of a terrified child—which was exactly what she was. Chad huddled against Karen.

Nothing was going to happen to his family, Frank told himself. They were all going to be all right. This was all crazy, couldn't even be happening. Guns going off and people shouting and screaming and cars crashing . . . that wasn't part of the tour. It just wasn't.

But he wasn't imagining the five grim-faced gunmen standing in the aisle of the bus, spread out and turned in different directions so that they could cover all the passengers with the weapons they were holding. Frank had seen guns like that before in movies. Uzis? Was that what they were called?

And why wasn't the bus driver doing anything?

Well, the man had done *something*, Frank reminded himself. A few minutes ago, he had killed the man who had broken out the bus window and shot up that police car. That didn't mean the bus driver was one of the good guys, though. Otherwise he would have stopped driving by now. Instead the driver was going faster and faster, swerving around all the slower-moving traffic, taking foolhardy chances, throwing the passengers back and forth with his wild maneuvers. The gunmen in the aisle had to constantly brace themselves to keep from being thrown off their feet.

Maybe one of them would fall and drop his gun, thought Frank, and then he could jump out in the aisle and snatch it up and . . .

And what, tough guy? Frank asked himself. He wasn't one of those action movie heroes. He was just a copier salesman from New Braunfels on vacation with his family.

The driver reached above his head and plucked a microphone from a holder beside the mirror. It was connected to the bus's public address system. The driver's voice boomed out of the speakers as he turned the microphone on and held it to his mouth.

"Everyone please relax. If you cooperate, no one will be hurt."

Well, that was just a lie, Frank thought. That cop had already been hurt, and so had the man who had shot him.

"I apologize for the inconvenience and want you to know that you'll be back at your hotel as soon as possible."

Frank didn't believe him, not for a second. He didn't know what sort of crime the driver and these other men had committed, or were trying to commit, but he was certain of one thing. He and his family, and all the other passengers on the bus, were hostages now. The driver wasn't going to let them go until he got what he wanted.

No matter how many of them had to die.

But not my family, Frank thought. *Not my family.*

Walker leaned forward anxiously as Agent O'Donnell sent the car screeching around a corner. He peered through the windshield, hoping to catch a glimpse of the bus up ahead. So far, though, it was nowhere to be seen.

The radio in the government car was tuned to the frequency used by the Laredo PD. That was how Walker, Trivette, and O'Donnell had been able to keep up with what was going on. They had heard reports that the bus had passed the Civic Center and was still proceeding north on Santa Maria. Suddenly, word came that the bus was turning again, this time heading east on Lafayette.

"Where will that take them?" Trivette asked from the back seat.

"Back toward the freeway," replied O'Donnell. "And on into the east side of the city if the bus keeps going. I still don't understand what they're trying to do."

"We'll find out soon enough," said Walker.

O'Donnell turned sharply right. "Maybe we can cut them off."

Alvarez was sweating. He *hated* to sweat. Growing up in northern Mexico, the weather had been hot all the time, so he should have gotten used to it, but he never had.

Just as he had never gotten used to people trying to deny him what he wanted. He had learned to crush them, sometimes openly, sometimes in secret. And any time he was unable to do so, any time his wishes were blocked, even as a child, he had seethed with anger for days, sometimes weeks. Rage had settled on him, and it was not safe to be around him during those times.

It was during those dark moments that El Diablo had been born. El Diablo, the Devil, too powerful for anyone to deny. Someday, he had told himself, someday he would have such power. No one could defeat El Diablo.

And from the child's fantasy had grown the man, ambitious and ruthless and cruel.

Alvarez lifted his arm, sleeved sweat from his forehead.

He saw the freeway up ahead, cars passing back and forth, their drivers blissfully unaware of what was happening on the side streets. Alvarez whipped the bus around two more vehicles, blaring the horn at them as he did so.

Lights flashing in the outside mirror caught his eye.

So, another police car had caught up to him, he thought as he looked at the mirror. This one hung back a little. No doubt its occupants had heard what had happened to the first cop who had tried to pass the brightly colored bus. They wouldn't close in until they had more help. They might not try to stop the bus at all; they could attempt to just herd it toward a roadblock.

They were still in for a surprise, thought Alvarez.

He pulled down the thick armrest that lowered beside the driver's seat. It was supposed to be solid, but while the other work had been being carried out on the bus, changes had been made here, too. Alvarez flipped the top of the armrest up like the lid of a coffin, revealing a double row of buttons and switches. The electrical wiring connected to them was concealed inside the seat, he knew. He selected one of the switches, thumbed it.

Even without seeing what was happening, Alvarez knew. He had gone over all the engineering drawings in great detail. On the back of the bus, a small panel had just flipped open, and flung from within it were dozens of small metal balls studded with razor-sharp spikes. Right about now, Alvarez told himself, they were bouncing all over the road, and that cop car would be running over them, causing all four tires to blow out . . .

The outside mirror showed Alvarez the result. The police cruiser suddenly veered crazily back and forth across the road, out of control. It grazed a parked car, rebounded, then clipped another one and went into a spin before slamming broadside into an oncoming delivery van. Alvarez even heard the crash. It was a satisfying sound.

There were plenty of other surprises just waiting for anyone who tried to stop him.

The young man with long brown hair put his hands over his face to cover his eyes. He didn't want to see what was happening. He had hoped that once more cops started to close in, the driver and all the gunmen would realize they couldn't get away and would surrender.

But that wasn't going to happen. After seeing what had happened to the police car pursuing the bus, the young man knew that now.

His friend leaned over from the other rear seat and said in a low voice, "What do you think they're going to do?"

The young man lowered his hands and repeated, "Do?" His voice shook a little. "They're probably going to kill us, you—"

One of the gunmen swung toward them and jabbed a pistol toward the young man. "Shut up!" he ordered. "No talking!"

"Okay, okay!" The young man held his hands up, palms out.

For a few moments, he and his friend sat in the same terrified silence that gripped the entire bus. Then, the one in the sombrero said quietly, "They really are going to kill us, aren't they?"

"I don't know, man. . . ."

"I'm not going to just sit here and let them shoot me. I'm getting out of here."

"How?"

"I'll take my chances with the emergency door."

"No, wait—"

It was too late. The young man in the sombrero stood up and lunged for the handle of the emergency exit located between the two rear seats. Leaping from the bus while it was moving at such a high rate of speed would be very dangerous, but he might survive the fall.

He never got a chance to attempt it. The handle of the emergency exit turned, but the door didn't budge. Meanwhile, the young man's movement caused the gunman who had threatened them earlier to jerk around and fire. The automatic weapon in his hand erupted with a sound like a giant bolt of cloth being ripped. Bullets tore into the young man and threw him against the emergency exit as more screams echoed through the bus.

The other young man caught his friend as he fell. At least three bullets had hit him in the legs, and he was whimpering in pain. Blood was everywhere.

"Nobody else move!" screamed the gunman. "The next person who moves dies!"

"Shots fired inside the bus," reported the radio in Agent O'Donnell's car. Walker, Trivette, and O'Donnell knew that the bus was being observed by unmarked police units now, since the last patrol car that had tried to close in had been wrecked in some fashion. Walker wasn't exactly clear on what had happened.

"What are they trying to do now?" asked Trivette.

"Trying to keep a bus full of scared people under control," said Walker. "It can't be easy."

"This is Lafayette," O'Donnell said as he turned right. "We didn't get here in time to get in front of them, though. That last report said they were just passing San Bernardo— *Up there!*"

Walker had already spotted the bus. It was a block and a half ahead of them, a large, brightly painted vehicle that should have been cheerful, not ominous.

A shadow suddenly passed over the car and swooped on down the street like a giant bird flying over them. Walker leaned forward to peer up through the windshield. "There's a helicopter," he said.

"Not the Vega Garcias again, I hope," said Trivette.

Walker shook his head. "It's a TV news chopper."

"Then there'll be more of them showing up in a few minutes," O'Donnell said. "If one of the stations knows what's going on, they all do."

"That might not be a bad thing," mused Walker. "If they spread the word about the pursuit, people will be more likely to get out of the bus's way."

"Do we want that?" asked Trivette.

"We don't want any innocent people getting hurt before we can figure out a way to stop that thing."

Trivette nodded, seeing Walker's point. A lot of law enforcement officers didn't care for the way high-speed pursuits so often became fodder for airborne TV news crews, but in some cases the publicity could come in handy.

More voices came from the radio: police units reporting that a roadblock had been set up at the intersection of Lafayette and Interstate 35. Walker grabbed the microphone and cut in on the chatter. "This is Texas Ranger Cordell Walker, in pursuit of the suspect vehicle. Use extreme caution in any effort to stop it. There are hostages in there."

"We copy, Ranger Walker," came the reply. "Don't worry, they won't get past us."

Walker grimaced as he hung up the mike. He wanted to stop the bus, sure, but not at the cost of dozens of innocent lives.

O'Donnell sped up a little, closing the gap between his car and the bus. "Careful," warned Trivette. "They managed to wreck the last car that got too close."

"The driver's trying for the freeway, no doubt about that," said O'Donnell. "Look, you can see the roadblock now."

Indeed, what looked like a sea of flashing lights was visible up ahead of the bus. It roared under an overpass and then veered toward the entrance ramp that would carry it up on the interstate highway. A police car was parked across the ramp, blocking it, and more cruisers were arranged across Lafayette to close it off.

The bus didn't slow down.

"Oh, my God!" exclaimed O'Donnell. "He's going to try to break through!"

Walker was certain of it now:

El Diablo was at the wheel of that bus.

211

TWENTY-FOUR

Alvarez's jaw was set tightly, almost as tightly as he was gripping the wheel. He peered through the bus's windshield at the police cars arranged across the road, their lights flashing. He could see dozens of cops crouched behind those cars, all of them holding guns that were pointed toward the onrushing bus.

Alvarez moved the bus into the lane that led onto the freeway entrance ramp. The roadblock was less than a hundred yards ahead now.

Spurts of bright flame came from behind the cruiser blocking the ramp. The cops behind it were firing at him now, as it became obvious that he wasn't going to stop. Their hope would be to take out the driver with a well-placed shot and let the passengers take their chances with a crash.

But the slugs from the police guns just flattened against the bullet-proof glass of the windshield. All the windows in this bus were bullet-proof, in fact. Alvarez was as safe behind the windshield as the Pope or the President would have been in their official vehicles.

Seeing that their shots were having no effect, the cops

switched to firing at the tires, but with the same lack of success. Those tires were self-sealing; it would take at least an armor-piercing round to puncture one of them, and even that might not make it go flat. And the shots that the police directed at the bus's engine never penetrated anything except the outer skin of metal, either. Armor plating had been installed underneath the regular body of the bus.

Alvarez might as well have been driving a tank. And he had almost as much firepower as a tank, too, he thought with a cruel smile as he thumbed another of the controls on the armrest beside him.

Firing ports on the front of the bus near the headlights flipped open, and a pair of small rockets streaked out, heading straight for the police car. They struck it fore and aft, exploding with a force that flung the car into the air like it was a child's toy. The cops using the vehicle for cover never had a chance. They were caught in the twin explosions and thrown into the air along with the car.

What was left of the police car's blazing chassis slammed back into the ground at the edge of the ramp, still partially blocking it. But Alvarez had plenty of room to maneuver around the wreck, and the bus roared unharmed through the flames that had spread from the explosion. The bus was protected against fire, too. El Diablo's mechanics had been very busy during those long nights of secret modifications.

Alvarez swung the wheel, piloting the bus through the long, sweeping curve of the entrance ramp. The freeway opened up in front of him, three lanes in each direction with a grassy median dividing them. He was heading north, with no real idea of where he was going. The idea came to him that if he could get well beyond the city and then leave the highway, he might be able to lose the pursuit in the vast open spaces of the South Texas *brasada*.

But shadows keeping pace with him on the ground told him that might be an impossible hope. There were helicopters up there, he realized. Probably TV news choppers at this point, but the authorities had aircraft available to them, too. They would be able to track him from the air, no matter where he went.

Unless he took out those helicopters some way.

He reached for the controls on the armrest again.

O'Donnell brought the car to a skidding stop before it could run over any of the debris that had been scattered by the explosions. "Lord have mercy," he breathed as he surveyed the destruction.

Walker threw his door open and got out of the car to hurry over to a knot of uniformed officers in riot gear. Trivette followed at a trot. "Texas Ranger," Walker said to the man who was in charge. Other officers were using portable fire extinguishers to try to put out the fires started by the blast.

The Laredo cop glared at Walker. "Do you know what the hell's going on here, Ranger? What's this all about? Who is that madman on that bus?"

"He calls himself El Diablo," said Walker, "but his real name is Jorge Alvarez."

The cop's eyes widened, and several of the other officers exclaimed in surprise. "Alvarez? The Mexican agent who's in charge of the antidrug task force?"

Walker nodded curtly. "That's right. He's really working for the cartel that's been smuggling heroin across the border."

"There's fifty million dollars' worth of drugs hidden in that bus," Trivette put in.

"That's crazy!"

"Alvarez would probably prefer to think of it as audacious," said Trivette.

"That bus is full of tourists, too," Walker pointed out. "Alvarez will use them as hostages if he's cornered."

The head cop took off his helmet and rubbed a weary hand across his face. "I don't know if we can stop him or not. He blew that car to kingdom come, along with three of my officers. Nothing we threw at him seemed to faze him.''

"The bus must be specially armored," said Trivette. "We know it's well-armed. That's no normal tourist bus."

"Alvarez has been planning this for a while," said Walker. "He wanted to make the biggest score ever along the border. He won't give up."

"Yeah, but he'll run out of gas sooner or later," said O'Donnell, who had come up to join the conversation.

"Then we'll have a standoff," said Trivette, "and him with dozens of hostages."

The loud drumming of a helicopter's blades and a sudden hard downdraft of air made the lawmen turn around. A chopper was landing on the highway embankment. The tail of it was emblazoned WEBB COUNTY SHERIFF'S DEPARTMENT.

A burly, middle-aged man in a Western-cut suit dropped down from the chopper's cabin and ran over to join the gathering of law enforcement officers. He held his Stetson on with one hand as he ran. As he came up, he nodded to the Laredo cop and raised his voice to be heard over the beating of the helicopter's still turning blades.

"Need a hand, Captain?"

"Thanks, Sheriff." The cop jerked his head toward Walker and Trivette. "These two fellas are Texas Rangers."

Walker quickly introduced himself and Trivette to the sheriff. He was all too aware that with each passing minute, Alvarez and everyone else on that bus were getting farther away. "We need to get in the air, Sheriff," he said.

"Come on, then. Any resources we've got are at your disposal, Ranger Walker."

A moment later, the chopper was lifting off and soaring once more into the air. The pilot sent it winging northward, following the interstate highway below.

The sheriff had insisted that Walker take the seat beside the pilot. He was in the back seat with Trivette, being filled in on what had happened so far. It had been an eventful day, thought Walker, and even more so for him and Trivette. They had had to deal with not only this pursuit of Alvarez, but also the fight at Cabeza de Oro, the destruction of the cartel's stronghold, and then the battle with the helicopter that had more than likely been carrying the Vega Garcia brothers themselves.

No wonder he was starting to get a little tired.

Walker leaned forward as he spotted the bus down below. Traffic on the highway was fairly light, and Walker wondered if some of the drivers had heard about the pursuit on their car radios and decided to get off the interstate and out of the way. He hoped so. It might be a good idea, in fact, to get some police cars ahead of the bus and clear the road completely.

He turned around in the seat and said as much to the sheriff, who reached for a radio console and said, "I'll get right on it, Ranger."

"Bring the units in from the sides of the highway," suggested Trivette. "Anybody in an official car who gets too close to the bus is in danger."

The sheriff nodded and got busy setting up the effort. Within minutes, Walker and the others in the helicopter could see the results. Laredo police and sheriff's deputies stayed off the highway, using side roads until they were well ahead of the bus, then raced out onto the interstate to begin clearing it of traffic. Soon there was open road in front of the fugitive vehicle, with a half-mile gap between it and the row of police cars with flashing lights. More cars were trailing the bus at a distance, also with lights flashing and sirens blaring, and from the air the bus looked rather lonely in the center of all that open highway, flanked front and rear by a police escort.

"Now what?" asked the sheriff, leaning forward from the rear seat. He echoed the sentiment expressed earlier by Agent O'Donnell. "That fella can't keep going forever. Sooner or later he'll run out of gas."

A couple of helicopters suddenly flew past the sheriff's

chopper, one on each side. They were flying at reckless speeds in an attempt to catch up to and keep pace with the bus.

"Damned news hounds!" the sheriff exclaimed. "They shouldn't be up here so close!"

Suddenly, a streak of fire shot upward from the bus. It was aimed unerringly at one of the news choppers, and a split second later, the two intersected. Fire bloomed in midair as the missile fired from the bus blew the helicopter out of the sky.

The shock wave from the explosion bounced the sheriff's chopper. The sheriff let out a blistering tirade of profanity that trailed away into a shocked silence. After a moment, Trivette muttered, "Surface-to-air missiles? What else has he got in that thing?"

"I'm afraid we're liable to find out," Walker said.

The targeting computer that had swung down from the bus's regular instrument panel told Alvarez that the strike had been successful. It had taken several minutes to set up, but once a targeting lock was achieved, the missile had flown straight and true. Alvarez didn't know if the helicopter he had destroyed had been from the cops or from one of the TV stations in town, but either way, everyone would think twice before overflying him again.

The police had cleared the road in front of him while he was working with the computer. He could see their lights up ahead in the distance, but they weren't setting up another roadblock. Instead they were keeping a constant space between themselves and the bus, and the same situation held true to the rear. The bus had the highway to itself for the time being.

That wouldn't last, though. The cops would make another try at stopping the vehicle. Even with all the demonstrations Alvarez had given them of the bus's capabilities, the cops wouldn't just let him go.

Earlier, one of the passengers had tried to get out of the

back door and had gotten shot for his trouble. Considering the circumstances—a crowded bus, itchy trigger fingers on the gunmen—the passengers were lucky no one else had gotten hurt.

Maybe it was time, Alvarez decided, to give the pursuers a vivid example of what was going to happen if they tried again to close in on him.

He turned and called to the nearest of the gunmen. The man backed up the aisle, still keeping his weapon carefully trained on the passengers in the front part of the bus.

"What is it, El Diablo?"

"Pick one of the passengers and take him to the back of the bus," said Alvarez.

"And then?"

"Then kill him and throw him out the emergency door," Alvarez ordered.

TWENTY-FIVE

Frank Dailey had his eyes closed. He was praying, something that he hadn't done in a long time. The first thing that made him aware of the situation getting even worse was the fact that his wife started trembling harder. Then Karen said shakily, "F-Frank . . ."

He opened his eyes to see one of the gunmen standing right in front of him and Karen and the kids. The man pointed the automatic pistol at Frank and said, "You. Stand up."

"No," Karen sobbed. "Please, no."

"On your feet, man, or I'll take this pretty wife of yours instead."

"Leave her alone," Frank grated. He was surprised at how strong his voice sounded to his ears. He had been afraid for a second before he spoke that the words would come out in a mouselike squeak.

Karen clutched at his arm as he shifted in his seat, ready to stand up. "No, Frank!" she pleaded. "You can't! You can't leave us!"

"It'll be all right," he told her, but now his voice sounded hollow to him. Just as hollow as the words themselves. Nothing was ever going to be right again.

Gently, Frank disengaged Karen's grip on his arm. Elizabeth had been sitting on his leg. He moved her to Karen's arms and then stood up and glanced around. All the other passengers were sitting with their eyes downcast, as if they were afraid to watch what was happening. As if they could pretend none of it was real and nothing would happen to them.

Frank stood up. "What do you want?" he asked the gunman.

The man jerked the barrel of his weapon toward the rear of the bus. "Back there," he ordered.

Frank nodded, stepped into the aisle. He tried to shut out Karen's frightened wails behind him as he started walking toward the back of the bus. He knew he didn't dare glance over his shoulder at her. The sight of her tear-streaked face would ruin his resolve.

The other gunmen moved aside to let him past. The man who had given him the orders was right behind him, and every so often Frank felt the barrel of the gun prod him in the back. As he approached the rear door, he saw that the young man who had been wounded earlier was stretched out in one of the last seats. Crude bandages made of strips of material from the serape he had been wearing were wrapped around his legs. He was pale and unconscious, had most likely passed out from loss of blood. He might even be in shock.

His friend was hovering over him. The long-haired young man looked up as Frank and the gunman approached. The gunman jabbed his weapon in Frank's back again, drawing an involuntary grunt of pain. "Open the door," the man ordered.

"It won't open," said the long-haired young man. "I think it's stuck."

"Shut up!" snapped the gunman. He prodded Frank again. "Open it."

Frank reached down and grasped the handle. He twisted

it. The handle turned, but the door remained shut.

Frank looked down. "It's got a second catch," he said, pointing to another, smaller handle lower down on the door.

"Then open it, too, you idiot!"

As Frank bent to turn the second handle, the long-haired young man hissed, "He's going to kill you!"

Frank just looked at him, the sure knowledge of his own death in his eyes. What else could he do?

Frank twisted both handles at the same time, and the emergency door popped open.

At that moment, the long-haired young man suddenly lunged toward him, driving a shoulder against him. Frank fell, sprawling on top of the man who had been wounded earlier. He heard a burst of gunfire and expected to feel bullets tearing hotly into his body. He caught his breath and squeezed his eyes shut in anticipation of the pain.

Instead, nothing happened. He heard the sound of a struggle and opened his eyes, turned his head to see the long-haired young man wrestling with the gunman in the aisle. The young man had his hands on the automatic pistol and was trying to keep it pointed away from everyone in the bus. The other gunmen were yelling, and one of them was hurrying down the aisle toward the back door of the bus.

Without thinking about what he was doing, Frank surged up off the seat where the unconscious man lay. He laced his fingers together and clubbed with both hands at the onrushing gunman. The man wasn't expecting the blow from someone who had seemed so thoroughly cowed only a few minutes earlier. The impact staggered him, made him slump against one of the seats.

Meanwhile, the long-haired man and the first gunman were still struggling on the brink of the rear door, and suddenly one of the gunman's feet slipped. He toppled toward the door, and his opponent broke free. With a scream, the gunman fell backward through the emergency exit. He struck the pavement of the highway headfirst with such force that his skull shattered like a watermelon. The gun went bouncing away across the asphalt.

The long-haired man had caught hold of both sides of the door to keep from falling out of the bus. He pushed himself away from the opening and turned in time to see the second gunman slash his weapon across Frank Dailey's face. Frank fell, blood streaming from a cut on his cheek. The gunman recovered his balance and aimed his automatic pistol down at Frank, then suddenly shifted the barrel and pointed it at the figure framed in the open doorway instead. He fired.

The young man was thrown backward by the slugs pounding into him. He went out the open door, mercifully dead before his body slammed to the pavement.

Frank lay in the aisle and tried not to whimper in pain. That young man had saved his life, he knew. . . .

But for how long?

"Damn it, what's that?" the sheriff had exclaimed as the first body came flying out the back of the bus. It was followed a moment later by a second body.

Walker had been afraid something like this was going to happen. "Alvarez is killing hostages," he said. "He wants us to know that he means business."

"How is murdering innocent people going to help him?" asked Trivette.

"He's already to blame for the deaths of several cops and the people in that chopper. A few more murders won't bother him if they get us to back off."

"I'm not backing off, blast it!" said the sheriff.

But in fact, that was what they had already done. The chopper had pulled back so that it wouldn't be the target of another missile attack, and the sheriff had gotten on the radio and ordered all the TV news choppers to fall back, too. The brightly colored bus was strangely alone now, with dozens of police cars a good distance behind it and ahead of it and a no-fly zone above it.

The bizarre convoy was well north of Laredo now. Walker said to the sheriff, "There are no towns of any size between here and Cotulla, are there?"

"Nope, just a few wide places in the road. A couple of truck stops. And Cotulla's not that big a town, nor Pearsall, either. The next real city is San Antonio."

Walker nodded. He had no idea how far the bus could go before it ran out of gas. Considering how much had been done to modify the bus—hiding places for all that heroin, armor, bulletproof glass, even missiles—Walker knew it was possible that extra gas tanks had been added to the vehicle, too. If the bus stayed on I-35, it would reach San Antonio in less than two hundred miles. Walker felt confident that it had at least that much range and probably more.

If the bus made it to San Antonio, stopping it would become that much more complicated, simply because there would be so much more traffic to deal with in the Alamo City. Out here where open ranchland stretched for miles on both sides of the highway, the only innocent people who would be at risk in any sort of operation would be the passengers on the bus. Of course, Walker didn't want to take chances with their lives, but it might come down to that.

If there were some way to slow the bus down, Walker thought, then the passengers would have better odds of surviving a crash. But Alvarez had turned the bus into a juggernaut. What could slow such a thing down? What was big enough and strong enough to even come close to approaching the bus on equal terms?

Suddenly, something the sheriff had said a few minutes earlier popped into Walker's head. He turned to the pilot and said, "We need to get ahead of them."

"You mean fly over them?" asked the pilot, clearly nervous by what had happened to the last chopper that had attempted that.

"Swing over to one side and go around," Walker told

him. "Give the bus as much room as you want, just get us ahead of them."

Trivette leaned forward. "You have an idea, Walker?"

Walker nodded and said, "Maybe . . ."

Alvarez wiped more sweat from his forehead. Just when he had thought he might have a way of making the cops back off—dropping dead hostages out the back door of the bus until they did—things had gone wrong again. One of the hostages was dead, true, but so was one of the men the Vega Garcias had sent to make sure the delivery of the heroin went smoothly. Now there were only four of the gunmen to keep the passengers under control. Luckily, the gringos were so frightened by everything that had happened that any more trouble from them was unlikely.

Still, there had been that momentary show of resistance which had resulted in the death of one of the gunmen. That was troubling.

The emergency exit was closed now and once again latched shut. One of the gunmen had done that following the brief flurry of deadly violence.

Alvarez's eyes flicked from gauge to gauge on the instrument panel. Considering how hard he had been pushing the bus, its engine was performing exceptionally well. The oil pressure and temperature were in fine shape. So was the fuel supply, for that matter. Alvarez could keep driving for a long time.

He hadn't given up on the idea of pulling off on one of the ranch roads, however. He and his men could abandon the bus and its passengers and try to get away through the scrubby brush that covered the landscape.

But that would mean abandoning fifty million dollars' worth of heroin, too. It would mean the end of Alvarez's plans, the end of his association with the Vega Garcias.

The end of El Diablo.

That might well turn out to be the price of his life, but Alvarez wasn't ready to take that step. Not yet.

One of the gunmen came up the aisle. He was a tall man with a pockmarked face, the legacy of some childhood disease. "Don Carlos and don Ramon will not be pleased about this," he practically snarled at Alvarez.

The last man who had thrown the Vega Garcias in his face had wound up dead, Alvarez thought. Obviously, this pockmarked gunman had forgotten about that. But with an effort, Alvarez controlled his anger and said calmly, "Everything will be all right."

"How?" demanded the gunman. "They might as well have us in prison right now! We are trapped out here on this highway."

"Then perhaps it is time we got off the highway," said Alvarez. He had just passed a sign that said there was an exit a mile ahead. If it looked promising at all, he would take it.

But when the bus reached the exit, a little less than a minute later, what Alvarez saw made him curse and pound his hand on the steering wheel in frustration.

An eighteen-wheeler was parked across the exit, completely blocking it. And the big truck was too massive to be blown out of the way with missiles, as the police car back in Laredo had been.

The gunman was right. They were caught in the jaws of a trap. . . .

TWENTY-SIX

A short time earlier, the Webb County sheriff's helicopter had descended out of the sky onto the parking lot of a large truck stop that sprawled across several acres along the interstate. The lot wasn't full, but it was so big that over a dozen rigs were parked there without filling it up. Walker was out of the chopper almost before its landing skids had settled onto the asphalt.

He hurried toward the building that housed a restaurant, a truckers' supply store, and showers. A sizable group of men had come out of the place to watch the helicopter land. Most of them wore jeans, work shirts with the sleeves rolled up, and ''gimme'' caps adorned with various logos. They were truck drivers, men who pushed the eighteen-wheelers over the ribbons of concrete that networked the country.

And right now, Walker needed their help.

''I'm a Texas Ranger,'' he said by way of introduction. ''Have you heard about what's going on out on the highway?''

''That's why we're here, Ranger,'' replied one of the truckers. ''The word came over all our radios that we were supposed to get off the road for a while.''

"It's playin' hell with my schedule, too," grumbled one of the other men.

Walker smiled faintly. "I'm sorry about that. We'll have the situation resolved as soon as possible. That's why I'm here. I could use a hand."

"From us?"

"That's right. Are any of you dead-heading?"

He got affirmative nods from four of the men. "Yeah, I'm runnin' empty," one of them said. "Why?"

Walker pointed to the exit ramp that led off the highway just south of the truck stop. "I want one of you to take your rig down there and park it across the exit."

Understanding dawned on the faces of the men. "You think that crazy bus driver's going to try to get off the interstate?"

"He might," said Walker. "I want him to keep going—for now."

"I can do that," one of them volunteered.

"What about the rest of us?" asked another man.

Walker glanced over at Trivette, who had come up beside him. "Trivette, you can handle a truck, can't you?"

"I drove one for my uncle back in Baltimore one summer when I was a kid," replied Trivette. "Why?"

"Because," said Walker, "we're going to borrow a couple of these big rigs."

It had been a while since Walker had been behind the wheel of an eighteen-wheeler, but he discovered it was just like riding a bicycle. Well, maybe not quite that simple, he thought with a slight smile as he looked over the instrument panel to familiarize himself with it.

The trucker, a tall man with a short, rust-colored beard, pointed out several things to Walker, then asked, "You're sure you can handle this, Ranger? I'd be glad to take the wheel."

"No, thanks, Mr. Burke. I've already asked you to risk your truck. I won't ask you to risk your life."

Burke, who was an owner-operator, shrugged his shoulders. "The truck's insured. I'm not worried too much about it. I just want you to catch that lunatic."

Walker nodded. "I'll do my best."

Burke stepped back and closed the door of the cab. Walker fired up the engine, let it warm up for a minute, then grabbed the stick and put the transmission in gear. He rolled slowly out of the parking lot onto the frontage road. In the big outside mirror, he saw Trivette pulling out behind him in a similar rig.

A county road crossed the highway here on a bridge, meaning that the interstate dipped down below the level of the frontage roads. Walker drove the truck past the intersection and then eased it to a stop. Trivette pulled in behind him. From the highway below, the two trucks would be partially visible but not very noticeable. Walker and Trivette had a good view of the interstate, however, and the frontage road turned into an entrance ramp right in front of them.

Walker and Trivette had each taken a walkie-talkie from the sheriff's helicopter. The one on the seat beside Walker crackled a little, then the sheriff's voice said, "Coming up one."

Walker had warned the sheriff to be careful about what he said, just in case Alvarez had a scanner in the bus. The way the bus was equipped, anything was possible. They didn't want to tip him off, hence the vague message directed to Walker and Trivette. It meant that the bus was still coming and was one mile south of the truck stop and the intersection with the county road.

The engine of the truck was idling smoothly. Walker flexed his hands, then wrapped his fingers around the steering wheel. This day already seemed as if it had been a year long, but Walker's instincts told him the action was coming to a head. A high-speed showdown with Alvarez was looming.

The police cars leading the convoy raced past on the highway. Thirty seconds later, the brightly colored bus itself appeared, zooming on by the exit ramp. If Alvarez had intended to take the exit, that idea had been scotched by the eighteen-wheeler parked there. And the next exit was nearly ten miles away. Walker had checked that on the map.

Meaning that these next ten minutes would be the best chance he and Trivette would have to stop Alvarez.

Walker put the truck in gear again and eased into motion, accelerating smoothly down the entrance ramp onto the highway. Trivette was right behind him.

Alvarez looked to both sides of the bus. The frontage road back there at the intersection had turned into an entrance ramp, then ended, so there was nowhere to go to the right of the highway lanes. The grassy median might be negotiable, though. The southbound lanes of the highway were empty; no doubt the cops had blocked them off somewhere up ahead and diverted all the traffic onto alternate routes. So if he could slow down and make it across the median, he might be able to make a U-turn and head south again. That would sure as hell take all the cops by surprise.

But before he could finish formulating that plan, movement in the outside mirror caught his eye. He looked and saw a truck coming up behind him. It was moving fast, as if the driver was trying to make up for lost time. How had the driver gotten onto the highway? Hadn't the cops warned him to stay off?

Alvarez's hands tightened on the wheel. There was a second truck back there, he realized. He had just caught a glimpse of it behind the first eighteen-wheeler. And it was coming on just as fast, almost like they were trying to catch up to the bus. . . .

Alvarez's lips pulled back from his teeth in a grimace. He breathed curses. Those truckers might not be truckers at all. They might well be cops, trying to use the big rigs to either force him off the road or make him stop. Hadn't they learned anything from what had happened back in Laredo?

Truckers or cops, it didn't matter. Alvarez reached for the special controls. If they wanted to play tag with him, they would find that the game was deadly.

Steadily, Walker increased the speed of the truck he was driving. It took a while to coax one of these big rigs up to high speed, but once it was there, it seemed to race along almost effortlessly. Bit by bit, he cut down the gap between his truck and the bus. It was less than a hundred yards in front of him now.

In fact, Walker was close enough so that his keen eyes saw the ports opening up on the back of the bus. Dark liquid suddenly spewed out of the ports, coating the roadway.

Walker wrenched the wheel to the right. The bus was straddling the centerline, so the oil that sprayed out landed on part of both northbound lanes. There was a wide shoulder on both sides of the highway, however, so Walker had enough room to maneuver the truck past the worst of the oil slick. The tires on the left side of the rig hit the edge of the spreading pool of oil, but Walker didn't lose enough traction to slow him down very much. Right behind him, Trivette alertly followed his lead and avoided the worst of the spill as well.

Oil stopped spraying from the rear of the bus. Alvarez had gained a few yards by this trick, but that was all. Walker wondered what else Alvarez had up his sleeve.

He didn't have to wait long to find out.

Another port opened on the rear of the bus. This time a stubby black cylinder protruded. Walker jerked the wheel, veering left this time. Flame spurted from the muzzle of the machine gun built into the bus. The slugs chewed up the pavement where Walker's truck had been a couple of seconds earlier.

Walker checked his mirrors, saw to his satisfaction that Trivette was hanging back now. They had discussed this ahead of time. It was Walker's job to draw Alvarez's fire. Trivette hadn't liked that idea, but he had reluctantly gone along with it.

Walker was driving mostly on the left-hand shoulder now. He saw more flame erupt from the muzzle of the machine gun, but the barrel couldn't swing far enough to the left for the slugs to reach him. The weapon's range of motion was limited by the cramped nature of its housing. Walker pressed down on the accelerator, sending the truck roaring ahead.

Fifty yards between truck and bus now. The angle made it impossible for the rear-mounted gun to threaten Walker. But Alvarez might have more surprises waiting in the side of the bus. Walker watched it closely as he drove.

With a puff of smoke from the launching mechanism, hundreds of the spiked balls were thrown from a hatch on the bus's left side. Walker saw them scattering all across the road in front of him and hauled the wheel to the right, cutting across the highway behind the bus. That took him back into the machine gun's field of fire, just as Alvarez must have intended. He heard slugs plinking off the hood of the truck's cab as he went into a controlled skid. For an instant, the rear end of the truck threatened to start fishtailing, but then it stabilized. Walker brought the truck under control and raced along the right-hand shoulder. He was past the spiked balls now and once again out of the line of fire from the machine gun.

But it had been close. If one of those slugs had found a tire, or the gas line, it could have meant disaster.

Walker wondered if Alvarez had any more missiles in the bus. There had to be a limit to how much armament could have been concealed in the vehicle. Walker leaned forward and gripped the steering wheel tightly as he waited to see what Alvarez would throw at him next.

That trucker was crazy! It had to be a cop at the wheel, Alvarez told himself. No normal truck driver would take such chances.

So far the bastard had been lucky. If he tried to get in front of the bus, he would regret it.

But deep inside his brain, Alvarez had to admit that he was running out of options. His firepower was limited now.

He had the men the Vega Garcias had sent. They were all armed, and those automatic pistols would be quite effective at close range. Maybe it would be best to slow down a little and let the trucker pull alongside him, if that's what the man wanted so badly. The gunmen could riddle that truck cab.

Alvarez turned his head and shouted to the men, "Get ready! When he catches up to us—*kill him!*"

Walker saw the bus's brake lights flare. He was only about twenty-five yards behind now, still on the right-hand shoulder. He reacted instantly, swinging the bus back to the left. If Alvarez wanted him to pass the bus on the right, then that was exactly what Walker didn't want to do. The change in course cost Walker a little distance. The bus was still slowing down, though, and Walker hadn't let off the pressure on the accelerator. The gap vanished in a matter of seconds, and suddenly Walker was alongside the bus.

Walker ducked a little as a slug whipped through the open window on the passenger side of the cab and sang past his ear. Again he heard bullets thudding into the cab and then into the empty trailer he was pulling.

Walker pulled even with the bus. He looked over at it and couldn't help but smile grimly as he saw shock appear on the face of the driver. They had recognized each other at the same moment. Jorge Alvarez—El Diablo—was indeed behind the wheel of the bus, and he was staring at a man he had believed to be dead in the cave at Cabeza de Oro. Walker took one hand off the wheel and sketched a little salute at the renegade Mexican cop.

Alvarez's features twisted in fury. He jerked the wheel and sent the bus veering straight at the truck.

TWENTY-SEVEN

Walker! *Dios mío!* It couldn't be *Walker....*

But it was, and as Alvarez looked at the Texas Ranger, a red rage such as he had never before experienced filled him. Walker was supposed to be dead, and it was as if he had come back from the fires of Hell itself to torment him.

Walker might not be dead now, but he soon would be, even if it cost Alvarez his own life. El Diablo made that vow.

And El Diablo kept his promises.

Frank Dailey had his arms around his wife and both children now, and he prayed as he had never prayed before. He had thought he was afraid earlier, but now he realized that he hadn't known the meaning of fear until this moment.

Just get us out of this, Lord. Please, just get us out of this....

Walker tromped down hard on the accelerator and turned the truck's wheel. The massive vehicle lurched ahead as it swung to the left, away from the bus. Alvarez kept coming, though, and the left front corner of the bus struck the right rear corner of the empty trailer. The impact jolted Walker and threatened to tear the wheel out of his hands, but he clamped down tighter on it and kept control of the speeding truck. The bus rebounded a little from the collision, giving Walker some breathing room. He tried to coax a little more horsepower out of the straining engine as he glanced at the big mirror mounted just outside the passenger door of the cab and saw what he had hoped he would see.

Trivette was coming up fast.

Alvarez veered the bus toward Walker's truck again. The rig was out in front now, just barely but that was enough. The bus missed. Walker cut the wheel hard to the right. That brought the truck directly in front of the bus.

A bad place to be if Alvarez had any more of those missiles just waiting to be fired. . . .

Alvarez was panting as he tried to control the careening bus. The passengers screamed and cried out prayers, too scared for any threats from the gunmen to quiet them now. Alvarez glared out through the windshield at the truck in front of him. The two vehicles were close, with only a few feet separating them.

There was one more missile in reserve. Alvarez reached for the button that would fire it and almost pressed down before he realized what a bad mistake that would be. The missile would destroy the truck, all right, but at this range the explosion would also turn the bus into so much scrap metal.

Damn it! thought Alvarez. Walker had outsmarted him.

And in the heat of battle, Alvarez had made another mistake. He had forgotten all about the other truck.

But he remembered it when it slammed into the rear of the bus.

The impact threw Alvarez forward in his seat and brought more screams from the passengers. Alvarez caught himself against the steering wheel and straightened. A glance in the outside mirror told him the other truck was dropping back a little now after running into the bus. Through the windshield of the truck, Alvarez saw the other Texas Ranger, Walker's partner Trivette. So both of them had survived the trap at Cabeza de Oro. Well, Trivette was in perfect position to die now.

Alvarez jammed his thumb down on the button that controlled the rear-mounted machine gun.

Nothing happened.

Alvarez's teeth ground together in frustration. The machine gun must have been ruined when Trivette crashed his truck into the back of the bus. Now there was no way to lash out at Trivette, nowhere to go because Walker was right in front of him, no way to win. . . .

Then they would all die. If El Diablo was going home to Hell, then he would take Walker and Trivette and all the passengers with him.

He reached for an unmarked button at the bottom of the armrest, the button that would detonate the explosives hidden on the undercarriage of the bus.

Red flames danced in front of Alvarez's eyes, the flames that awaited his damned soul.

But they weren't flames at all, he realized as a pair of shuddering impacts threw him forward, then back, jerking him violently in his seat before he could push the fatal button.

They were brake lights.

Walker practically stood on the truck's brakes. Smoke rose from the tires as they left rubber in black streaks hundreds of yards long. Alvarez had had no chance to avoid crashing into the back of the truck, and Walker had felt the second impact as Trivette once again slammed his truck into the rear of the bus, pinning it between the two eighteen-wheelers. Walker snatched up the walkie-talkie from the seat beside him and shouted over the wailing of tires on concrete, "We're bringing the bus to a stop! All units close in! Close in!"

There were still the passengers on the bus to think of, Walker reminded himself. He was hoping, however, that he and Trivette could get on there quickly enough once all three of the big vehicles were stopped to minimize the danger to the passengers.

Shuddering and sliding, the truck finally came to a halt. Walker had killed the engine and dropped out of the cab almost before the eighteen-wheeler stopped moving. He ran along the trailer, pulling the pistol the Webb County sheriff had given him from behind his belt. Trivette was coming from the other direction, also with a gun in his hand.

Suddenly, an automatic pistol was thrust out of one of the windows. Walker threw himself down and to the side as bullets erupted from the gun. He rolled underneath the truck trailer, scrambled on hands and knees to the other side. As he emerged from under the truck, one of the gunmen from the bus slammed out through the doors of the vehicle. The man jerked his weapon toward Walker, who dropped to a knee and triggered twice.

The slugs drove into the man's chest and threw him backward. Trivette had crawled underneath the bus and came out into the open to cover the fallen man.

More gunfire sounded inside the bus. People were screaming. Walker leaped for the doors, fearful that Alvarez and his men were murdering the passengers.

Walker took the steps in one bound. The driver's seat was empty. Where was Alvarez? Walker didn't see him, but he did see several of the passengers struggling with their former captors. Clearly, some of the hostages had finally seized the opportunity to strike back. A couple of bodies were sprawled in the aisle, and Walker didn't know if they were passengers or some of Alvarez's henchmen. The passengers appeared to be winning the fight now, though. One of them wrenched a gun out of the hands of another man and started beating him over the head with it.

"Texas Rangers!" Walker called loudly. "Everyone drop your weapons! On the floor! Down! Down!"

People cowered in their seats and covered their heads with their arms. Walker kept looking for Alvarez as he went down the aisle, swiveling the gun from side to side. The fight was over now, and one of the men who had overcome a gunman looked up at Walker with a proud grin on his face and a bloody gash on his forehead. "I got this one for you, Ranger," he said as he pointed the gun in his hands down at the man he was kneeling on. "Pretty good for a copier salesman, huh?"

"Give me the gun, sir," said Walker, reaching out to take the automatic weapon from the former hostage. "Have you seen where the driver went?"

The man shook his head. "Isn't he up front?"

Walker didn't take the time to answer. Sheriff's deputies and highway patrolmen were pouring onto the bus now from the dozens of units that had closed in on the scene at Walker's order. The surviving gunmen were handcuffed, and paramedics began checking on the wounded. Everything was under control.

But where was Alvarez?

"Walker!" Trivette hurried up to him. "Alvarez isn't on the bus!"

Walker's expression was both grim and puzzled as he nodded. "I know."

"But where the devil could he have gone?"

That was the question Walker wanted answered.

Stay calm, Alvarez told himself as he walked quickly along the shoulder of the highway. No matter how much he wanted to, he could not break into a run. That would draw attention to him, especially since he was walking away from the trucks and the bus. Most of the other officers were hurrying toward the locked-together vehicles. Alvarez even nodded curtly to some of them as they passed him, as if they were friends of his.

Alvarez wanted to look like a man on the way back to his car for something he had forgotten. He had peeled out of his uniform jacket as soon as he dropped through the escape hatch right behind the driver's seat, then taken his badge from his pocket and pinned it on. He was wearing slacks, a white shirt, and a tie, and with the badge prominently displayed, he looked like one of the officers who had responded to the emergency on the interstate.

Walker had to be wondering where he was by now. Alvarez had slipped out of the bus while Walker was right outside it, but he had closed the hatch behind him, and it might take Walker a while to locate it and discover the ruse Alvarez had pulled off. By that time, Alvarez would be long gone.

Sooner or later, though, he would be back. He understood now why Carlos and Ramon del Vega Garcia felt the way they did about the Texas Ranger. Alvarez burned with the desire to settle the score with Walker.

Someday, he told himself, someday El Diablo would return.

One of the sheriff's deputies had been in such a hurry to get to the bus that he had gone off and left his car running. Considerate of him, thought Alvarez. He had almost made it to the vehicle, and still there was no outcry behind him. He resisted the urge to glance back. Again, he wanted to look like a man who knew exactly what he was doing and had nothing to hide.

He reached for the door of the cruiser, lifted the handle, swung the door open . . .

A booted foot came out of nowhere, kicked the door closed.

And Ranger Cordell Walker said, "You're under arrest, Alvarez."

Walker was ready as Alvarez spun around with a roar of rage and insane hatred. He blocked the blow Alvarez swung at him and threw a punch of his own, a hard right cross that caught Alvarez in the jaw and knocked him back against the sheriff's car. Alvarez rebounded from the vehicle and used that momentum to launch himself at Walker. His arms went around the Ranger in a diving tackle. Both men went down on the shoulder of the highway.

Walker rolled over and heaved Alvarez to the side. Alvarez recovered quickly, came up on hands and knees, then surged to his feet at the same time Walker did. Alvarez wiped the back of his hand across his mouth and glared at Walker as he said, "How . . . ?"

"I found the driver's jacket under the bus and knew you had to still be around here somewhere. It was just a matter of spotting you, Alvarez." Walker paused, then added, "Or should I call you El Diablo?"

The Ranger's mocking tone sent Alvarez charging forward like a maddened bull, just as Walker had intended. Walker met him with a kick to the stomach and tried to follow it with another, but Alvarez recovered quickly and grabbed Walker's leg instead. He heaved, upending Walker, then tried to throw himself down on top of the Ranger.

Walker rolled aside and twisted, coming down on top of Alvarez instead. He looped an arm around Alvarez's neck. One quick twist would break Alvarez's neck, and that was surely no less than he deserved.

Instead, Walker pushed himself to his feet, dragging Alvarez upright with him. Alvarez was still struggling, but he was weaker now that Walker had cut off his air. Walker released his grip and shoved Alvarez away from him. Trivette and more than a dozen cops were standing by, watching the showdown between Walker and Alvarez, and Walker was content for them to take him into custody now. He was about to say as much when Alvarez, still gasping for breath, swung around toward him and lifted the little pistol he had taken from somewhere inside his clothes.

Walker came completely up off the ground, twisting and spinning and lashing out with his foot. The gun in Alvarez's hand cracked wickedly, but the slug went whining off harmlessly. A split second later, Walker's kick crashed into

Alvarez's face and sent him flying backward. Alvarez landed spread-eagled in the middle of the highway, out cold, his jaw broken in at least two places.

El Diablo was finished.

EPILOGUE

"So that's what happened, Manuel," C. D. said as he looked down at the small boy in the hospital bed. "The bad fella who was responsible for you gettin' sick won't ever be hurtin' any more little boys."

Manuel Rodriguez smiled up at the adults standing around his bed. He was still weak, but his eyes were bright. "That is good, señor C. D."

"And as soon as you get to feelin' better," C. D. went on, "I want you and your mama to come over to my place for a big ol' bowl of chili."

"Wait a minute, C. D.," said Trivette. "You don't want to put Manuel right back in the hospital along with his mother this time, do you?"

"Dang it, Jimmy, I've told you and told you, my chili never put anybody in the hospital . . . unless they, uh, had somethin' else wrong with 'em to start with. . . ."

With a grin on his face, Walker angled his head toward the door and opened it so that Alex Cahill and Phyllis Harrison could step out into the corridor with him, leaving Trivette and C. D. to entertain Manuel and Silvia. He heard both the boy and his mother laughing as the wrangling continued.

"I'm glad to see that Manuel's doing so much better," Walker said to Phyllis.

"Yes, he looks like he's going to make a complete recovery, thank God. He was lucky . . . and so was I," Phyllis added somewhat ruefully.

Walker looked at Alex. "Mrs. Harrison won't spend any time in jail, will she?"

"No, the arrangement with the district attorney's office calls for probation," said Alex. She laid a hand on Phyllis's arm. "Provided, of course, that you stop practicing medicine without a license and prescribing illegal medications."

"You don't have to worry about that," Phyllis said solemnly. "I've realized now that I'm just an old woman who's outlived her usefulness."

"I wouldn't say that," Walker told her. "In fact, I was just talking to a friend of mine who runs a free clinic in South Oak Cliff. He's in desperate need of a competent nurse."

"As a matter of fact," added Alex, "I know the same doctor. I told him to give you a call, Mrs. Harrison."

Phyllis looked back and forth between them, hope and gratitude on her face. "But how . . . when did the two of you have time to cook this up, Ranger Walker? You just got back from all the uproar in South Texas."

"Well, actually, it was Alex's idea," began Walker.

"No, Walker suggested it," Alex said.

Phyllis smiled. "It doesn't matter. I just . . . thank you so much."

"You can do a lot of good, Phyllis," Walker told her. "Those young people trust you."

"I won't let them down," Phyllis vowed. Wiping away a tear, she went on, "I think I'd better go back in there and referee that chili argument."

"You'll be wasting your time," Walker warned her. "I've been doing it for years, and they're just as bad as ever."

When the door of the hospital room had swung shut behind Phyllis, Alex turned to Walker and asked, "What about the Vega Garcias? Have you heard anything more about them?"

"Their hacienda was deserted when the Mexican authorities—the *honest* Mexican authorities—got there." Walker shook his head. "I have a feeling we'll be hearing from them again someday."

"Well, Alvarez will be lucky to ever see the outside of a prison again, that's for sure. And good riddance, if you ask me. There's nothing worse than a crooked law enforcement officer."

"Yeah," said Walker, resting the palm of his hand against the door. "I'm just glad we caught up to him when we did."

He pushed the door open a few inches and heard C. D. saying, "And not only that, but chili's actually *good* for you, especially mine. It'll open your sinuses right up."

"It'll open up something, all right," countered Trivette, "but I'm not sure it's your sinuses."

Walker let the door ease shut and then slipped his arm around Alex's shoulders. "Let's go down to the cafeteria and get a cup of coffee instead," he suggested.

"I'm with you, Walker," she grinned back at him, and together, they walked down the corridor.